PROXY WAR

Vietnam GZ Thriller Series
Book Twenty-Nine

Eric Helm

SAPERE
BOOKS

PROXY WAR

Published by Sapere Books.

24 Trafalgar Road, Ilkley, LS29 8HH

saperebooks.com

ISBN: 978-0-85495-403-2

PROLOGUE

Hidden deep in the bowels of the Pentagon, in a room with a vault-like door and access controlled by a senior NCO sitting at a desk and armed with a Colt .45 1911A1 ACP, was a select group of senior officers. The highest ranking of the men was the Army Chief of Staff, General William C. Westmoreland, who had been the senior officer and overall commander in Vietnam for several years. Next to him was Major General David Kincaid, a senior intelligence officer who was virtually unknown to anyone outside of the Army. Across the table was Major General Steven Walker, an expert in asymmetrical warfare who had been one of the first of the Green Berets and who had served three tours in Vietnam advising both the Army of the Republic of Vietnam and the local indigenous forces. The last man, and the lowest ranking of them, was Captain Leslie Newman, who was there as the classified briefing officer.

Newman, a young man who had just returned from Vietnam after a special mission into Laos, stood behind a lectern with a remote control for a slide projector in his left hand. He waited as the generals settled into their seats, plush high-backed chairs, poured themselves either coffee or water, and turned their attention to him. He was more than a little nervous because he had rarely been in any room with a general officer and certainly not alone in a room with three of the highest-ranking generals in the United States Army.

Westmoreland sat back in his chair, raised his glass almost as if it was a badge of rank and said, "You may begin, Captain."

Newman hesitated, then gestured toward the screen where the first slide reinforced the importance of the briefing. He said, "Gentlemen, I guess I don't need to mention that this briefing is classified at the highest levels and that nothing said in here is to be discussed outside the confines of a properly secured room or with those not cleared to hear it."

With that, he pressed the button on the remote and the slide changed, showing a group of armed men in the distance. Although it was difficult to make out, given the poor quality of the photograph, it seemed that some of the men towered over the others. It was a group of European men with a group of either Vietnamese or Laotians, though their identity was almost impossible to make out.

"This photograph was taken by an Australian journalist and smuggled out of Laos several months ago. It seemed to suggest Caucasian men working with members of either the North Vietnamese Army in Laos, or members of the Laotian Army or a combination of both those organizations."

Westmoreland looked at his watch and said, somewhat impatiently, "We know this. Move on."

Newman changed the slide. It was an enlargement of part of the first photograph, but it was centered on one of the taller men. "Although we've lost some contrast, we were able to identify some of the decorations and rank insignia on the uniform. We had originally worried that the men might be defectors from the U.S. military, but that wasn't the case. That man is a Russian."

Kincaid interrupted. "We have known for a long time that there were Soviet advisors in North Vietnam. There is intelligence suggesting that Soviet fighter pilots have engaged in aerial combat with our Air Force and Navy pilots. We have recordings of the air-to-air chatter."

"Yes, General," said Newman. "We've ignored that, as has the U.N. and our allies. They have been afraid of widening the war which could escalate into a nuclear conflagration. We have avoided attacking the North Vietnamese ships in Haiphong Harbor because of the risk of sinking one of those ships."

"Captain," said Westmoreland, "we are not here for a history lesson."

"Yes, General. I wanted to set the stage. I wanted to ensure that the point is not lost."

"Then get on with it."

"Certainly, General." He clicked on the next slide. It was clearer — clear enough that the unit insignia worn by the Caucasian men could be identified.

Westmoreland asked, "Where did you get that picture?"

Walker spoke for the first time. "We put a team into Laos to investigate. HALO insertion. They then walked out, over the border into South Vietnam. They brought the pictures."

"I hope that you decorated that team, General," said Westmoreland.

"Of course."

Newman clicked on the next slide and said, "We can see these Soviets, and it is clear that they *are* Soviets, are engaged in training the local troops. Change the location, the uniforms and you could be looking at our Special Forces training one of the indigenous populations in South Vietnam."

"Yes, yes," said Westmoreland.

"General, what we're suggesting here is that the Soviets are training those people to engage in combat operations with our forces in South Vietnam."

Westmoreland was about to ask about the importance of that when he realized what was being said. He held up a hand to stop Newman from continuing as he digested what he had just been told.

"They're turning the tables on us. They are training a force to engage us in Southeast Asia."

Newman nodded. "Yes, sir. They're replacing the Viet Cong with another military force being trained in a neutral country to deploy in South Vietnam."

Westmoreland stood up suddenly and said, "General Walker, I'd like to see you in my office. General Kincaid, I'll want to know more about this."

"Yes, General."

"Captain Newman, that'll be all. Thank you."

CHAPTER 1

Major MacKenzie K. Gerber, U.S. Army Special Forces and known as Mack to his friends and a few of his enemies, sat in the semi-airconditioned office in a single-story building in Nha Trang, Republic of Vietnam. He sat behind a battered desk that had an actual bullet hole in it, though it was from an American-made M-16 and not a Chicom-made AK-47. He was wearing jungle fatigues with the sleeves rolled to the halfway point between his shoulder and elbow and he was sipping on a warm Pepsi from a can. With his feet propped on the lowest drawer, he was reading the weekly incident report that had been handed to him by Sergeant Major Anthony B. Fetterman, also a member of the Army Special Forces and assigned to the same office as Gerber.

Fetterman was an older soldier; in his late forties, he was smaller than the average NCO, but Gerber had never met anyone tougher or more dangerous than Fetterman. He had been a paratrooper in World War Two and had combat experience in both Korea and Vietnam. The sleeves of his jungle fatigues were buttoned at the wrist because, for some reason, he had become concerned about skin cancer caused by exposure to the blazing tropical sun.

Like Gerber, he was drinking a Pepsi from a can and didn't care that it was warm. He waited for Gerber to finish the incident report and then asked, "What'd you think of it?"

"New A Team at Song Be seems to be having some trouble."

"I wouldn't say that sporadic mortar attacks are much trouble."

"I see that they're reporting limited damage and no casualties. More harassment than enemy action," said Gerber.

Fetterman shrugged and set the can on the corner of Gerber's desk. "You think we should go take a look?"

"Well, that would get us out of here and into the field."

Now Fetterman grinned. "But here we have an all-night generator, movies, clubs that have actual food, and nurses. There are none of those things in the field or at Song Be."

Gerber raised an eyebrow and said, "Nurses ... or nurse?"

"I don't know what the problem is, Major. I can look at a nurse or two."

"Does this nurse or two have a name?"

"I'm not sure that I understand this interrogation, Major."

"I am following the finest traditions of leadership here. I'm taking an interest in the welfare of the soldiers assigned to my unit."

Fetterman looked as if he was deep in thought and then said, "I would believe that a nurse is safer than a reporter. The nurse would be inclined to help while the reporter is only interested in gathering information that will ultimately harm us."

"Aren't we moving into a personal arena here, one that is far above your pay grade?"

"I was just suggesting a difference in the occupational outlooks for various vocations that could affect our missions," Fetterman replied.

"But the question remains, Sergeant Major. Does the nurse have a name?"

Hoping to change the subject, Fetterman asked, "Did you see the report from Johnny's team?"

"Indeed I did but I wonder, now that he's a captain with his own team, if we shouldn't refer to him as John or Captain Bromhead,"

"It might be interesting to visit young Captain Bromhead, which also gets us out of here."

Gerber took a long pull at his Pepsi and tossed the now empty can into the waste basket, also known throughout the Army as the circular file. "I think Johnny —"

"You mean Captain Bromhead?" interrupted Fetterman.

"I dislike being interrupted, especially when you're right. I think Captain Bromhead is capable of handling his team. We trained him well. I'd like to see how this new guy is handling his team at Song Be. We can always visit Bromhead later."

"When would you like to go?"

Gerber looked at his watch. "Well, there is no sense in going this afternoon. We can have a good meal, get a good night's sleep and head out in the morning."

Fetterman nodded. "Mode of travel?"

"C-123? There are flights down toward Saigon and Cu Chi or maybe Tay Ninh," said Gerber. "We might be able to arrange something."

"Can they land a C-123 at Song Be?" asked Fetterman.

"They've got a good runway outside the camp. That shouldn't be a problem and if not, then we can catch a helicopter from one of those places to Song Be."

Now Fetterman smiled cautiously. "We going to tell them we're coming or are we just going to drop in on them?"

"Nope. We're not on an inspection tour. We're just going to check out the situation and see if there is something we can do for them. We'll just show up and see what we can see."

"Are you going to arrange the flight?"

"I'll go over to operations and see what's scheduled. Once I know that, I'll let you know when to be there. Of course, I need to know where you'll be."

"Nice try, Major," said Fetterman. "Just wake me in the morning in time to catch the flight."

Gerber dropped his feet to the floor. "I say we call it a day. I'll leave a message with the CQ for you, giving you the flight time."

"And where will you be?" asked Fetterman.

"Unlike you, I won't be chasing wild women and probably drinking intoxicating beverages."

Fetterman laughed. "Are you ill?"

"No, I'm just a little tired and figured that one night of good sleep is worth it." With that he stood up. "See you in the morning."

There was no rule about the wearing of civilian clothing after duty hours. Fetterman, having fallen in love with Hawaiian shirts, had bought six before he had deployed to Vietnam. He found them comfortable and perfect for the stifling humidity that was accompanied by the high temperatures of Vietnam. He found the loudest of them that contained bright reds, greens with splashes of yellow. If nothing else, he would stand out in a crowd.

Although there were officers' clubs and NCO clubs and enlisted clubs, the Special Forces had one open to all military personnel regardless of rank. The only requirement was to have earned a Green Beret, though that rule was sometimes bent for helicopter pilots who had pulled a team from a near fatal encounter, or medical personnel who had saved a life or two. The club wasn't overly exclusive, but you did have to earn your way through the doors one way or another.

Fetterman entered and was immediately hit by the cold air of an overactive air-conditioning system. After the heat outside, it was downright chilly in the club. He walked past the racks for weapons, which were not allowed in the main part of the club. Fetterman wasn't carrying a rifle but he did have a personal 9mm automatic tucked in a holster inside the waistline of his khaki pants and was hidden by the tails of his shirt. Fetterman just couldn't surrender all his weapons even if the rules required it. His philosophy being that it was better to have a weapon and not need it than to not have it and need it.

This attitude was developed during Tet in 1969. Although not covered with the same enthusiasm as the attacks a year earlier, there had been widespread engagements throughout South Vietnam. There had been a large spike in casualties, but that had dropped off in the days following Tet. The media was too busy searching for horror stories of American atrocities rather than the assaults on American and South Vietnamese installations.

Fetterman had been in Saigon, his M-16, locked in a rack at his camp. He had been in Saigon for a briefing that provided no real information when one of the attacks had been launched. He was seated in a briefing room when he heard shooting outside. Unlike some of those who were stationed in Saigon, who thought of themselves as safe, he understood the danger. Rather than sitting there, looking at the others, Fetterman had pushed himself out of his chair and walked to the door.

One of the senior officers had said, "Where are you going, Fetterman?"

"I thought I would see what is happening out there."

"There is no need for that. We have MPs guarding the entrance."

Fetterman, pulling his pistol from the small of his back where it had been hidden, said, "Yes, sir. I saw them when I came in."

"Then you know there is no reason for you to leave this room."

Another of the officers said, "That weapon is illegal. Carrying a concealed weapon is against Army regulations."

Fetterman ignored them both and opened the door. He stepped into the hallway and saw the guard kneeling against the wall, his rifle pointing down the corridor. The MP was a young Spec Four who probably had less than two years of service and probably only a few months in Vietnam. He might have never fired his weapon at another human being.

Fetterman asked, "What's happening?"

"I don't know. There's shooting out there, but I don't see anything."

"Stay here and don't let anyone get close to the door who isn't in uniform. I'm going to check this out. Make sure of your target before you shoot."

The man looked up at Fetterman and nodded.

Fetterman then walked slowly down the corridor, his back against the wall and his eyes on the end of the hall. Through the glass doors, he could see two MPs, crouched down, their weapons pointing at the empty parking lot. As he reached the door, one of the MPs opened fire on full auto. Fetterman couldn't see what he was shooting at and didn't like the way the soldier was burning through his ammo. He probably didn't have more than two or three spare magazines, meaning he had fewer than a hundred rounds.

When he reached the door, he took cover on one side, against the wall and looked out. He could see no threat, but heard firing off to the right, out of his line of sight. He didn't really want to enter a firefight with only a pistol and two spare magazines in his pocket. He needed an M-16, even if it wasn't one that he had zeroed.

A stray round shattered the glass of one of the doors. Fetterman had no idea where it had come from. He only knew that it hadn't been aimed at him. It was the classic golden BB. A round fired that finds a target by luck rather than skill.

He dropped to one knee and then saw three men dressed in black pajamas running across the parking lot. He was about to shout at the MPs, when one of them turned and engaged the enemy. Two went down and the third turned to run.

"That stopped them," shouted the MP. He sounded like the runner who had just scored an improbable touchdown. He hadn't expected the result, but he had engaged anyway.

"Can you see anyone else?" shouted Fetterman.

They both shot a glance back at him. "No. Just those three guys, but there's a hell of a lot shooting out here."

Fetterman stepped through the remains of the glass door and knelt behind one of the decorative plants. It was in a large pot that provided both protection and cover. "Who else is around here?"

"Our platoon has deployed, and I think they're engaged off to the right. We were told to protect this entrance."

That had satisfied Fetterman for the moment. He had no real authority here, other than the six strips sewn to his sleeve. He said, "I'm going to pull back now." He had thought about giving them instructions, but it seemed that both knew what they were doing. At least they were smart enough to remain under cover while keeping an eye on the area around them.

He slipped back down the hall to where the young Spec Four had been waiting. He asked, "What's going on out there?"

"Harassment," said Fetterman. "I think the MPs have it covered."

When he entered the conference room, he saw that everyone was sitting right where they had been when he left. He was surprised by that. He would have thought that some of the officers would want to take charge. He supposed it was the difference between a combat veteran and the guys who had spent their careers out of the combat arena and behind a desk.

One of them said, "I'm going to have to report that violation of regulations, Sergeant Major."

Fetterman let down the hammer on his pistol carefully and asked, "What are you going to do, send me to Vietnam?"

There had been no repercussions. Fetterman hadn't thought there would be. Everyone he knew in Vietnam had unauthorized weapons. Pilots had AK-47s and the crew had M-79 grenade launchers; soldiers with .357 Magnums and even a chaplain or two had carried pistols.

So, here he was, at the club with the pistol hidden under his Hawaiian shirt. He had two spare magazines in one of his pockets. No one in the club would care that he was armed, and he figured ninety percent of everyone in the club had a weapon of some sort. The exception would be the nurses and he guessed more than one of them had some sort of weapon too.

Sitting at a small table, near the back of the club, was a lone nurse. Fetterman was surprised that no one had approached her. She was blonde, which he found strange because her name was Carmen and that suggested a raven-haired woman. She was on the short side, only about five-four, but was surprisingly strong.

He slipped into a seat opposite her and said, "I thought you would be surrounded by admirers."

"I chased them away. They're good boys, professional."

The waiter showed up. Unlike the other clubs, there were no Vietnamese working here even though the Status of Forces Agreement required it. Without Vietnamese, whose loyalty was sometimes for sale, there were no fears of spying. The most innocuous statement, overheard by a waiter or bartender, could compromise a mission. The loyalty of the American soldiers who spent some of their time as the waiters and bartenders was without question. Nearly everyone around had a security clearance, which didn't prove loyalty but certainly was an indication of it.

"Just bring me a beer," said Fetterman.

When the waiter was gone, Fetterman asked, "How are your parents?"

"They're fine. They ask if I ever run into you. I told them that we had a beer or two once in a while."

"Must be hard on your father," said Fetterman. "His little girl in a combat zone drinking beer with an old NCO."

She grinned at that. "He thinks of you as my protector. I told him that we are rarely mortared and I'm not in all that much danger."

The waiter returned and set the beer down in front of Fetterman. He handed the man a fifty-cent Military Payment Certificate, the so-called Monopoly money used by the U.S. armed forces in Vietnam.

"You want me to send him a letter?"

"I don't think that'll help. He's been there and understands how it works. I think he wishes he was here, and I was back home."

"Well, you can't blame him."

She was quiet for a moment, sipped her beer and asked, "What was it like? He never talks about it."

Fetterman waved a hand around and said, "Not much different than this. Rear areas that are shelled. Soldiers in the field engaged in combat operations. Periods of intense excitement spread through longer periods of boredom."

"Just like here?"

"Yes," said Fetterman, "just like here."

"He never told me how you met."

Fetterman closed his eyes for a moment and was about to say that her father had been the first sergeant, so they hadn't really met, but then he was thinking about standing knee-deep in a flooded field, in the dark, wondering just where he was because the anti-aircraft fire had set an engine ablaze and they had bailed out early. The pilot had sounded the bell and the light on the side door had turned green. He was telling them to get out before the aircraft exploded. Fetterman made it out the door with half a dozen others. He watched the C-47's left wing, now gloriously on fire and spreading toward the fuselage. Moments later the plane had exploded, killing the aircrew and most of the paratroopers still on board.

He turned to his left and looked at the apparition about twenty feet away and recognized him as the company first sergeant, Steven Anderson. Fetterman was smart enough not to call out but began moving toward him. The man waved toward the hedgerow fifty yards away. There would be cover there and they'd have a chance to figure out what they needed to do.

Once there, crouched in the foliage, Anderson said, "We're pretty much on our own here."

Fetterman nodded but didn't move. "You know where we are?"

"We're hell and gone away from the drop zone. I think we're a couple of miles short of it, but I'm not sure. We may be close to one of the beaches. I'm inclined to remain here for a few minutes until we figure out what to do."

That had been Fetterman's introduction to Carmen's father. A tall man who had been in the Army prior to the beginning of the war. Fetterman had faith in him. He had learned a lot from

18

Anderson, who had been calm and cool even when the battle plan had been so badly botched and the D-Day invasion seemed to be a bad idea.

The trip down memory lane was interrupted by a soldier. He stood near Carmen and asked, "What are you doing with this old man?"

Fetterman looked at him. He was tall but thin. Fetterman didn't recognize him but there had been a few Special Forces soldiers assigned recently and he didn't know all of them. Given the nature of the club, Fetterman thought he had to be Special Forces, but he was uncommonly rude for a Green Beret.

Before Fetterman could say anything, Carmen said, "Go away." She smiled briefly.

The man reached for the back of the nearest chair as if to pull it out to sit down. Fetterman caught his wrist and held it there. He said quietly, "Join your friends."

"You going to make me, old man?"

As Fetterman slid back his chair, another soldier appeared at the table. He grabbed the man by the shoulder and said, "Sorry, Sergeant Major. He's new and doesn't understand. Come on, Jerry, let's go."

Jerry tried to shake the hand from his shoulder, but his friend held on and said, "You don't know what you're doing." He spun him around and pushed him back toward the rear of the club.

"That happen much?" asked Fetterman.

"Only if someone is new and impolite."

Fetterman said, "You want to have dinner here?"

"Sure, and you can tell me more stories about my dad when he was a soldier."

Because the aircraft was designed for the military and would be carrying more cargo than people, the soundproofing was not the best. It was impossible to carry on a normal conversation when they had to lean close to one another and shout into each other's ears.

To make it worse, the seating was red canvas tightly strung between two metal pipes. It was not comfortable and after an hour or so, the stress of sitting there began to wear on the passengers. But Fetterman didn't care about that. Once they were off the ground and climbing to altitude, he unbuckled his seat belt and stretched out, going to sleep. The only other passengers were on the other side of the aircraft, ignoring both Gerber and Fetterman.

Gerber didn't like taking naps early in the day. Sometimes he'd take a nap in the middle of the afternoon if nothing was going on and he was bored. But in the morning, on an aircraft, he'd rather stay awake. He pulled a paperback from one of his pockets and started to read.

There was a change in the engine noise and Gerber knew that they were making a landing approach. He looked over at Fetterman, who was now awake, but he didn't sit up. Gerber shouted, "We're landing."

Fetterman sat up and swung his feet to the deck of the aircraft. "Figured," he said. He buckled his seat belt, leaned his head back and looked as if he had gone to sleep again.

Before Gerber could respond, there was a bounce, and then a rumbling as they touched down on the gravel runway outside of the Special Forces camp at Song Be. The engines roared as the pilot reversed the thrust. He stood on the brakes to slow the aircraft. When it stopped the crew chief opened one of the side doors and signaled Gerber and Fetterman.

"Grab your ruck, Tony." Gerber slipped his arm through one of the straps and hoisted his rucksack to his shoulder and then picked up his weapon. There was a magazine inserted but no round chambered. He didn't expect a firefight on the aircraft and if there had been any enemy contact near the camp, they wouldn't have landed.

Gerber stepped into the bright sunshine and the staggering humidity. For a moment it was almost impossible to breathe. He moved away from the aircraft and its spinning propellers quickly. His attention was drawn to a jeep that had left the camp and was racing down the side of the runway. There were two men in it.

"Welcoming committee?" asked Fetterman.

"Well, at least we don't have to walk."

The jeep stopped near them. It carried two NCOs, both wearing their berets. The passenger grinned and asked, "Need a ride soldier?"

Gerber tossed his ruck into the jeep and climbed up on the rear. Fetterman did the same thing. Once he was settled, the driver started up, turned, and drove back to the camp. As they approached the gate, the engines of the plane revved. Gerber watched as it began its take-off roll. It raced down the runway and lifted off, turning to the south as it climbed out. The sound of the engines faded as the plane disappeared.

At the gate, the jeep stopped, and two men walked up to it. As Gerber got off the back of the jeep, the soldiers saluted. One of them said, "I'm Captain John Martin, sir. How can I be of service?" He was about thirty, just a hair under six feet tall. He was wearing tiger-striped fatigues and carried an M-16. Unlike many of the soldiers in Vietnam, he had no mustache.

Fetterman said, "We're from the government and we're here to help."

"Tony," the other man said with a nod. "You should have called."

"You know this man, Sergeant Major?" Gerber asked.

"Yes, sir. I thought they had tossed him out of the Special Forces a long time ago."

"Tony, you wound me." He turned his attention to Gerber. "I'm Sergeant Davis, sir." He held out a hand. Davis looked like a typical Green Beret. Young, in great shape, now deeply tanned. His hair was cut close to the head and bleached to the point where it was nearly invisible. Unlike Martin, Davis's boots were highly polished, suggesting that he paid close attention to detail.

Gerber shook his hand. "Gerber. Captain. Shouldn't we get out of the line of fire? One grenade can get us all."

Now Martin laughed. "Haven't heard that in a day or two."

"It is the unofficial slogan of the Special Forces," said Fetterman.

"Let's go to the team house," said Martin. "You can fill me in on the purpose of your visit."

They walked through the gate. On both sides was a berm about chest high that would protect the defenders in the event of a ground attack. There were hootches aligned in the area for the Vietnamese strikers assigned. There was an interior redoubt designed for the last stand if the perimeter was breached. The mortar tubes were there and both fifty- and thirty-caliber machines were mounted in small bunkers.

They entered the team house, which seemed luxurious compared to some that Gerber has seen. It was air conditioned with ceiling fans spinning to circulate the air. There was a large refrigerator next to what was a makeshift bar made of plywood that had been colored by a blowtorch. The grain of the wood had been highlighted by the heat, giving the bar an almost camouflaged appearance.

"Drop your rucks by the door," said Martin.

He took them over to a table that was surrounded by ten or twelve mismatched chairs. "Anybody want coffee, juice, soft drink?"

Fetterman said, "I could use a cold Pepsi if that refrigerator works."

"If we're lucky," Davis said, "it won't be frozen into a solid chunk of ice. That refrigerator takes its job very seriously."

"Coffee for me," said Gerber.

Davis left them for a moment. He returned with the drinks and said to Fetterman, "You're lucky, Tony. I think it's in liquid form. Just be careful when you open it. Sometimes they spray."

Once everyone had a drink, Martin said, "So, Major, what brings you here?"

"I've been reading the incident reports and noticed that you seem to have more than your share of mortar attacks."

Martin shrugged. "It's really nothing, sir. Couple of rounds every other night, every two nights. Ten rounds a week and they do very little damage."

"Countermortar?"

"We try, but they're well concealed. They fire three or four rounds and then run. Seems like a waste of ammunition to fire countermortar."

"Aviation support?"

"Well, sir, I'm not sure how that would work. If they staged out of here, then they'd be the targets and that sort of defeats the purpose. There's nothing close enough, so that by the time they got here, the tubes would be broken down and the crews scattered."

Martin took a long sip of his coffee. "You really here to talk about our countermortar efforts?"

Gerber grinned. "My mission —" he looked at Fetterman — "our mission is twofold. First, I thought we might be able to figure out a way to make it risky for the VC to throw the mortars at you. And second, I was getting bored hanging around Nha Trang, and this was a good excuse to get into the field."

Fetterman broke in. "I thought we should check out the defenses at Vung Tau, but the major wasn't thrilled with going to the beach."

"Well," said Martin. "We did try to get gunships standing by, meaning, orbiting south of the camp where they would be handy if something happened, but the VC seemed to know they were there. No luck."

"Patrols?"

"I'm a little worried about sending out a patrol that could be ambushed. Send them out in the morning and have them in the area, but again, the enemy just never picked those nights to hit us."

Gerber nodded. "They're either watching the camp, or they have someone on the inside signaling those outside."

"You know as well as I do that there is VC in the strike force."

"How about a longer patrol. Out three or four days?"

"Same results. They just know what we're doing."

"Okay, how about a fast mover high overhead. Out of earshot and out of sight. Could roll in faster — two or three minutes."

Martin nodded but said, "First, we'd have trouble getting a dedicated team. Air Force doesn't want to commit two or more jets to orbiting around here night after night, especially to take out a mortar team of five or ten guys and a mortar tube or two. Just not cost-effective."

"I can understand that," said Gerber. He didn't like it, but he understood it. He scratched the top of his head.

"I'd say we put in the patrol from another camp. Insert them several klicks away and let them walk into the area." He looked at Davis. "Have you tried to coordinate something like that?"

"No. Ties up a lot of assets. Both aviation and personnel. I'm sure we could borrow a platoon or two from one of the other camps. Considering the damage done, the risk just seem to be justified."

Fetterman finished his Pepsi and carefully set the can on the table. "I suppose you have an idea where they set up for these attacks."

"Sure. Not the same place every time. They move it around."

"Mechanical ambush?" asked Fetterman.

"I don't like to use those," said Martin. "Too many farmers and local hunters in the area. I'm more likely to get them than I am the bad guys."

Gerber said, "It seems to me that there would only be a limited area for them to set up the mortars. They've got to be in a clearing so that they can fire their weapons."

"True," said Martin. "I think they sometimes pick the worst spots, which is why their aim is so poor. Keeps us guessing."

Gerber looked around the team house. The only other person there was another American soldier. He was sitting by himself reading a week-old newspaper and paying no attention to them.

Lowering his voice, Gerber said, "I think the first thing we need to do is figure out how the intelligence about your patrols are being spotted. Since there have been aviation assets involved, there must be some sort of signal. If we can spot that, we can turn this around."

"How do we do that?" asked Martin.

"No offence, Captain, but I think we bring in a team from one of the other camps, or rather deploy them around here to see what they can see."

"You mean sneak them in here to spy on us?"

"With the luck you have been having with your countermortar, we need to try something a little more radical."

Martin raised his coffee cup in a semi-salute. "Seems like a lot of effort for a problem that isn't all that great."

Now Gerber smiled. "But sometimes it's the small victories that are the most satisfying."

CHAPTER 2

Captain George Smith sat in a tiny office on the third floor of the Pentagon and studied the papers sitting on the desk. Smith had graduated from ROTC at the University of Iowa, had accepted his commission, and was called to active duty immediately. He had attended his basic course in infantry and then been assigned to the Pentagon. He had also gone to jump school because it was almost necessary to have completed jump school to advance a military career. The exception seemed to be those officers who had gone to flight school or were commissioned in specialties such as law or medicine.

He had been handed a contingency plan for a HALO infiltration into an unidentified tropical environment. Smith wasn't dumb. He knew that the tropical environment would be Southeast Asia, though the exact location and country were not mentioned. He was the tenth or eleventh person to review the plan and by this stage, he was simply looking for typos, grammar errors and logical inconsistencies. He wasn't going to change it or modify it or comment on the practicality of it. His review was to ensure that there were no obvious errors in it.

The insertion was to be made by HALO and that confused him. He knew what HALO meant, in a general sense, but he didn't understand the precise operation. To be accurate in his assessment, Smith wanted to know more about it. He closed the folder and took it into the outer office where there were other officers who had similar tasks. There were a half dozen desks in the room, each with a telephone, a lamp and a chair that was uncomfortable. All were young men who were from a variety of military branches including artillery, aviation, military police, signal corps, and intelligence.

Thinking about it, he turned and asked the others, "Any of you know anything about HALO?"

A second lieutenant stood up. He was short, stocky, and looked as if he had slept in his uniform. His hair was cut so short that it looked like a shadow on his head. Above his left breast pocket, he wore the National Defense Service Medal, an Army Commendation Medal and jump wings. He asked, "What do you want to know?"

"Come with me." Smith turned and walked into the small office he had been using. He sat down behind the desk and put the folder he had retrieved from the safe, in front of him. He said, "HALO?"

"Yes, sir," said Jerry Kimball. "What do you need to know?"

"I know that you jump out of an airplane at high altitude and free fall for tens of thousands of feet and that about covers it."

"You know about the temperatures and the oxygen levels?"

Smith shook his head. "I know about jumping out of an airplane but nothing above fifteen thousand feet, which is the extreme."

"Okay," said Kimball. "There is special gear needed. The temperatures at that altitude can run somewhere around forty-five or fifty degrees below zero depending on the weather conditions. You need special clothing to prevent frostbite and you need a pressure suit, not to mention that you need to flush the nitrogen from your system by breathing pure oxygen for about half an hour before the jump. You can't smoke, drink, or take drugs before a jump."

Smith nodded and said, slowly, "Okay."

"You have to understand that jumping at HALO altitudes require supplemental oxygen. At about thirty thousand feet, your useful consciousness is about ten seconds."

Smith held up a hand. "Wait a minute. You have people climbing Mount Everest and that's just under thirty thousand feet…"

"They spend days, if not weeks, acclimating themselves to the altitude and even then, they have supplemental oxygen. I've heard that the area around the summit is littered with discarded oxygen cylinders."

"So, you need special training to make a HALO jump?"

"Yes, sir. It's not like normal parachuting. Once you jump out, you have to be careful because it'll take a minute and a half to two minutes of free fall before you deploy your parachute. You have to pay attention, or you just keep going until you splatter yourself all over the countryside. It takes four weeks to go through the course at Fort Bragg."

"How many are trained to do this?"

"I couldn't tell you, sir, without doing some research. There aren't very many because of the hazards."

"What about equipment drops?"

"They can be done, but the problem is that at high altitude it is difficult to exactly position the loads. While the soldier can manipulate his chute, the load has no human control. And sometimes the chutes don't open, leaving a crater in the ground filled with broken equipment."

Smith rubbed a hand over his head. He looked at the document on the desk and back at Kimball. "What sort of mission uses HALO?"

"Mostly short-term. They can't carry much in the way of supplies and they have to have water and ammunition, depending on the mission. You have to extract them or get to them in two or three days."

"You don't have a company of soldiers to deploy with a HALO jump?"

"That sort of defeats the purpose, sir. It's all about sneaking in. You drop at night from high altitude hoping that the aircraft noise is dissipated because of the altitude. You drop four, five, six guys because when you begin dropping more people the rate of detection goes up. It's all about getting in and out without anyone seeing you."

Smith sighed and said, "I have a plan here that seems to demand a HALO insertion, but the numbers wouldn't work out. I mean, you must prepare by breathing pure oxygen, and then, I suppose, you must take the oxygen with you or the nitrogen seeps back into the blood stream. These HALO operations aren't as easy as some suggest."

"No, sir. They're not used very often. What's going on here?"

Smith shrugged and stood up. "Thanks for the information."

As Kimball left the little room, Smith decided that there was more to this than he had thought.

The real power here was in working at the Pentagon and working in a section that was small, but powerful based on their assignment. There were people who knew about the unit but didn't know what it did. Only that the operation was highly classified and that they had a priority. Almost any request was granted, and if there was a problem, then someone from the Secretary of Defense's office would call to eliminate the problem. When Smith decided that he needed to travel to Fort Bragg, that afternoon, on one of the courier flights that originated at Andrews Air Force Base, he was given the option on which flight would be most convenient for him.

He made his choice, picked up a copy of the generic orders for the flight to Fort Bragg. The shuttle to Andrews had already left, but Smith was able to schedule a staff car along with a driver. In rank-heavy Washington, a captain scheduling a car and driver would be impossible, except in special circumstances. Smith, wrapped in the mantle of his position and the Office of the Secretary of Defense, had those special circumstances.

Smith stepped into the outer office and looked at the master sergeant who was the chief of the admin section. He was an older soldier who had served in both World War Two and Korea. In Korea he had been assigned to a corps headquarters after the breakout at Pusan and hadn't been involved in the fighting. Now he was nearly at mandatory retirement, was outranked by nearly everyone in the office, though the lieutenants knew not to question him. His knowledge of the administration details was encyclopedic, and when the regs were consulted, the master sergeant was found to be right nearly all the time.

Smith stepped to his desk, waited while the master sergeant finished writing a note and looked up. Smith said, "I need to catch the afternoon shuttle to Bragg, and I need a car."

"It's getting late in the day for that," said the master sergeant.

"I know, but I've called Andrews Operations and I have time to get there, if I can get a car."

The master sergeant picked up the telephone, dialed a four-digit number and said, "General Kincaid needs a car and driver for a trip to Andrews." He listened for a moment and said, "That won't do. We need it at the main entrance in ten minutes." He listened again and said, "Thank you, Sergeant."

Now he grinned at Smith. "I've got a car coming for you but it's not one of those for senior officers. Might be a little dirty and beat up."

"Don't really care, Master Sergeant, as long as it gets me to Andrews."

The master sergeant reached into a draw and pulled out a set of preprinted papers. He flipped through the stack, extracted one and said, "Here are your orders. Will you need more than one copy?"

"Two would be better, but I think one will do it."

Extracting another sheet from the stack, the master sergeant said, "There you go, sir. Does the general know about this?"

Now it was Smith's turn to grin. "No, but I'm working on something for him."

"And where will you be, in case he asks?"

"Enroute to Andrews, enroute Bragg, then either at Eighteenth Headquarters or with the Special Warfare Commandant at Mackall."

"Will you RON?"

"Depends on how things go at Bragg. I'm getting a late start, so I'll probably spend the night there and be back tomorrow morning."

"You need to swing by your quarters?"

Smith noticed, as he had in the past, that the master sergeant rarely said "Sir," to company grade officers. That was reserved for field grade and above, though some majors didn't rate it either.

"I've got my go bag here. Not a problem."

"Then grab your gear and the car should be waiting at the main entrance."

"Thank you, Master Sergeant."

"You're welcome."

Smith went to his locker, found his go bag. He then went to his desk, put the contingency plan in his briefcase, closed it and locked it. As he walked to the door, he said, "I'll see you all tomorrow." With that he walked out.

As promised, the car was waiting, with the driver standing beside the rear door. Smith hurried down the steps and noticed the driver was less than pleased to see a captain without a general in tow. He had assumed that Smith was the general's aide.

The driver saluted. "We're going to Andrews?"

"As quickly as the law allows," said Smith. "Need to catch the courier flight."

The driver, a buck sergeant as opposed to a Spec Five, just said, "Yes, sir," and closed the door when Smith slipped into the rear seat.

It was a typical military sedan. There was nothing in the car that suggested luxury. The seats were vinyl, there were no power windows, AM radio and several decals telling the passengers to fasten their seatbelts, that the car would not drive above fifty-five miles an hour and to not engage the driver in unnecessary conversation.

Smith sat back and looked out the window. Washington, D.C. was filled with monuments, statues, and large government buildings. Smith had lived in the area for more than a year but about the only site he had seen was the Pentagon and only because he worked there.

They crossed the Potomac River and Smith could see the Washington Monument. He hadn't realized that it was so close to the Pentagon. He drove in from one of the northwestern suburbs, usually in the dark. He was busy dodging traffic, so he didn't have time to look around.

As they drove to the southeast, they passed signs showing him the way to the Capitol Building and the National Mall where the Washington Monument and the Lincoln Memorial were located. When he got back from Bragg, he'd have to take a Saturday or Sunday and just walk around the area. It would be a reconnaissance, something that he should have done when he had been assigned to the Pentagon several months earlier.

They reached the front gate and the guard there looked at the car but saw no general officer license plate and no flags mounted to the fender. There was an officer sitting in the back, but he had no real status given the appearance of the staff car. The guard came to attention, saluted, and passed the car through.

"Airfield Operations," said Smith.

"Yes, sir." The driver made a turn and then headed down a street, driving at the required twenty miles an hour on the base. A few minutes later, he pulled up in front of the Operations Building.

Smith opened the door before the driver could get out of the car. He reached back in and grabbed his go bag. He saw the driver walk around the front of the car. He said, "Thanks for the lift. Take a commendation medal out of petty cash."

"Have a good trip, sir."

"Thanks." Smith turned and entered the building. There was a counter that looked like those in a civilian airport manned by several enlisted soldiers. Behind them was a scheduling board that listed the various flights, destinations and take-off time.

Smith stepped up and said, "I need to get on the courier to Fort Bragg."

The clerk turned, looked at the board and saw that the flight had not left. She then checked the manifest and said, "I'm sorry, sir. The flight is full."

"You'll need to bump the lowest ranking soldier."

"I'm sorry, sir, but I can't do that."

"If you would look at my orders, I think you would have a better understanding of the situation."

She repeated her answer and was becoming annoyed.

Smith knew that the argument was about to go around and around. He said, reasonably, "Let me talk to your supervisor."

"He'll tell you the same thing, sir. We must maintain the schedule and we can't alter it for someone who shows up late."

Smith knew that wasn't true. If he was a colonel or a general, they'd work to accommodate him, but as a captain, they didn't really care that much. He said, "Please advise your supervisor that I have a question."

She took a deep breath and went through a door at the back of the room. She returned in a moment with a master sergeant who looked as if he had been around the military for his entire adult life. He stepped up to the counter and said, "How may I help you, sir."

"I need to make the courier flight to Bragg."

"The manifest is set, sir, and we can't change it at this point."

"Let me show you my orders."

"I don't need to see your orders," said the master sergeant. "The manifest is set."

"My orders will provide some context."

The master sergeant finally took the orders and read them. "Anybody with a mimeograph machine could have created these orders."

Smith stared at him. "Are you seriously suggesting that I have a set of forged orders? Might I suggest you call the Pentagon and talk with the master sergeant there and if that won't do it, then you need to call Major General Kincaid."

"Can you wait a moment, Captain?"

"Certainly, but please remember that I have to get on the flight to Bragg."

The master sergeant left the room and then came back quickly. He didn't look at Smith but said to the clerk, "You need to bump Sergeant Forbes and schedule him for the next flight."

"Are you sure?"

"Just do it."

"Yes, Master Sergeant."

Smith said, "I don't want to make trouble here, but it is important that I make it to Bragg."

"Yes, sir."

The flight was pleasant and landed on time. Smith was one of the first off the aircraft and walked into the Operations Building. He saw a sergeant working the counter and asked, "How do I get over to Smoke Bomb Hill?"

"Are you being assigned there?"

"No. But I need to get over there as quickly as I can."

"There's a shuttle to Bragg in ten minutes. You can arrange transport from there. Shuttle's loading now."

Smith looked at the sergeant for a moment and realized that the woman would not be intimidated by him or his orders. She probably dealt with irate colonels and generals daily so an Army captain she didn't know and who had just arrived wouldn't phase her. He thought about asking for a taxi, but it would be quicker to take the shuttle to Bragg and work the problem at that end.

Smith left the building and spotted an Army bus that had seen better days. It was dented, the paint was chipped, but someone, and Smith knew that someone was probably several low-ranking airmen with cans of wax and all day to work, kept it shining. The windows were open, meaning there was no air conditioner, but the weather wasn't all that bad. The ride wouldn't be uncomfortable.

Smith climbed on board and the driver, who looked to be a high school student but who wore staff sergeant stripes, asked, "Where to, Captain?"

"Ultimately, Smoke Bomb Hill but almost anywhere on Bragg would do it. Maybe the officers' club."

"I can get you over to Smoke Bomb Hill, sir. Not a problem."

"Thank you, Sergeant. Take medal out of petty cash."

"Sir?"

"Just a joke. Not a good one, but a joke."

"Yes, sir."

The driver closed the door, ground the gears and the bus lurched forward, belching a black cloud of smoke that smelled heavily of diesel. Smith leaned back and looked out the window as they left the airfield and headed from Pope Air Force Base toward Fort Bragg.

Smith was the highest-ranking man on the bus. The driver, catering to him, took him to Smoke Bomb Hill and dropped him in front of the headquarters of the Special Forces. He got off the bus and walked to the front door. Inside, he found the commandant's office and entered. A senior sergeant saw him, seemed unimpressed and asked, "How may I help you, sir?"

"I'd like to see the Commandant," said Smith.

"You and about fifteen others, sir. He's not here. Can I be of assistance?"

"I need a briefing on HALO operations."

"The purpose?"

"I'm involved in a research project and need some specific information."

One of the clerks sitting at a desk in the rear of the room asked, "Are you Captain Smith?"

Smith turned and looked at him. The young soldier was dressed in jungle fatigues with camouflage insignia on it. He was young, no more than twenty-four or twenty-five and had a scar on the side of his face that crawled up into his hairline. It was white and looked fresh.

"You have a question for the Captain?" asked the first sergeant.

"Yes. Are you Captain Smith?"

"I am."

"We received a message for you about thirty minutes ago." He looked at the first sergeant and then back to Smith.

Surprised, Smith asked, "What is it?"

"Return immediately."

"That's it?"

"Yes, sir. Apparently, something has come up and you are required to return to your home unit as quickly as you can."

The door opened and a man wearing a green beret and lieutenant colonel silver leaves entered. He looked at Smith and then asked, "What do we have here, Sergeant Major?"

"Captain Smith is here, and we have a message from the Pentagon ordering him to return."

The officer walked to Smith and held out a hand. "I'm Colonel Hendrickson. And you're here, why?"

Smith said, "I am doing research on HALO operations."

"Because?"

Smith thought about it for a moment and then said, "Contingency plans."

Hendrickson said, "Let's go into my office." He looked at the first sergeant and asked, "Is the Commandant here?"

"He's over at the Corps Headquarters."

"Let me know when he comes in." Hendrickson said. Then to Smith he added, "Follow me."

In the office, Hendrickson said, "Grab a seat and tell me what is going on?"

"We're developing contingency plans and one of them calls for HALO operations. I need to learn a little more about how all this works."

"You understand that much of the HALO technology is classified. And, come to think of it, wasn't there someone at the Pentagon who could have answered your questions?"

Before Smith could answer, the telephone on Hendrickson's desk rang. He held up a hand to stop Smith from answering and picked up the phone. "Okay. Got it," he said into the receiver and hung up. Now he looked at Smith. "Well, Captain, that seems to conclude our business."

Smith looked puzzled. "Sir?"

"I have been instructed to order you to return to Washington as soon as possible and that no further assistance is required from us. I am to provide you with no information about any of our operations here. Frankly, Captain, it sounds of if you have stepped on your dick, jumped up and down on it, and your superiors are now extremely unhappy with you."

Smith sat quietly for a moment, unable to think of a response. Hendrickson said, "It's none of my business, but this is a first for me. I have never received a telephone call from a general officer at the Pentagon ordering me to conclude my business with an officer without some sort of explanation. Obviously, if a general gives me an order, I am obligated to obey that order."

Smith stood up. "I'm sorry to have bothered you, Colonel."

Hendrickson couldn't help but grin. "You've been no bother. Instead, you have provided a bit of entertainment on a routine afternoon. I will forget that you mentioned HALO, which hints at what you are doing, and ask if you need a ride back to Pope."

"That would be most kind, sir."

"I don't know what their schedule is, but there are flights out of there at all hours, along with the normal courier flights. You should be able to get back to Washington tonight without too much trouble."

Captain George Smith arrived at his office in the Pentagon just after 2100 hours, or late enough that many of those assigned to the office and to the Pentagon had left for the day. The night crews had taken over, and because they had no real-world assignment that required the office be manned twenty-four hours a day, everyone was normally gone by 1800 hours at the latest.

Only the master sergeant was still there, but it was clear that he believed he was off duty. His shoes sat on the floor next to his desk, and he was reading a paperback novel rather than dealing with military paperwork. He looked up when Smith entered and said, without preamble, "The general will see you now, Captain." He stressed the word captain.

"The general is still here?" asked Smith, surprised.

The master sergeant closed his book, set it on his desk and then nodded. "Yes. I believe he was annoyed at your sudden departure without proper authority and the utilization of military resources that could have been deployed in a more beneficial nature."

Smith was tempted to grin at the assessment, but because the general had waited, he knew there was nothing amusing about it. "Where is he?"

"Upstairs in his office. I'll let him know that you're on your way up."

"Thank you, Master Sergeant." Smith set his briefcase and go bag on a chair near the door. Before he left, he said, "I image you're on your way home now?"

"No, sir. The general asked that I wait."

Smith snorted. "That does not bode well for me."

The master sergeant said nothing. He just picked up his book.

Smith made his way to General Maxwell's office and was surprised to find the reception area to be dark. The day staff was gone, and the only light was a small lamp sitting on a table to the right. The typewriters were covered, the desks were clear of paper and files and Smith suspected the drawers on those desks would be locked.

He walked across the plush carpeting, stopped at the general's door, and hesitated. It was a military tradition that an officer, called to an audience with a general, one who had waited hours, would not go well. In that moment, Smith wondered what he had been thinking.

He knocked on the door and heard, "Come on in, Captain."

Smith opened the door, walked directly toward the general's desk. He stopped three feet in front of it, came to attention, and saluted. "Captain George Smith, reporting as ordered."

For nearly a minute, General Maxwell stared at him and finally returned the salute. He then asked, in a conversational voice, "Just what in the hell were you thinking?"

Smith took a deep breath. "I was attempting to do my job."

"Your job was to review a contingency plan. Your job was to make sure the commas were used properly, that there were no misspelled words, and that the language made sense. Your job was not to assess the feasibility of the plan, which you are not qualified to criticize."

"General, I found what I thought was a flaw in the plan."

"Then you should have brought that to the attention of the original author and not make an unscheduled trip to Fort Bragg. You overstepped your authority."

Smith realized that there was nothing that he could say that wouldn't dig the hole he was in any deeper. He had wanted to correct the flaw with additional information but that hadn't been his job.

The general touched the telephone on the desk. "If you needed additional information, that was the tool to use. Thirty minutes on the autovon and you would have learned what you wanted to learn and not spend hours away from your desk bothering others who had important jobs. And you wouldn't have been bumping people from the courier flight."

"Security, General. I was worried about a breach of security."

"Did it occur to you that there were officers assigned here that could have answered your questions? I understand that you did talk to one of the lieutenants about this and he provided the information you wanted."

Smith didn't speak for a moment and then said, quickly, "I just got lost in the weeds, sir."

General Maxwell took a deep breath and then shook his head. "I don't know whether to be angry with you or to be pleased that you went that extra mile. I suppose anger wins because there were ways to do it without causing trouble."

Smith felt relief but then the general said, "I do have a report from Flight Operations at Andrews about you pulling rank to bump a passenger from the courier flight. You made some people over there unhappy by interfering in the operation of their mission."

"Yes, sir."

"That was over the line. You had no authority to do that. From this point on, you'll coordinate these activities with the master sergeant in your office and with the sergeant major in this one. There will be no taking off on a whim. Is that understood?"

"Yes, sir."

"And one other thing. We already knew that HALO operations required specialized training, and that large scale, meaning company sized infiltrations using HALO tended to defeat the purpose of them, not to mention that there are not that many HALO-trained soldiers in the Army. It's a contingency plan, like all those others in which scenarios are devised that have virtually no possibly of being needed."

That caught Smith by surprise. He hadn't thought about the possibility that the contingency plans would cover events that were unlikely to happen. But in that moment, he understood what that meant. Someone would think up something that might happen and to be prepared for it, a contingency plan would be created. It might not cover the event, but it would provide a starting point or a framework on which to build a plan. He said, "Yes, sir."

"Get out of here now. I don't want to see your face around here for a while and I'll consider what the ramifications of your trip are."

Smith saluted. "Yes, sir. Thank you, sir."

CHAPTER 3

Kapitan Aleksei Petrov stood in the shade of the only two-story building on the camp and was still uncomfortable. He had grown up in a small village near Murmansk and was used to cold weather. He despised the hot, humid weather of the jungles. It made his skin itch, made him sweat heavily, and oppressed him because there were no relief in sight. Had he known that he would be sent into southern Laos to train the locals, he would have avoided the Spetsnaz altogether. He thought the Spetsnaz was an elite unit and that the missions would be of high value and high risk. Now, he was in Laos on a training mission that didn't seem to fit with the overall mission of the Spetsnaz.

He had arrived two weeks earlier, with the rest of his team of eleven men. Only four of them could speak the local language. They had collected, which is to say, they had abducted two hundred military age men from the surrounding countryside to form the first of the company of freedom fighters who would then train others until they had a battalion-sized force.

Now, he had surrendered his Soviet Army uniform for the jungle fatigues favored by the Americans in South Vietnam. He carried a Colt 1911A1 ACP in .45 caliber, attached to web gear of American manufacture. He wore the black jungle boots with the green nylon inserts, along with what the American soldiers called a boonie hat. Because he was tall with blue eyes, he could pass as an American soldier if he wasn't required to engage in a long conversation in English.

He watched as the recruits were lined up in platoon formation. They were not wearing uniforms, but the clothing they had brought with them. These men, boys really, were short and thin, with jet-black hair and skin tanned brown by the tropical sun. The formation was ragtag, and they were in various states of standing at attention, none of it quite right. They had been freedom fighters for three weeks and hadn't adapted to their new life in the military.

Leytenant Grigoriy Fedorov walked up. He was a shorter but more robust man who was dressed the same way but carried an M-16 rather than an AK-47. He stopped next to Petrov and said, "They don't look much like soldiers."

"No, they don't. But the Americans have made good soldiers from villages in the South. I don't know why these men would be any worse."

"What's on the training schedule?"

Petrov shrugged. "Major Semenov has not confided that in me. He briefed the NCOs and made it clear that he wanted to see progress. It's been a couple of weeks."

"Maybe conscription isn't the answer."

Petrov turned and looked into Fedorov's eyes. "These men are volunteers. You would be wise to remember that."

"Yes, sir. I just meant that there was no real warning about the changes we were about to introduce to their lives. There might be some resistance to that."

"We're dealing with peasants here. They live in huts without electricity. They don't live in the twentieth century. They have never held a weapon, driven a car or listened to the radio. We must teach then everything." Petrov stopped, realizing that he had said more than he should have to a junior officer.

Changing the subject, Fedorov said, "Sure is hot."

"I'm not interested in discussing the weather with you, Leytenant. Don't you have something you need to do?"

"No, sir. Not yet."

"Then find something," said Petrov. "Do it now, before I report you to the major and let him provide you with guidance."

Fedorov turned and walked back to the sandbagged hut that was the operations center. It had a field generator sitting outside it, but the generator was quiet. Sunlight could illuminate the interior and they wouldn't need to use the radios or other equipment until later in the day.

Petrov was still standing in the shade watching the formation when Major Leonid Semenov walked up. Petrov came to attention, but he didn't salute. They tried to avoid that in the field because it tended to identify the officers for any sniper who might be around. Petrov didn't expect a sniper, but it didn't hurt to be cautious. Besides, he wasn't convinced that Semenov had been through all the training demanded of those assigned to Spetsnaz.

"Good morning, Major."

"Good morning, Aleksei."

Semenov was a shorter man, with a barrel chest, short legs and huge, almost deformed hands. Petrov sometimes wondered if he had been assembled by parts left over. He looked that strange.

He was wearing American-made jungle fatigues, but they had been tailored so they fit better than those of the other Soviet soldiers. On his collar was the yellow oak leaf of an American major and the crossed rifles of the American infantry. Petrov knew that the insignia were incorrect. The Americans had switched over to black and dark gold years earlier. The mistake would reveal Semenov for the imposter that he was, if confronted by American forces, but the odds of that happening approached zero. Petrov said nothing about the error.

"Have you thought about a patrol or two?" asked Semenov.

"The men aren't ready for anything that complicated. They are having trouble with close-order drill and there is still some resentment among them. They believe it is unfair that they have been brought here."

"What do you plan to do about that?"

Petrov shrugged. "Communication is the key, but we only have four men who speak their language and none of them speak Russian. They have been isolated here for their entire lives. I'm not even sure they know that there is a war being fought for control of the region."

"The Americans seem to be able to communicate with their allies in the South, regardless of language."

"Yes, sir. But their mission is different than that of ours. We are a quick strike force working behind the enemy lines and creating chaos. They are training an army."

Semenov waved a hand to indicate the local soldiers in front of them. "That is our mission here. A company, then a battalion and eventually a brigade."

"But that should be the mission of someone else. Not Spetsnaz. It should be the mission of the Army and not us. We are not trained for this sort of activity."

"Your mission here, is to create the cadre necessary to build a fighting force. Are you incapable of that?"

Petrov saw the trap immediately. He could be pulled from the field and assigned to something else, or he could be sent for reeducation and end up in prison for disobeying his orders. He said, "No, sir. I'm just suggesting that our time could be better spent on raids into South Vietnam and Cambodia and the training of these men could be conducted by regular army units."

"Is that your only complaint, Kapitan?"

"I don't mean to be critical, Major. I just worry about many things."

"Such as?"

"The camp is not easily defended. The arrangement of the structures does not allow for mutual support in the event of attack. There is no berm around us and no concertina wire to inhibit enemy attack."

Semenov sighed and spoke slowly, as if to a child. "This is a secret installation, hidden from American spy planes. To change the village significantly, to add berm and wire would alert the Americans to our presence here. Our defense is based on the loyalty of the Laotian government and the neutrality of the country."

"Still, I find it disturbing that we are not establishing a defensive perimeter."

"If there is something that you think we need, you are encouraged to submit the proposal to me. But remember, we don't want anything that would be obvious from the air."

"I'll give it some thought, Major."

Semenov pulled a white handkerchief from his rear pocket and wiped the sweat from his face. "It is getting hot around here," he said. "It's cooler in the communications hut."

He stood quietly for a moment. "And with an eye to your concern, I would think that daylight patrols into the jungle around here would be a defensive move. Find the enemy away from here, if there is any enemy to find. You might want to lead one of those yourself."

Although said in the form of a suggestion, Petrov knew it was an order. The major was punishing him for suggesting that Spetsnaz soldiers should be used in a different mission.

"Certainly, sir," Petrov said. "I'll get with the NCOs and put together a patrol."

"You are dismissed," said Semenov, though it wasn't necessary for him to say that. He was reminding Petrov who was in charge.

Petrov turned and walked toward the formation. Sergeant Mikhail Volkov was standing behind the formation, watching as two other NCOs worked their way among the recruits. Volkov was the youngest of the Soviet Spetsnaz assigned to the training mission. He was thin but muscular, had light hair, blue eyes and stood just over six feet tall. He had an M-16 slung over his shoulder, and like the other Soviets, wore an American-made pistol belt holding a Colt 1911A1. Though he would never say it, he believed that the Colt was a superior weapon to the Soviet-manufactured handguns. He preferred the Kalashnikov AK-47 to the M-16. It was a thirty-caliber weapon, designated as 7.62mm while the M-16 at 5.56 was only slightly larger than a child's twenty-two. He believed the larger and heavier bullet would put down an enemy more effectively than the lighter M-16 bullet.

As Petrov approached, Volkov came to attention but didn't salute. He waited quietly. He was frightened by officers, even those he knew. Officers, in his limited experience, always meant bad news.

Petrov asked, "What is your assessment of these soldiers?"

Volkov was surprised by the question. He assumed that officers had all the answers and that was why they were officers. He took a deep breath and said, "They are learning."

"Anyone stand out?"

"What do you mean?"

"Has anyone shown a natural talent for soldiering. Anyone shown to be a good shot or understand the basics of small unit tactics."

"Well, sir, there are a couple who seem to be natural leaders. I noticed that the others looked to them when they had questions."

"Here's the problem, Sergeant. Tomorrow morning, you and I will be taking a patrol out. I believe this to be more of a training mission than an actual search for the enemy. However, it will give us an opportunity to study the capabilities of several of the soldiers. You should prepare a list of ten soldiers who you believe will benefit from this training."

Volkov rubbed his eyes as if the sun was bothering him. "How long will we be in the field?"

"I'll have the operations order in about an hour. Basic load of ammo, canteen, one field meal. We'll be back no later than dusk."

"Yes, sir."

"We'll also need one of the NCOs who speak the language. Let me know who you think will be the best man for that job."

Although Petrov didn't expect an answer, Volkov said, "I believe Sergeant Sidorov communicates with the soldiers the best, sir. They seem to understand what he wants them to do and follows his orders."

"You've seen this?"

Volkov waved a hand at the formation. Sidorov was walking among them, shouting his displeasure at them. When he stopped in front of one of the soldiers, said something, there was an immediate reply. Although Petrov didn't understand what was said, it was clear that both Sidorov and the soldier understood one another.

"I'll be in the operations hut. Have Sergeant Sidorov report to me when he finishes his instructions."

"Yes, sir."

Petrov stood for a moment, his hand up, shading his eyes, watching Sidorov as he continued to provide instruction. Finally, he turned and walked toward the operations hut.

The members of the patrol were sitting in the shade of two of the huts which, in theory, would have prevented photographs from high-flying spy planes revealing the armed men. Sergeant Ilya Sidorov was standing just inside the doorway of the hut. He was looking up, into the bright blue sky as if looking for one of those spy planes, though there was no way that Sidorov could have seen one of those spy planes, even if there was one flying over.

Sidorov was nearly thirty, had served first in an armor division but wasn't as mechanically inclined as he could have been. He didn't like the claustrophobic nature of being inside a tank. He had read, as a youngster, the stirring accounts of the massive tank battles as the Germans invaded the Soviet Union. He had thought, at the time, nothing could be better than being assigned as a tank commander.

But older and climbing into the cramped interior of the modern battle tank, Sidorov realized that it was not something he could do. He had gone to the first sergeant and mentioned that his father had been assigned to the Soviet embassy in Laos and that he, Sidorov, had learned the language. He couldn't speak it like a native, but he was fluent enough to make himself understood. He could read and write the language. He wondered if there might be a way to use his skill.

The first sergeant had shrugged, as if he didn't care and wished that Sidorov would just go away. Sidorov returned to his unit and continued his training in the tank. He was using car wax on the exterior, shining the green painted metal to a glow for an upcoming parade to display the might of the Soviet Union. The company clerk approached, said nothing but handed Sidorov a stack of orders. He was to report to the Spetsnaz training camp outside of Moscow.

There he learned other skills and he was subjected to an intense language program where his ability to speak Laotian was improved. When training was completed, he was assigned to a special unit that learned more about the Laotian culture, the country and the people. While he didn't understand the purpose of the training, he was glad to be out of the tank division.

He lowered his eyes and saw that Kapitan Petrov was walking toward him. He was followed by Sergeant Volkov. Both were wearing their American jungle fatigues, carrying M-16s, and were equipped with American web gear that included both canteens and first-aid kits. Petrov had two American hand grenades wired to the shoulder straps of his web gear. Sidorov knew that was more for show than necessity. They would not be engaged in any combat operations.

He stepped out of the shadow, spoke quietly to the men around him who all stood up. When Petrov got close, Sidorov said, "Good morning, sir. We're ready."

"You've briefed them on this mission?"

"Yes, sir."

"Then let's get this show on the road. Sergeant Volkov will take point with one of the Laotians shadowing him. You'll need to be near the center to pass along instructions and I'll bring up the rear."

Sidorov turned, facing the Laotians and told them to check their equipment and prepare to move out. He assigned one man to stick with Volkov and one to stay with Petrov. He then pointed to a spot in the jungle only about fifty meters from the edge of the hut. They would be exposed in the open for the shortest time, though he didn't believe there was anyone to see them.

Rather than crossing the open area quickly, Sidorov walked out into the bright sunlight and glanced up into the deep blue of the sky. There was no sign of aircraft overhead. No vapor trails and no sound. If there was an airplane over them, it was so high as to be invisible.

Sidorov didn't use hand signals but shouted at the Laotians, telling them what he wanted as he walked along one of the rice paddy dikes. He knew that in South Vietnam, there might be a land mine, or a booby trap hidden there. He knew that American and South Vietnamese soldiers avoided the dikes when possible.

Looking back, over his shoulder, he saw that the rest of the patrol were following, now outside of the cover of the cluster of huts. He reached the jungle and halted for a moment. The patrol was disciplined, spread out five or ten feet apart, their heads swiveling right and left as if searching for signs of an enemy ambush.

Once the majority of the patrol was in the jungle, he stepped off, following a game trail. That was something he would have avoided in a real combat environment. The enemy, and North Vietnamese and the VC, sometimes arranged mechanical ambushes on the trails. It could be something as simple as a grenade anchored by a tree, with a pin partially pulled attached to a thin cord. If someone walked by and caught the cord on his shoe, the cord would tighten, the pin would be pulled, and the grenade would detonate. The trouble with mechanical ambushes was that civilians and larger animals could trip them and that was bad in a public relations aspect. It caused the civilians to distrust the military.

Sidorov kept the pace slow because of the heat and humidity and because it reduced the noise made by the soldiers. Patrolling in enemy territory required noise discipline, something that the Laotians had been told repeatedly but not understood. Both Petrov and Volkov could make the soldiers near them understand the need to be as quiet as possible. Following the rules here, in training and in the safe environment of Laos, it wasn't as important as it would be in South Vietnam. It did, however, teach the recruits the importance of noise discipline.

After an hour, still deep in the dim green of the triple canopy jungle, Sidorov raised his arm to halt the patrol. He turned and watched as the men dropped to a knee, facing in opposite directions so that no one could sneak up on the patrol. They had moved off the path, using the bushes and trees for cover. It wasn't perfect, but it provided some concealment.

Petrov left his position in the center of the patrol and leaned close to Sidorov, keeping his voice low. "I'm impressed with these guys."

"These were the first we recruited. They've had about six weeks of training before you got here…"

Sidorov trailed off and stared out, to the right. He cocked his head as if listening intently, then moved rapidly toward the rear of the patrol. He found one of the men sitting on the ground. Sidorov kicked him in the side and grabbed at the man's right hand. He pulled the cigarette from it, burning himself on the glowing ember.

"That is the quickest way to get us all killed," he hissed. He threw the cigarette at the man's chest and watched as it bounced off. "At night, the glow of a cigarette can be seen for miles over open territory. An astute enemy will smell the burning tobacco from a long way off which gives away your position. While you're smoking, he's creeping up on you to slit your throat. Give me all your cigarettes."

The man still sat on the ground, rubbing his side where he had been kicked. He stared up at Sidorov who held out a hand. When the man didn't move fast enough, Sidorov kicked him again, but not as hard. The man tried to scramble away, but Sidorov followed, still holding out his hand. Finally understanding, the man surrendered the cigarettes and watched as Sidorov shredded them slowly.

Petrov, who had watched the whole exchange, asked, "That happen often?"

"Not as often as it did before. They're beginning to understand what patrolling is all about."

"Shouldn't we get moving?" asked Petrov.

"If you say so, sir."

"It's your patrol, I'm just observing."

Sidorov walked back to the point and then switched the man who had been with him with another. The idea was to get everyone some experience on point.

They continued on, now four of five klicks from their base. They reached the edge of the jungle that opened into rice paddies with farmers' huts scattered around. It wasn't exactly a village, but just a cluster of huts made of mud and straw.

Sidorov crouched on one knee and leaned against the huge trunk of a tree. He held his weapon in his right hand, the barrel pointed up, into the sky. In front of him was a scene that bothered him and then he realized the problem. There were no people around. There were rice paddies to be tended and there was smoke from a cooking fire, but there were no people. The only living creature he could see was a water buffalo tethered to a pole near one of the huts.

When Petrov and Volkov joined him, he said, "This is the end point of the patrol. From here we return to our camp, using a different route, of course."

"Where are the people?" Petrov asked. "There should be people."

"That bothers me, too," said Sidorov.

Then, suddenly, there was a ripping sound of an M-16 on full automatic. It came from the right and Sidorov looked in that direction but couldn't see who had fired. The water buffalo stood from a moment and then toppled over.

"Find the man who fired," ordered Petrov.

Sidorov was on his feet but hesitated until he remembered this was a training exercise. There were no Americans or South Vietnamese anywhere near him. He shouted, in Laotian, "Who fired? Who fired?"

He reached the end of the line and said, "Tell me who fired, or I will begin to count rounds. Whoever fired will be short." And then he spotted the brass near one of the men. These were the ejected cartridges and Sidorov knew who had fired. He stepped close to the man, grabbed his rifle from him and then hit him with the butt.

The man fell back, a hand to the side of his head and a look of hate on his face. He reached to his side and pulled his combat knife.

Sidorov just laughed. "You think you're going to win a fight with me?" He dropped the man's rifle to the jungle floor and then chambered a round in his own. "You make a move toward me and you're a dead man." He stared at the man.

There was a sound behind him, but Sidorov did not look to see who it was. He said, in Laotian, "Hold your position or you're next."

Petrov said, "I don't know what you said, but I have your back here."

The man on the ground took his hand away from his knife but he didn't look away.

"I'm not going to lecture you here," said Sidorov, "but when we get back to camp, I'll explain in great and painful detail what you have done."

Petrov said, "Maybe we should get moving."

"Yes, sir. At the double. Let's run these guys into the ground so that they all understand that they work as a unit and the punishment for the offender will be spread among them all."

"Maybe you should have shot him on the spot," said Petrov.

"I thought about it, sir, but it might be counterproductive. I thought it might be best if some night soon he just disappeared."

Petrov didn't comment. He just turned and walked back to what had been his position with the patrol. He wasn't looking forward to the long jog back. He understood the reason and knew that he, along with both Volkov and Sidorov, would be able to do it.

CHAPTER 4

Sergeant Major Anthony Fetterman stood on the northeastern side of the Song Be Special Forces Camp staring into the jungle. He held a beer in one hand, had his M-16 hanging from his right shoulder and was wearing a Colt 1911A1 ACP in a holster attached to his web gear. He and Gerber had been at the camp for a couple of days.

Fetterman said, "I think it's about time that we headed back to Nha Trang, sir. There really isn't much more for us to do here."

Gerber was armed in much the same way as Fetterman but held a Pepsi instead of a beer and had a second-generation starlight scope with him rather than his rifle. "I'm thinking of this as something of an R and R, Tony. We're away from the grind in Nha Trang without someone breathing down our neck. The best part is that we set our own schedule."

Standing next to Gerber was the A-Team leader, Captain Martin, who also held a beer and was wearing a pistol, but had left his M-16 in his hootch. He was listening to Gerber and Fetterman.

"We could be doing the same thing in Saigon, where there are more opportunities for entertainment," said Fetterman.

"If you can think of an excuse for us to be there, then we can head off to Saigon in the morning," said Gerber.

Fetterman grinned. "I can supply all sorts of reasons that we need to go to Saigon. We can confer with MACV-SOG for one thing. We could ask for a briefing from the theater intelligence officer, which will help us formulate our strategies for the next several months. We could pretend that we needed to be there and head downtown."

Before Gerber could respond, Fetterman pointed and said, "There. Did you see the flash?" He added, unnecessarily, "Incoming."

The round fell short, detonating in the wire on the northside of the camp. There was a second pop followed by a third.

"Maybe we should head to the bunker," suggested Martin.

Gerber had leaned forward so that he was partially protected by the berm. He raised the starlight scope. "I don't think we need to. That's a 60mm mortar…"

"Which can kill you just as quick as a grenade or rifle shot," said Fetterman, grinning.

"It's just more of the harassing fire that Captain Martin talked about."

Ignoring that, Martin asked, "You have it spotted?"

Fetterman pointed toward the tree line. "Maybe five hundred meters away."

"My exec should have called for countermortar, but the gun team is too far away. Be fifteen or twenty minutes before they can get here."

"What about your mortar teams?"

At that moment one of the mortars fired. Gerber glanced toward the mortar pit that was barely visible inside the redoubt. He then looked back at the jungle. He saw the detonation and said, "You're about a hundred short and fifty to the right."

There was a second round and then a third fired by the team's mortar crew. The rounds walked toward the spot where the enemy had set up his mortar. There had only been three rounds and nothing more.

"I think we're clear. They just blew up some wire," said Martin. "The exec did a nice job of getting the rounds on target."

"I think we need to patrol that area tomorrow," Gerber said. "Get a fix on that location."

"We've mapped the area," said Martin. "I've marked the most likely spots for them to set up. But it really doesn't take much time to set up a sixty-millimeter mortar and then break it down. Three or four minutes."

"Have you registered the spots? Make your countermortar more effective," said Fetterman. "And you can coordinate with the arty at the fire support bases around here to put some heavier stuff on them."

"We've tried to anticipate their placement, but they don't need much in the way of a clearing. Makes the registration difficult." Martin grinned. "What I keep hoping is that one of their rounds will hit the branches of one of the trees and explode, killing them."

"Not much chance of that happening," said Gerber.

"No. But it would be rather funny."

Gerber said, "Tony, you want to take a patrol out there and see what you can find?"

"Some time in the morning?"

"I would think that would be best. I doubt they have set up an ambush, but why risk it."

Martin said, "I'll get with the team sergeant, and we'll have a patrol ready at first light."

"That sounds good, sir," said Fetterman. "I'd like your heavy weapons guy, and Sergeant Davis, to go with us."

"Not a problem," said Martin.

"If I'm going patrolling tomorrow," said Fetterman, "I'd better get some rest."

Grinning, Gerber asked, "You entertained now, Sergeant Major?"

"No, sir, but then I'm not bored either."

Sitting in the team house, just before dawn, Gerber was eating a breakfast of fresh scrambled eggs, a thick slab of ham and orange juice that had been made from a powdered mix. It wasn't bad orange juice. It was cold, but it just didn't have the flavor of fresh squeezed or even frozen concentrate.

Fetterman entered carrying his M-16 and wearing his web gear. He dropped into a chair opposite Gerber. "I don't think I like the idea of this patrol," he said without preamble.

Gerber put down his fork. "Getting old, Sergeant Major?"

"I thought that was obvious, Major, but no. I don't see the purpose. The tube will be gone, the enemy will be gone, and we'll learn nothing of importance."

"I will assume here, risking the cliché, that you have an alternative plan?"

"Why, yes, sir, I do. I'm thinking we could recon the area by helicopter. We could cover more ground faster and we wouldn't be at risk of an ambush."

"But we don't have a helicopter," said Gerber, picking up the glass of orange juice.

"I checked with their ops guy, and we made a request. Seems we can get a single bird in here in a couple of hours."

Now Gerber grinned. "Let me guess the rest of it. You believe that the local team can handle any patrol without your guidance."

"Yes, sir. Davis is a good man. Knows his stuff and this isn't his first tour. I've talked to a couple of other guys. I'm a little surprised I don't really know them, but the Special Forces has expanded so much that there are probably a great many of the new guys I don't know."

"But you think they're competent enough to run this patrol."

"They are, but I'm not sure the patrol is necessary. If Charlie knew what he was doing, there'd be nothing for us to find. It doesn't take much to carry off the tube, base, and anything else they brought with them."

"Well, it's not my job to tell Captain Martin what to do. If you don't think you'll learn anything by going out with the patrol and would rather ride around in the back of a helicopter, who am I to dissuade you?"

Fetterman looked over at the Vietnamese soldier who was standing near the stove. He wore tiger-striped pants, a white T-shirt and what looked to be a chef's hat. Fetterman raised a hand, and the man came over.

"You want breakfast now?"

"Same same as the major."

"Yes, Sergeant."

Gerber resumed eating. "We really aren't doing much here, are we?"

"No, sir. We understand what is happening and why Martin hasn't been able to suppress the mortar fire. But then, it's not very accurate mortar fire so it's really not all that important. We understand what was in that incident report."

Martin walked in, signaled the cook, and then sat down at the table with Gerber and Fetterman. "Good morning."

Fetterman nodded and Gerber said, "Good morning."

"Sergeant Major, I understand you conferred with my ops people this morning about a helicopter?"

"Yes, sir. I hope that I haven't stepped on any toes."

"Not at all. Just wondered about it."

The cook arrived with Fetterman's food and with a bowl of cereal, a plate of toast, and a cup of coffee for Martin. Martin said, "Thank you, Tran."

"After thinking about it, I thought it would be more effective to fly over the area for a quick recon."

"You aren't suggesting that I cancel the patrol?"

"No, sir. That's up to you. I thought that Major Gerber and I might be able to see something from the air that had escaped those on the ground."

Martin took a sip of the coffee and turned in his chair. "Tran, this stuff is terrible. Put on a new pot."

"Yes, sir."

"Then you wouldn't mind my accompanying you on the flight?"

"No, sir. Probably is a good idea."

Gerber, having finished eating, pushed his plate to the side and drained the last of the orange juice. He said, "The sergeant major meant no offense, Captain. I will note that we did drop in because of the incident reports and wondered what was happening. I can't think of much I would do to stop the harassment. Anything too extreme would only offend the local population."

Martin rubbed his face, as if he had just gotten out of bed. "I think I might have given the wrong impression here. I was just curious about the change in plan is all. Besides, I'm always looking for a good excuse to take a flight around here."

"Well, as I say, sir, never walk when you can ride and never ride when you can fly. You shouldn't walk through Vietnam when you can fly over it."

The patrol gathered at the north gate, spread out just in case of enemy action. Sergeant First Class David Williams, the Song

Be team's heavy weapons specialist, crouched near the gate and was inspecting his equipment before moving into the field. The rest of the patrol, made up of the local, indigenous soldiers, were waiting to move out.

Williams was twenty-eight, stood just over six feet tall and was stocky, more muscular than fat. He had dark hair cut short, but it was almost hidden by his green beret. Like the other soldiers, both American and local, he wore tiger-striped fatigues. The only way to tell him from those soldiers was that he was much larger than any of them.

Williams then walked over to where Davis waited, and asked, "Is there something else that we should be doing?"

Davis shrugged. "I don't know what it would be."

"Then we're ready to go."

"I'll fall in at the rear of the patrol," said Davis. "If I spot something, I'll let you know."

Williams said, "Okay. Here we go."

He walked to the gate, turned, looked at the soldiers, and then waved them forward. He pointed to one of the men and said, in Vietnamese, "Take the point. Head straight to the jungle, at those four tall trees."

The man nodded, and then worked his way through the wire. Once through, he headed straight for the trees. He was followed by the others, who had spread out and who were looking right and left, searching for the enemy. The open area, known as the killing zone, extending some five hundred meters from the camp, had been cut down so that the vegetation was only ankle high.

Davis fell in with the last couple of soldiers. He saw nothing that would suggest any enemy were nearby. He was certain that their path to the jungle would be clear. He had been up early, searching the jungle with binoculars for any sign of movement that would indicate anyone was out there. Those who had fired the mortar rounds the night before, were long gone, along with their mortar tube.

The local soldiers seemed to know what they were doing, watching all around and carrying their weapons as if they were needed instantly rather than looking like hunters on a casual stroll through the woods.

After an hour, Williams called a halt. Half the soldiers formed a perimeter while the other half sat down, drank from their canteens and relaxed. After ten minutes the roles were reversed. Once everyone had an opportunity to rest, they began again, but Williams switched the point with those who had been in the center of the patrol.

They stayed off the trails, both human and animal, had flankers out, and a rear guard that would provide warning if attacked from that angle. The pace was slow but steady in the humidity and heat of the jungle. Although he, along with the other Green Berets were sweating heavily in the environment, the Vietnamese were adapted to the climate. They hadn't grown up in a world that was periodically cold with snow and ice. They didn't have air-conditioning and didn't have the electricity to run it even if they had an air conditioner.

They halted again but this wasn't a rest break. Williams moved forward to the point and found Davis crouched there. There was a wide place in the jungle that had a narrow opening to the sky. Williams recognized the situation. He was looking at a rocket-launching site, set up for an attack. Of course, the launching apparatus was two thick poles crossed to hold up the rocket. Given the location, the opening in the jungle canopy, and the orientation of the poles, the likely target was the Special Forces camp at Song Be.

Williams stood and was about to walk forward.

"Halt," said Davis. "This could be a trap."

Williams dropped to one knee and looked at Davis, who said, "They might have set this up as a mechanical ambush. They'd know that the farmers wouldn't go near it, but soldiers, especially those in the camp, would be inclined to rush forward to destroy it."

Williams said, "I think we have a training opportunity here. Let's see how Minh or one of the other NCOs handles this."

"Okay," said Davis, "but let's not take any chances."

Williams looked back, spotted Minh kneeling to the right, facing into the jungle, searching for the enemy. It was a standard tactic that the Vietnamese sometimes overlooked. He walked toward him and said, "Sergeant Minh, why don't you take charge of the situation here. What do you think we should do?"

Minh stood up, looked at the distribution of the patrol. He said, quietly, "We have security established. A rocket-launching site is rather primitive." He thought for a moment and then said, "I would leave it intact, but I would rig a mechanical ambush."

"Wouldn't you be afraid of farmers, or any of the local population accidentally tripping such an ambush?"

"I believe the locals would stay away from the site. They would know that the VC are in the area, and this is something they created. They would be afraid to get near it. They would be afraid of the VC."

"What, exactly, would you do, Sergeant?"

Minh crouched down and examined the area. There were only two of the "X's" set there and nothing more. The VC would be bringing in the rockets to launch. In fact, if they knew what they were doing, they could set it up so that the rockets would launch thirty minutes or an hour after they left the area. The rockets had no guidance system. They were aimed in the general area with the hope that they would hit the camp and do damage. It was just as likely that the rockets would land nowhere near the camp.

"Conceal grenades in locations where they would be bumped. Pins pulled with the safety levers held in place against the ground. Somewhere near the launching point." Now he grinned. "With any luck, the grenade would detonate and destroy the rocket. Big win for us."

Williams said, "Get it done."

"Yes, Sergeant."

Davis, who had been standing nearby said, "Bright guy that Minh. Wonder why he isn't an officer."

"No political connection. We'll have to work something."

Davis looked at his watch and then glanced up into the sky. It was nearly noon and would take two or three hours to return to the camp. They hadn't found much in the way of locations for a mortar crew to set up and he just found the rocket-launching point to be more of a joke than a military tactic.

"Let's take a break here, have our lunch, and then work our way back to the camp."

Williams nodded and gave orders to the Vietnamese. He then said, "This hasn't accomplished much."

"Other than we see how well trained our strike force is."

Williams grinned. "Well, it was something to do."

The helicopter pilot contacted the communications hootch at the camp and said that they were inbound, about ten minutes out. The communications NCO acknowledged the call and asked, "Do you want smoke?"

"I think I can find a camp in a large open field without benefit of smoke." The sarcasm was obvious.

"Roger. No smoke."

Staff Sergeant Derek Willis left the communications hootch, heading for the team house. Willis was on his first tour in Vietnam and felt fortunate that he had the opportunity. Clearly, President Nixon was winding down American participation in the war and American troop levels were being reduced. Willis knew that a combat tour with the Special Forces would look good on his record.

He worried about his record because he had not been an outstanding soldier. He barely made it through his "Q" course, and had he not been a HAM radio operator while in high school, he suspected he wouldn't have made it at all. But he *had* made it and his orders for Vietnam had come through quickly, as a replacement for the Communications NCO at Song Be who had been sent home because of bleeding ulcers.

He found Captain Martin, along with Gerber and Fetterman, relaxing in the team house. He interrupted the conversation and announced, "Have the helicopter about ten out."

"Thanks, Derek."

Martin stood and said, "Why don't we go out to the helipad?"

Gerber nodded and grabbed his web gear and weapon. "Right behind you."

As they reached the gate, they could hear the approaching helicopter. It came from the south and landed in a blowing cloud of red dust and loose debris. Once sitting on the skids, the whirlwind of rotor wash dissipated, the pilot looked out at the welcoming party. Martin sliced a finger across his throat and the pilot nodded, shutting down the engine.

The aircraft commander and the co-pilot climbed out of the cockpit. One was a warrant officer and the other a first lieutenant. The warrant officer looked as if he belonged in high school rather than flying a Huey in Vietnam.

Martin stepped forward. "Welcome. I thought we'd talk about the mission before we take off. Give you an idea of what we want to do."

The warrant officer, whose last name was Russell, turned and said, "Tom, take a quick look around and then relax. We probably won't be more than ten minutes."

Tom said, "Sure."

They walked through the gate and headed for the team house. Martin took charge once they were inside. "Before we get started, does anyone want something to drink?"

Russell said, "I'm good.

The others followed his lead. Martin then spread a map out on the table, looked at the first lieutenant, whose name tag said "Gaines," pointed to an area to the north and east of the camp. "We're looking for anywhere the VC might be able set up a mortar tube, a rocket launcher and clearings that we can use for landing zones."

Gaines said, "You need to talk to Russell. He's the aircraft commander."

Martin looked at Russell and snapped, "How old are you?"

"Old enough to be the aircraft commander," only slightly annoyed by the question.

"I don't understand."

Russell sighed. "AC status is based, not on rank or age, but on time in-country, number of hours, and skill as a pilot. Lieutenant Gaines has been in-country for about two months and has two hundred and twenty hours. I have been here eight months and have nearly eight hundred hours, of which five hundred is as an aircraft commander."

"I'm sorry," said Martin, "but you look as if you should be in high school."

"Eighteen months ago, I was in high school," said Russell. "I met the requirements for warrant officer candidate flight training, completed that training and was sent to Vietnam immediately. As I said, I have met all the requirements and training and am an aircraft commander…"

Fetterman was barely able to conceal his grin. "I believe that we can assume that Mister Russell is a competent pilot."

Russell looked directly at Fetterman. "I'm better than competent. I'm fucking amazing."

Gerber laughed out loud. "Thank you, Russell. Captain Martin?"

"I apologize," said Martin, "I didn't mean to question your ability. I was just struck by how young you look."

"Age doesn't translate to competence," said Russell. "We have one lieutenant who has been here for six months and still has not made AC. He is good as a peter pilot but just has trouble being the aircraft commander."

"I think we've lost the train here," said Gerber. "Captain Martin, you were pointing out areas of interest?"

Martin pointed at the map and said, "There is a cluster of hootches in this area. There is VC in there, so we need to stay away from them…"

"Why not take them out?" asked Russell.

"Because there are more civilians than enemy fighters. We know they're there, armed with old Japanese rifles and an SKS or two. They don't pose a threat to us, so we leave them alone."

"Propaganda value," said Fetterman.

Martin rubbed a hand over his head. "Really not much. Sure, we could take them out, but I think that would create more bad blood than is necessary. The farmers there have pointed out booby traps to us, though I suspect we would have spotted them anyway. It's sort of a wash."

"We could fly over and take a quick look," said Gerber.

"I don't see the point, Major. It's really a situation where they don't bother us."

"They could be gathering intel on you here."

"They're too far away to do that."

"Okay," said Gerber. "That's your call."

They spent the next fifteen minutes looking over the map and plotting the flight path. Martin provided information about what he wanted to know and both Fetterman and Gerber added to that. Russell didn't say much, just nodding and of all of them, Gaines was the quietest.

"I think we've got it," said Russell. "We'll go crank the aircraft and be ready to take off in five or six minutes."

"Preflight?" asked Gerber.

"Done before we left the base camp. Crew chief gave it the once over after we shut down here. We're good."

Once the pilots were gone, Fetterman laughed and asked, "How old do you think Russell is?"

"Certainly no more than twenty," said Gerber, "and he might be nineteen."

"Is that possible?" asked Martin.

"Right out of high school and right into flight school. I wouldn't be at all surprised. Those warrant officer pilots are all on the young side. Early twenties and no more than twenty-four or twenty-five. Army thought that high school grads would make good pilots."

"Well, I suppose if he's survived eight months here, he must be doing something right," said Fetterman.

They had flown over half a dozen clearings and open spots in the jungle. There had been nothing interesting in any of them. Russell mentioned that it was not a good idea to fly over the same place too often. If there was someone below them, repeated overflights gave the VC time to respond.

They were nearing a cluster of hootches. It wasn't really a village, just seven hootches all built near one another without any discernible pattern. There was a pen for a water buffalo, a pen for hogs and what looked to be a well. The vegetation was beaten down and red, bare ground was visible where the grass had been worn away. There were no rice paddies nearby.

Although it was just afternoon when they flew over, there was no sign of people and no smoke from cooking fires. They would have thought it was deserted if it had not been for the hootches. They looked to be well kept with no sign of decay.

Gerber was about to suggest they make a low-level pass when there was a ripping sound. He knew that it was an AK-47.

The aircraft banked to the right and dived for the treetops. As they skimmed over the trees and away from the hootches, they began a rapid climb to fifteen hundred feet.

Russell began to orbit south of the hootches, out of sight of them. Over the intercom, he said, "Ask one of those guys what they want to do."

Gerber's voice came back, the door gunner having loaned him his helmet. "What do you recommend?"

"Depends on what you want to do. We can just fly off. Nothing hit the aircraft and I didn't see anyone on the ground. Just heard the shots. Or we can fly back over and let the door gunners attempt to engage."

"Let me talk with Captain Martin."

"Time is of the essence here, sir."

A moment later Gerber said, "We have the location marked on the map. I'm thinking that Martin might send a patrol out later to look around."

"Yes, sir." It was clear from the tone of his voice, even filtered through the intercom, that he was disappointed.

Russell asked, "Either of you see where that fire came from?"

"No, sir," said the crew chief. "I didn't see a thing."

Martin said, "Let's head to the camp. I can get a patrol out there."

"It'll be dark before the patrol can get there," said Fetterman. "Whoever fired at us will either be long gone or have hidden his weapon by the time a patrol can get there."

"Then we're done here?" asked Russell.

Martin said, "Yeah. Let's head for the barn."

Gerber and Fetterman, along with Martin and his team, were gathered in the team house. Both Williams and Davis were there to describe what they had found during their patrol.

Williams said, "I think we need to point out that neither Davis nor I provided anything more than basic instructions. The striker NCOs were in charge and led the patrol."

"How'd they do?" Martin asked.

"It was textbook. Proper spacing, flankers out, rear guard, point and slack. Kept their heads on a swivel, and when it was time for a break, half remained alert and they switched out without any trouble."

Gerber interrupted. "Would you be confident that they would perform that well without members of your team there for guidance?"

"The NCOs know what they're doing, sir. They all get a passing grade in marksmanship. They all have the basic skills.

We have outstanding strikers here and they are taking over the leadership positions. They're very good, sir."

Martin, holding a can of beer, said, "Continue."

Williams mentioned the length of the patrol and that he sometimes felt that he was micromanaging the situation. "I would say something to one of the NCOs, but he had already thought of it."

Gerber grinned at Fetterman and said, "Sergeant Major, I think we need to arrange a flight to Saigon in the morning."

"You mean our work here is done?"

"I can't think of a thing that Martin and his team could do to alter the situation without seriously destroying any rapport he had with the locals."

Fetterman shrugged. "I think I need another beer, then."

CHAPTER 5

Although Kapitan Aleksei Petrov had overseen the creation of the rifle range just east of the camp, he was unaware of several flaws in the design. The range, facing the north, looked to be set on level ground. The land dropped away so gently that it looked level but was not. When standing at the firing positions, it was impossible to detect the slope down toward a small stream.

There was also a flaw in the measured distances to the targets. The first target was only five meters short of the hundred-meter range. At the five-hundred-meter range, the difference was nearly sixty-five meters. Training the recruits in marksmanship wasn't adversely affected by the mistake, it was, nonetheless, an error.

Petrov believed that the bank of the stream, on the opposite bank was higher than the firing positions, it was not. It was nearly five feet lower, but over the distance to the firing positions, it seemed to be higher. Petrov had ordered a sandbagged wall built on that bank in the belief that it would stop nearly all the rounds fired down range. The AK-47 had an effective range of three to four hundred meters, but the round could travel twice that far. This meant that a poorly aimed shot could fly over the berm and into the jungle. No one lived in that area, but farmers were sometimes seen in the jungle. The berm was inadequate and had Petrov or Semenov known about the problem, they would have ignored it.

Behind the firing line they had created a shaded training area that would look, from the air, just like any of the other hootches built in the small cluster. Inside, they had set up a table at one end for the trainer. The recruits sat on the ground, watching.

Sergeant Mikhail Volkov was behind the table with an AK-47 on it. He waited for the eighteen recruits to fall silent. He then held up the weapon, and said, "This is the AK-47, known as the Avtomat Kalashnikov, which is a gas-operated, magazine fed weapon, firing the 7.62 round. It was introduced in 1947 to the Soviet Army and was issued to selected units in 1949."

He waited for Sergeant Ilya Sidorov to catch up with the translation, knowing that the recruits wouldn't care about the finer details. It was the way he had learned in his basic training, so it was the way that he was going to teach the recruits.

When the translation was finished, he began to break down the weapon into its component parts, explaining the purpose of each. Then, he put it back together, again showing each part and explaining how it fit into the entire assembly. With that done, he asked three of the recruits to come forward. The idea was to have them repeat the process.

That didn't work out. Each seemed confused by the training. Finally, Volkov said, "Follow my lead. The rest of you come forward and watch." He knew this was going to take longer than he had thought. The recruits had no real mechanical skills, and he was asking them to disassemble and then reassemble the weapon.

The first couple of groups had trouble with the reassembly, but the last groups had it all figured out. They had seen the operation and Volkov worked with them slowly, showing them again and again how it was done. The last group looked like they had been working with the weapon for months.

With that finished, they moved toward the firing line. Again, there were tables set up with weapons on them, spare magazines and metallic boxes covered in stiff metal sheets that when peeled back exposed the ammunition.

Volkov stood in front of the table, looking over it at the recruits. "There are some rules that we much discuss. First, we treat every weapon as if it is loaded. It doesn't matter if you watched someone remove the magazine and clear the weapon when it is handed to you, it is your responsibility to ensure that it is not loaded. Mistakes are sometimes made."

He picked up one of the weapons, clearing it by working the action, showing that it was not loaded and there was no round chambered. He then said, "Second, be aware of the muzzle." He touched the end of the barrel to show them what he meant by muzzle.

"Third, never point the weapon at anything you do not plan to shoot. While we might tolerate some horseplay when dealing with other aspects of your training, we will not tolerate anyone playing around with a weapon. Keep that in mind at all times."

He touched the front of the barrel again. "Always keep the muzzle pointed down range when on the firing line." He pointed toward the target area. "No one will walk beyond the firing line until the all-clear is given, all weapons have been cleared, and all weapons have been brought back here."

He looked at each of the recruits and then asked, "Are there any questions?" He didn't expect any because they never asked questions. Asking for questions meant that the instruction had been concluded.

Leytenant Grigoriy Fedorov joined him then. He had been standing at the rear of the lecture listening to what Volkov said and the translation added by Sergeant Sidorov.

As the recruits picked up a weapon, they were handed a magazine that held only fifteen rounds. They were to fire those to familiarize themselves with the rifle, the noise, and the kick. They were told about all that, but there was nothing better than to fire the weapon. While they were shooting, the second group would be standing nearby, waiting to assume their duties of a coach. The last group would be loading additional magazines. It was an assembly line that they would use as the training continued.

The first group, holding the weapon, walked to the firing line, and were instructed in the prone position. They stretched out, on the ground, the AK-47 pointed down range. Once everyone was situated, Sidorov told the coach to hand one magazine to the shooter. The shooter inserted it in the well and then charged the weapon.

The only targets erected were those at the one-hundred-meter range. They were the easiest to hit and the theory was to build the confidence of the shooter. If their first experience had been to hit near the bullseye, or at least put the round through one of the rings, it would inspire them to do better.

Then, giving the commands in Russian, Volkov said, "Ready on the right. Ready on the left." He glanced in both directions and then said, "Ready on the firing line. Fire!"

There was a hesitation and then a single shot, followed by a volley as everyone who held a weapon fired down range. The rounds were slamming into the dirt berm and sandbags. Volkov had no way of knowing if any rounds were flying over the sandbags, but he didn't care.

The rattling of the weapons slowly tapered and ended. Volkov said, again in Russian, "Cease fire. Cease fire. Shooters and coaches make sure the weapon is clear. Remove the magazines and work the bolt to eject any round that might not have been fired."

When all the weapons were cleared, the shooter handed the rifle to the coach and then with Volkov and Petrov, walked down range to examine the targets. Volkov provided patches so that the shooter could cover the holes they had made in the targets.

Petrov examined the targets and was unimpressed. There were few holes in the black, center rings and there were many holes outside the whole target area. That was the result of inexperience. Once they'd had the opportunity to understand the weapon and get used to the kick when they fired, the recruits would hit the center target more often. Petrov had seen the same thing with Soviets who had never held a weapon before they reached basic training. They didn't know what to expect and the first few times on the firing range would increase their accuracy.

Back on the firing line, those who had been loading the magazines, moved forward to become coaches. Once the shooters were in the proper prone position and the coaches were sitting next to them holding the loaded magazine, they began the ritual again.

Once everyone had the opportunity to fire, they all moved back to the tables and cleaned the weapons. They broke for lunch and a new group of shooters was brought in to go through the training in the afternoon.

With the last group of shooters on the firing line, late in the afternoon, Volkov was thinking that it had gone very well. They hadn't hit the targets with any great skill and none of them would have passed had this been at the end of training rather than the beginning.

Volkov was watching the last group at the end of the live firing, when one of the shooters came to his knees, looked at the weapon and then at the coach. He said something in

Laotian and then swung the weapon around so that the muzzle was pointing down the firing line rather than down the range.

Volkov yelled and began running toward the man. Another of the Russians did the same and a Laotian fell in with them. The shooter looked up in surprise, realized what he had done, but didn't react fast enough. The weapon fired, hitting the shooter at the next position in the head. He dropped his weapon, spasmed and was still.

Volkov grabbed the weapon of the shooter, flipped it so that it was again pointing down range and kicked the man in the head. He slumped down unconscious. Volkov turned to the wounded man and knew that he was dead. Volkov could see part of the brain.

In Russian, he screamed, "This is what happens when you don't listen. You were told to keep the muzzle pointed down range."

Others in the camp ran out. The medic, carrying his first-aid kit, knelt by the injured man but didn't bother with the kit. He put his fingers against the man's throat but there was no pulse. Had he been near a fully equipped operating theater, he couldn't have done anything. The damage to the head and the brain was too extensive. The man was dead before he dropped his weapon and fell to his side.

Most of the Soviet soldiers sat around the large table. Major Semenov was sitting at the head and looked at each of the men in turn. From his face, it was clear that he was more than a little annoyed. Normally, these meetings were started with a round of vodka and a toast or two. That was Semenov's way of connecting with the soldiers. They were stationed in the middle of nowhere with a difficult job and he believed that these little things would build comradery.

But he was angry. He slammed a hand to the table as if to reinforce his anger. He looked directly at Volkov and demanded, "What in the hell happened?"

"Round cooked off," he said.

"What do you mean the round cooked off?"

"It happens. The firing pin strikes the primer but that doesn't fire the round. It's a delayed reaction, which is why I had stressed that the muzzle be always pointed down range. It can also be caused by the heat in the environment. We have been using the same weapons all day. This was the last round in the weapon. The man thought the weapon was empty."

"But it was not."

"No, sir. He didn't count the rounds and the coach didn't tell him. He just turned to ask a question and the weapon fired. His finger was not on the trigger at the time."

Semenov glared at Volkov without blinking. When Volkov shifted his gaze, Semenov asked, "So, the recruit was not to blame?"

"No, sir. Had the weapon been pointed down range, the only thing would be surprise that it fired. But he didn't follow instructions."

"Did anything like this happen at another time today?"

"No, sir. We weren't firing the weapons continually so that they had some time to cool down, but the temperature was high, and this particular rifle had been lying in the sun rather than under cover."

"So, you are to blame as well?"

Now Volkov felt the color drain from his face. He took a deep breath. "No, sir. The recruit did not follow his orders. Had he done so, this accidental discharge would have resulted in nothing other than the last round missing the target."

"Kapitan Petrov, you were there?"

"Yes, sir, but I wasn't on the firing line at the time. I was supervising the loading of the magazines and ensuring that no one slipped a round or two into his pocket."

Semenov cocked his head to one side. "Why would any of the recruits take a round? The weapons are all counted and locked up each night. They have no access to them."

Petrov laughed. "From the beginning of time soldiers have been stealing weapons and other things that might be of no use to them. A soldier never knows what might come in handy."

Semenov waved a hand as if to wipe a slate clean. "The real question now, it seems, is what do we do with the recruit who killed his fellow recruit. We have established that the fault is his."

Now Leytenant Fedorov spoke up. "But it was an accident, sir. He is, after all, just a recruit. He didn't know better."

Semenov turned his attention back to Volkov. "Did you or did you not instruct the recruits to keep the muzzle pointed down range?"

"As each group took their position on the firing line, I explained the importance of muzzle awareness and keeping the weapon pointed away from their fellows. I was quite clear on the point."

Semenov looked at a document in front of him, studied it for a moment, and then said, "We have established that the recruit was at fault. He had been given the proper instruction, it was reinforced, and he still turned his weapon on a fellow recruit. Volkov, you have suggested that the round cooked off, but I wonder how you know that."

Volkov looked uncomfortable. "I have assumed that he wouldn't have pulled the trigger with the weapon pointed at a fellow recruit. The only explanation for the delay in firing was that the round was defective in some fashion or that the heat caused the problem."

"But you don't know if the recruit had a vendetta against the recruit he shot. Maybe he was using that as an excuse to kill a man he didn't like, for whatever reason."

Sidorov joined in the discussion. "I have noticed no conflicts among the recruits. If they are angry at anyone, it is us. If they were going to murder anyone, I believe it would be one of us."

Semenov turned his attention to the sergeant. "Maybe you should go ask the recruits about that."

"Now, sir?"

"Of course, now."

He waited until Sidorov had left the room before he spoke again. "We'll wait for the answer before we discuss this further. I would like a shot of vodka while we wait. Who would like the honors?"

Volkov slid back his chair and said, "I'll pour, sir."

"And bring the pepper grinder as well."

That brought a burst of laughter from the others. Semenov said, "There are just certain things that must be done for the sake of civilization."

They sat in silence once the drinks had been poured, waiting for Sidorov to return. Finally, Semenov, having drained his glass and set it upside down on the table said, "It shouldn't be long now."

"What, exactly, is the plan?" asked Volkov.

Before Semenov could answer, Sidorov returned. He sat down and then looked at the commander. "There seemed to be something of a fight between the two recruits days ago, but it had been resolved, according to those I interviewed."

"At best we have a fatal accident and at worst we have a case of murder. Recommendations?"

Petrov began to speak but Semenov waved him to silence. "Who is the junior sergeant here?"

Volkov raised his hand. "I believe I am, sir."

"Recommendations?"

"Punishment is required."

"How severe?"

"If he shot the recruit on purpose, then he should be executed."

Semenov turned to Sidorov. "Is it your opinion that this was an accident?"

Sidorov looked down at the table for a moment and sighed. "I would like to believe that it was an accident, but I can't be sure. The recruits were reluctant to talk to me about it. I have the feeling that it might have been something more than that."

"Then punishment is required, regardless of intent."

Sidorov was again reluctant to answer. He waited as the silence grew, knowing that he would have to say something. Finally, quietly, he said, "There should be punishment."

Not wanting to draw the discussion out any further, Semenov said, "So, confinement or death?"

No one was surprised at the choice. They had all believed it would come down to that. One recruit had killed another and, in the end, it mattered little if it had been intentional or accidental. The recruit was dead at the hands of a fellow recruit.

Petrov said, "You've been leading us to this all along."

"Yes. Discipline is necessary and we must maintain it with an iron hand. We must convince the recruits that we will not tolerate any deviation from the course we set and if they kill, regardless of the circumstance, then the punishment will be severe."

"What do you recommend, Major?"

"Tomorrow morning, just after dawn, the recruit will be escorted into the jungle, to a suitable location where he will be instructed to dig a hole five meters long, three meters wide and one meter deep. Once he has completed the task, he will kneel at one end of the hole and be shot in the back of the head. He will be covered by the dirt and all traces of the grave will be obliterated. He will disappear from here and no one will speak of him again."

"Isn't that overly harsh?"

"It is what is necessary."

At dawn, Semenov and three of the Soviet team including Sidorov, stood outside one of the recruit hootches. He waited as Sidorov entered and ordered the recruit out. When he emerged, Sidorov had the recruit with him. The man looked scared but wasn't resisting. He walked with his head down, avoiding looking at each of the Soviets near the door.

"I want ten recruits as witnesses," said Semenov.

"Is that a good idea, sir?" asked Petrov, who looked as if he was about to be taken out into the jungle himself.

"If we are going to enforce discipline," said Semenov, reasonably, "there must be those to spread the word."

Sidorov, along with Volkov, entered the hootch and returned with ten men. They were all dressed as local peasants. They weren't wearing anything that could be construed as a uniform. They lined up near the door.

Semenov said, "Tell them that they are to witness the punishment of one of their fellows who failed to follow instruction. That failure resulted in the death of another recruit and such a circumstance requires punishment."

After Sidorov translated the words, one of the Soviet soldiers handed the recruit a shovel. They all then left the central area, walking into the jungle just north of the camp. They crossed the stream, climbed the bank, and made their way to a clearing about five hundred meters away. It was a large, open area, covered in short grass and looking almost as if it was some sort of park.

Semenov pointed near the center. "Tell him to dig here."

While they watched, the recruit began to dig. The soil was soft, but it was filled with roots. He chopped through them with the edge of the shovel. He stopped after ten minutes and leaned on the shovel. He was covered in sweat and breathing hard.

Sidorov said, "Get back to work."

The recruit glanced at him and then started to dig again. He tossed the dirt to the side and worked his way down the long axis. He was in no hurry to finish the job.

Although it was hot, the recruits stood at attention, watched the progress. The Soviet soldiers stood behind them but not at attention. They were just standing without talking or smoking.

It was taking longer than Semenov thought it would. He thought the recruit was digging as slowly as he could. He was tempted to have the other recruits help, but they only had one shovel. They hadn't even brought water and Semenov was not going to let anyone go back to the camp to get some.

Although the hole wasn't as deep as he wanted it, it was long enough and wide enough. He called a halt to the digging and ordered the recruit out of the hole. Then, he ordered him to kneel at one end.

He said, "I believe that if I'm going to order the death of one of the men, it is my duty to carry out the execution. No one wants to do something like this, but it must be done."

Before Sidorov could translate, Semenov said, "I said that for the benefit of the soldiers, not these recruits who are not worth our effort. It is enough that they see the price for failure. I don't have to explain the reasons to them."

He walked up on the kneeling man who, at first looked at him and then turned so that he was looking down, into the hole he had just dug. Semenov didn't hesitate. He drew his pistol, one of the Colt .45 ACP weapons they carried. The round was already chambered. He put the muzzle close to the recruit's head and pulled the trigger.

There was a spurt of blood from the wound that hit Semenov. The recruit fell forward in a loose-boned way and was dead before he hit the bottom of the hole. Semenov turned, wiping the blood from his hand and holstered the weapon. He showed no emotion. It was as if he had shot a rat.

"Cover him," he ordered.

He did not watch as the recruits buried the executed man. They said nothing to one another. The Soviet soldiers just stood quietly, waiting for the opportunity to get out of the jungle and away from the execution site.

CHAPTER 6

Captain George Smith had nearly forgotten about his attempts to learn more about HALO operations. He sat with his feet propped on the bottom drawer of his desk and held a Seven Up in one hand. He was staring at the map of Southeast Asia attached to the wall but wasn't actually seeing it.

He was now emersed in the review of a contingency plan that dealt with a Cambodian invasion of Thailand. Smith knew that such an invasion was not something that would happen in the near future. There was talk about the possibility that if South Vietnam fell, the communists would then target Cambodia and Thailand and other sovereign nations. This was the domino theory that had seemed to require American assistance to South Vietnam to stop the spread of communism throughout Southeast Asia.

Smith wasn't worried about the political situation or if the theory was accurate. His job, once again, was to read the contingency plan, but not discuss the strategy during his review. He was looking at grammar and punctuation and poorly constructed sentences. That didn't mean he wasn't paying attention to the strategy; it meant that the strategy wasn't his job.

This contingency plan called for intervention on the western border of Cambodia to stop communist forces from moving from areas in Vietnam, through Cambodia, to attack Thailand. Smith couldn't see how that could happen, not with the current political climate. He found himself searching for what he thought were incorrect and inaccurate information to support the use of American troops to protect Thailand.

What he had failed to understand was the contingency plans did not necessarily reflect the current political situation but a situation that might exist at some later date. Contingency plans sometimes addressed situations that had little or no possibility in the real world. He had seen one that suggested an armed conflict between the United States and Australia over the small island of East Timor. Both American soldiers and Australia soldiers were stationed on the island and the conflict rose from a bar fight between the soldiers of the two nations. There was little chance of anything like that ever happening, but there was a plan to cover it just in case it did.

Thinking about it, he wondered if there was a plan to deal with an alien invasion. Was there someone planning to fight aliens even though they would command space and no one on Earth would be able to engage their forces while they were in space. But someone, at a higher level, had asked a question about that and a plan was drawn up to cover the situation.

He had learned his lesson with the HALO plan, however. He wasn't going to challenge the conclusions or the response by the United States if the communists were on the western border of Cambodia, posed to strike Thailand. If a general thought they needed a plan in case that happened, and even if Smith had seen a flaw in the plan, he wasn't going to say anything about it.

Instead, he corrected spelling, added commas, and suggested that some of the sentences were overly long. He noted that the active voice would make the document more dynamic and removed the passive voice when possible. But he was getting bored with the whole process. He was tired of reading contingency plans that had no real value other than someone had wondered about an obscure possibility.

The sergeant major approached him and asked, "Are you doing anything important, sir?"

"I'm just reviewing one of the contingency plans."

"Well, it doesn't really matter. General Maxwell wants to see you."

"When?"

"Now. He asked for you to come up at your convenience. That means just as soon as you can get up there."

"I'm aware of the military protocol at work here," he said. He dropped his feet to the floor and pushed the drawer closed with his foot. He stood up, closed the folder on his desk, making sure that the secret cover sheet was in place. He said, "I'll need to put this back in the safe."

"Yes, sir."

Smith walked to the safe and pulled open one of the drawers. He put the plan in it and pushed the drawer closed but didn't lock the safe. Everyone in the area had the clearance necessary to read anything in the safe.

Before he left the office, he checked himself in the mirror to ensure that all the insignia on his uniform were in place, that his ribbons were in the correct order, though there was no way for them to have shifted. He checked his gig line and then, happy with his appearance, left the office.

He walked down the hall to the general's office. He entered the outer office without knocking. To the clerk, he said, "The general has asked for me."

"Yes, sir. He said for you to go right in."

Smith was suddenly worried. The summons had been unexpected. He had thought he would have to wait but that didn't happen. He feared that the general was angry about something else. He didn't want to enter the office but walked to the door and knocked on it three times.

"Enter."

Smith entered, walked to the desk, stopping three feet away and saluted. "Captain Smith reporting as ordered, sir."

General Maxwell returned the salute. He was in a khaki uniform that only had the general stars of his rank on his collar and a name tag above his right breast pocket. He was wearing none of his awards and decorations and Smith was surprised that he was in a Class B uniform.

"What have you been doing, Smith?"

Smith didn't know how to answer the question. He had been trying to stay out of the spotlight since his trip down to the Special Warfare Center. He said, "I was reviewing a contingency plan about the invasion of Thailand by communist forces that had staged in Cambodia, General."

"I have been thinking about your recent interest in HALO operations."

The general saw that Smith was going to protest and held up a hand to stop him. "While it is not within our area of operations, there is an operation that is based on one of the contingency plans. It would be interesting, illustrative, and important that we, and by we, I mean you, see how the contingency plan is translated into action in the field."

Before Smith could respond, the general pointed at one of the chairs and said, "Have a seat."

Smith was suddenly relieved. If the general was telling him to sit down, then this was not some kind of a verbal admonishment. This was something else. He dropped into the chair and looked up, at a framed lithograph with a brass plate under it that said, "The Wagon Box Fight."

He had wondered about the Wagon Box Fight and finally looked it up. The fight was between a small force of U.S. Army soldiers from Fort Phil Kearny and the Oglala Sioux. The

Oglala had lost the fight though they had outnumbered the soldiers. The soldiers had repeating rifles and new breach loaders that increased the rate of fire, holding the Oglala at bay until reinforcements arrived. The Army had many such paintings hanging in offices and lining corridors at all their installations.

The office walls were paneled in dark wood, with a conversation area near a floor-to-ceiling bookcase filled with military history and tactics volumes. The carpeting was thick and dark green that fit with the rest of the décor. There were two chairs and a couch with a coffee table set among them. Near the desk were two leather chairs for visitors if the conversation area was too informal.

The general said, "There are several proposed operations that would involve a HALO component, all being mounted in South Vietnam. We'll cut orders sending you to Vietnam on TDY for a period of sixty days which means you'll probably be there for parts of three different months, meaning combat pay for those months. I mention this because regulations say that if you spend one day in a combat zone, you are entitled to hazardous duty pay and are exempt from federal income taxes for that month. Arrive several days into one month, spend the entire next month in Vietnam and return several days into the third month and you are good to go."

Smith was a little surprised by the assignment and the explanation. He would get credit for a tour in Vietnam, even if it wasn't the standard one-year tour. He would benefit from the various rules and regulations and even draw what he, and nearly everyone else thought of as combat pay.

"You'll be working out of Nha Trang but will be authorized travel to any location in Vietnam that is required by the assignment. You'll have the ability to extend that duty if necessary."

Smith, without thinking, said, "But I don't really know all that much about HALO operations, sir."

"You already know the essential information. You'll be able to evaluate the benefits of a HALO operation and you'll see what the shortfalls might be."

"When would I go?" asked Smith.

"A week. Ten days. Time to get your shots, get briefed on what to expect in the combat zone, code of conduct and the like."

There were things that he wanted to ask, but the only thought was that he was going to Vietnam. Temporary duty was a plum because it involved additional pay and he'd be avoiding income taxes for a few months. But he just wasn't ready. He hadn't qualified with the M-16 and the last time on the pistol range, he'd had to fire twice just to pass at the lowest level. He had been awarded the marksmanship badge, which meant nothing. Officers just didn't wear weapons qualification badges. It was assumed that they all were experts in the weapons they were assigned.

"You look confused," said the general.

"Overwhelmed," said Smith. "This comes out of the blue."

"I want someone to observe these HALO operations. You're not married, you have reviewed some of the procedures and that makes you our resident expert."

Smith started to say that he had learned most of what he knew from a lieutenant but then thought better of it. He had fallen into an old Army tradition. He had expressed an interest, or had made a suggestion about something, and was labeled as the resident expert. It didn't really matter how much or how little he actually knew. He had been identified with the topic at hand.

"The sergeant major will have copies of your orders and a packet of information for you. There will be a schedule for the briefings you need and an appointment for the shots."

"This is sudden," said Smith.

"The opportunity arose, and I want to take advantage of it. You know that sometimes the mission requires that we move fast."

"Yes, sir." Smith felt that there was something that he should ask or a comment that he should make but he didn't know what it would be. He sat there, staring up at the Wagon Box Fight while the general waited. Finally, Smith stood and asked, "Will that be all?"

"That's it, George. See the sergeant major and I'm sure will have a chat before you go."

Smith saluted, waited for it to be returned and said, "Thank you, General."

Sergeant First Class Eric Mendes wasn't fond of the heat, especially when the humidity was pushing one hundred. But he was sitting in front of a fan that kept the air circulating so that he wasn't all that uncomfortable. It was that the noise of the fan made it difficult to hear those talking and the breeze tended to blow around the papers that he needed. Mendes was rarely happy about anything and in Vietnam, there was always something to annoy him.

The office was typical of that in Vietnam: plywood floor and plywood halfway up the walls, with a screen above that. The screen was to allow for the cooling breezes but there were no cooling breezes. There was a ceiling fan that was spinning that squeaked with each revolution and a flare parachute hung from the ceiling that blocked the view of the exposed rafters.

Mendes was in his late twenties and had been one of the first to qualify for HALO operations. He had then trained others and had made ten HALO jumps. He had been in the Special Forces for five years and had two tours in Vietnam. He was skilled in the use of small arms and radio operations. He spoke Vietnamese as well as several of the dialects of other local languages.

He held up a piece of paper that contained a message telling him that an officer was coming to study their HALO operations. To no one in particular, he said, "This is all we need. Some Pentagon puke coming here to stick his big nose into our business."

Staff Sergeant Ian Morgan, who was also HALO qualified and also a Green Beret, looked at Mendes. Morgan was a year younger than Mendes, had only a single tour in Vietnam and was a heavy weapons expert and cross-trained as a medic. He had never thought of making the Army a career until he had become a Green Beret.

"He's just here to observe."

"All well and good, but we're planning a jump into a hostile environment. Who knows what trouble he could cause." Mendes, finally annoyed by the noise of the fan, reached over and turned it off.

Morgan rocked back in his chair. "Look at the message carefully. This isn't an inspection or a fact-finding mission. He's coming in as an observer."

"He's coming from the Pentagon and that can't be good. Someone coming from the Pentagon suggests that we're in some sort of trouble or they're looking to find some sort of trouble."

"He's a captain, for crying out loud. A fucking captain. If we were in any trouble, he'd be at least a lieutenant colonel and probably a full bull colonel."

That made sense to Mendes. He relaxed slightly. "Where's the rest of the team?"

"On their way. I told them that there was no hurry. This is just a prelim before we get to the brief back."

Mendes looked at this watch. "It's getting late in the day. I'm up for a beer. How about you?"

"I could use a taste," said Morgan.

"Cold beers are in the refrigerator in the team house. Bring me one too."

As he stood up, Morgan said, "Why am I not surprised?"

"Because you are an astute NCO looking to be promoted soon."

As Morgan reached the door, Sergeant Bruce Penrick was about to enter. Hendrick was the youngest member of the team and the last to go through HALO training. He had only made a handful of jumps but lived for the thrill of falling thousands of feet for two minutes or more. He had to be careful. He sometimes got so wrapped up in watching the changing landscape that he'd nearly forget to deploy his parachute.

Unlike the other members of the team, Hendrick was slight and thin. Although he didn't appear muscular, he had a wiry strength that surprised the others. He also had nearly three years of college and had majored in anthropology with an eye on manned missions to Mars. Had you asked what anthropology had to do with Martian exploration, he would have had no answer. He just believed that the military would need someone with a background in anthropology and there wouldn't be many available with that qualification.

Hendrick dropped into the chair that had been vacated by Morgan and then reached over and turned on the fan. "Hot in here," he said.

"You are supposed to ask before you alter the environment of a superior," said Mendes.

"You weren't hot?"

"The noise was getting to me."

Staff Sergeant Thomas Crockett entered and took a place at the table. Although he had never researched his family history, he told all who would listen that his great-great-grandfather had died at the Alamo. There was a family tradition that there was a family connection to David Crockett, but it was more along the lines of a third or fourth cousin rather than a direct link.

Like the other three, he was HALO qualified, had made ten or twelve jumps but rather than finding them exciting, he was terrified of them. There was so much that could go wrong and if the failure was in the oxygen system, there was very little time to recover.

Crockett was old to be only a staff sergeant, but he hadn't joined the military until he was nearly thirty. The draft had passed over him, he had a marriage which didn't work out, and had no real job skills. He was a passable carpenter but hated the work. He'd been a short-order cook with no flair for the culinary. He tried out as an apprentice mechanic but found he didn't like working on engines. As a last resort, he'd talked with an Army recruiter who had steered him to the infantry with a suggestion that he might find the Special Forces more to his liking. The Green Berets had become the darling of the Army after John Kennedy had authorized the wearing of the berets and then John Wayne made his movie in 1968.

Without waiting for Morgan to return, or to ask where he was, Crockett said, "I am here under protest, so let's get this show on the road."

"Why under protest?"

"I have decided to do everything under protest. I figured it might get me out of some lousy assignments."

Mendes grinned and said, "Won't work this time."

Morgan returned, set beers in front of the others, and sat down in the last available chair. When Mendes looked at him, he said, "I figure the others would show up and that you wouldn't want them worrying about why we had beer, and they did not."

"What if they didn't want a beer?" asked Mendes.

"Then I figured you'd be happy to drink it. But I don't know of anyone around here who wouldn't want a beer. That's almost un-American."

"Point taken." Mendes took a sip and said, "I have been alerted to a mission requiring our unique set of skills..."

"Meaning HALO," said Hendrick.

"Well, I hadn't wanted to be quite that blunt, but yes, HALO. We're not to discuss this mission with anyone other than the commander and this expert coming from the Pentagon."

"What expert?" asked Crockett.

"Some captain being sent to observe our operation," said Morgan.

Hendrick laughed. "We jump out of perfectly good airplanes at high altitude. What's to be observed?"

Mendes took a long pull at the beer and carefully set the bottle on the table. "Well, there isn't any such thing as a perfectly good airplane but overlooking that, I think this

HALO concept is attracting some attention at higher levels. Maybe too much."

"Why now?" asked Crockett.

"We're drifting a little far afield here. I want to give you the preliminaries of our mission. We will be jumping into enemy territory with a sneak-and-peek mission. We'll be in the field for several days before we move to a site for pick up by helicopter."

"Resupply?" asked Crockett.

"You're getting ahead of yourself here. We are going to be observing an enemy installation for those days with an eye to identifying the men running it, who all is there, and gathering intelligence about their overall mission."

Crockett began to speak again, but Mendes held up a hand to silence him. "Here is the problem. We're going to be in a static location for as much as ninety-six hours. We are to finally make our way to the pickup point that has yet to be designated but will be some thirty to fifty miles away from the target."

"That's going to take two to three days depending on the distance, terrain, and weather, not to mention the jungle to get to the extraction point. We're going to need resupply."

"That's one of the things that we're going to discuss. Resupply, basic load of ammunition — remembering that our mission is not to engage but to flee — and what is the absolute minimum that we take with us."

"I don't like it," said Crockett.

"Well, no one said that you had to like it, Thomas. You just have to do it."

"When do we go?" asked Morgan.

"A more germane question. Inside a week. The observer should be here by then. He'll sit in the planning sessions and the discussions, but we are not obligated to listen to any suggestions he might make."

"How do you know that?" asked Morgan.

Mendes held up the message. "There is nothing on this that says we must listen to him, only that we have to let him observe. I'm not worried about him compromising the mission because he doesn't know anyone here and he comes to us loaded down with security clearances. There isn't much that we do that he wouldn't be cleared to know."

"What are we supposed to plan?" asked Morgan.

"At the moment, I just want to know what you'd carry into the field given the length of the mission. Food and water are going to be our main concern, though depending on our location, water might not be much of a problem if you don't mind the chemical taste."

Mendes drained his beer and then looked at his watch. "Let's take a few hours to think about this and meet back here after we eat. Any questions?"

There weren't any, just an annoyance with the scant information supplied.

Major Gerber turned toward Sergeant Major Fetterman. "I see a HALO mission on the schedule, or, I suppose, I should say that there is some sort of HALO mission being contemplated in the future at some unspecified time into an unidentified location."

"Yes, sir. I just love these sorts of things."

"Do you suppose it has anything to do with that suspected camp located in Laos?"

"I would say that is a real possibility, though I think we're not supposed to know about it yet."

Gerber held up a sheet of paper. "I have here, in my hot little hand, a suggestion from the Puzzle Palace, that we consider a clandestine raid into the hinterlands to eradicate this camp. But we are not supposed to do it ourselves."

"Meaning you and me personally, sir?"

"Meaning, I suspect, U.S. Army assets of either the regular Army or the Special Forces or Marine Recon for that matter."

"That would mean the local indigenous forces," said Fetterman.

"I believe that local indigenous forces is somewhat redundant, Sergeant Major. They haven't supplied any real guidance. They have just suggested that we plan on a clandestine mission involving two or three hundred of these unspecified indigenous forces and that they attack an undesignated base somewhere in Southeast Asia."

"Is there a time frame?"

"No. There really isn't much for us to do, right now. Without a location, I can't even plan on which Mike Force to tap for this. Song Be might be the closest, but Bromhead's might be the better trained. It all depends."

Before Fetterman could answer, they heard the flat bang of a large explosion. Gerber cocked his head to one side, listening, but there wasn't a second detonation. He asked, "What's the EOD schedule?"

"I don't know but it sounded as if it came from that area."

"That's almost as bad when the artillery opens fire. Sure teaches you the difference between incoming and outgoing."

"Changing the subject," said Gerber, "we do have a briefing tomorrow about this latest boondoggle."

"Couldn't we do it somewhere more exciting?"

"What could be more exciting than being right here?"

"Let's go see the colonel," said Fetterman. "Pump him for information about this upcoming assignment. Get a leg up on it."

Gerber took a deep breath and looked as if he was going to say, "No," but then thought about it. "Why not? And when that fails, we can go in search of chow. I'm not up for eating in the mess hall tonight."

They left their office, walked down a short hall that had been painted off-green. It looked as if someone had spilled a dark green paint into a can of canary yellow and rather than throw it all out, they had used it to paint the hallway. It was a color that neither remembered ever seeing on a military installation.

They caught the colonel, Alan Bates, as he was leaving his office. When he saw them, he said, "Nope. I'm through for the day. Come back tomorrow."

"But, sir," said Gerber, "we have an important question for you."

"No, you don't. You're just looking for an excuse to go to Vung Tau for a day or two. I know you too well."

"Why, no," said Gerber. "But if there is something that needs to be done at Vung Tau, we'd be happy to do it, wouldn't we, Sergeant Major."

"Yes, sir."

"What do you want, Mack?"

"Wondered what more you might know about this upcoming assignment of ours. Location, maybe? Time frame? Anything that would help us."

"You know as much about it as I do. Briefing officer is coming in from Saigon and will provide the details. Besides, we shouldn't be talking about this in the hallway. Too many people might overhear."

Gerber shrugged. "And then they'd be as confused as we are. We don't know anything other than there will be a mission to do something at some point. The VC can guess that much."

"Mack, I've got to go see General Maxwell. He's waiting and I suspect it has something to do with you two. I'll be at the briefing tomorrow. We can talk then."

Bates pushed past them and hurried down the hall. Gerber said, "Well, that was helpful."

Fetterman nodded. "Maybe we should go find those HALO guys. I'll bet they know something we might like to know."

"I thought of that," said Gerber, "and then I thought, it'll wait until tomorrow."

CHAPTER 7

The flight from Washington, D.C. had taken much longer than Captain George Smith thought it would. They had landed in San Francisco and then traveled by bus to Travis Air Force Base. They'd flown to Hawaii where they were allowed off the aircraft for about an hour. Once the aircraft was refueled and the flight crew replaced, they flew on to Okinawa where they spent four or five hours on the ground. No time to do much, other than walk around the base and wait to get back on the airplane. The last leg was into Saigon, landing in mid-morning.

Smith sat quietly as the others got off the airplane. He was in no hurry. If he had been allowed to, he would have stayed on the aircraft for its return to the World. He understood the advantage he held, which was he had earned the combat pay for the month and he wouldn't be paying federal income tax for the month, but suddenly he wasn't sure it was worth the monetary reward. He'd be much happier in the land of the giant PX and the all-night generator.

For some reason, he thought the sun was brighter, as he walked down the stairs that had been rolled up to the aircraft. There was a line of soldiers, sailors, marines, and airmen walking toward several busses. Smith wasn't sure that he was supposed to get on one of the buses, to enter the terminal or find the Theater Headquarters somewhere near Tan Son Nhut. In fact, he wasn't sure he should even be in Saigon. He had been ordered to Nha Trang and knew only that it was somewhere north of Saigon though he didn't know how far.

He thought about getting on a bus but wasn't sure that was the thing he should do. As he stood there, in the bright sunlight, sweat popping out on his forehead and under his arms, a sergeant wearing a green beret walked up. He didn't salute. No one exchanged salutes on the flightline.

"Are you Captain Smith?"

"Yes. How did you know?"

The sergeant grinned. "I just looked for an officer who looked lost and figured it must by you."

Smith didn't know if he should be insulted or if he should laugh. "You know where I'm supposed to go?"

"There is a flight leaving for Nha Trang in about an hour. You have a priority seat on it, which means you get to move to the front of the first come, first serve line."

"And where is that aircraft?"

"I have a jeep waiting."

"My baggage?"

"We'll pick it up at the terminal. You have a weapon?"

"No. I thought I would draw one in Nha Trang, if I needed one."

"No offense, sir, but you should always have a weapon. You just don't know when you might need it." He didn't explain where Smith should have drawn a weapon or how he would have carried it onto the aircraft. Instead, he pointed to a single story, white building and said, "I'm parked over there."

The jeep was the standard issue with a canvas top to protect the driver and passengers from the sun. There was a chain welded to the floor that was looped through the steering wheel and sealed with a padlock.

Smith said, "That doesn't look all that secure."

"Keeps the Vietnamese from stealing it. The GIs know how to defeat the chain, but it would do them no good. Just cause them all sorts of trouble and see them sent to LBJ."

"LBJ?"

"Long Binh Jail. Doesn't get them a ticket home, just a stay in LBJ which sometimes doesn't count for time in-country. They still must finish their tour and get sent home with a bad conduct discharge. Young guys don't understand that a bad conduct discharge is really going to fuck up their lives, but we don't really have many soldiers stealing jeeps."

Feeling out of place in his green uniform, feeling like a target, Smith climbed into the passenger's seat. The canvas was hot, but not like it would have been had it been in direct sunlight. The sergeant unlocked the chain and dropped it to the floor. He started the jeep, shifted into reverse, and then backed up as if he was about to escape an ambush. He stopped, ground the gears, and took off in what he thought of as a burst of speed. Smith found it annoying but said nothing.

They stopped at another short building. The sergeant said, "Your gear should be in there. This is sort of the customs building for VIPs. Don't want you mingling with the enlisted pukes."

Smith looked at him. "You understand you're a sergeant in the Army and one of those enlisted pukes?"

"Yes, sir. But I live here in Saigon, I don't have to work too hard, and I have not been out of the city and into the jungle since I got here. Besides, I'm a master sergeant, a senior NCO and not an enlisted puke. I just see how everything runs and keep my nose clean and I'm golden. Besides, I'm short."

"Short?"

"Yes, sir, just forty-seven days and a wake up and I'm outta here."

"Short," repeated Smith.

"Nearly everyone knows exactly how many days are left in his tour. I am what is known as a double-digit midget because I have less than a hundred days left in this hellhole."

Smith climbed out of the jeep without another word and walked to the door. He pulled it open and saw a huge room, divided into long areas but very few people in it. A Spec Four carrying a clipboard approached and asked, "May I help you, sir?"

"I need to collect my equipment."

"Yes, sir. Your name?"

"Smith, George…"

"Yes, sir. If you'll follow me."

They entered a long, narrow room with a counter at one end. The walls had been painted white and once might have looked clean, but now had an old appearance. There was a sergeant there and behind him were racks for suitcases, duffle bags, briefcases and some other odds and ends. There were two huge fans standing at one end of the room and blowing at full blast, circulating the air. Smith wasn't sure how effective it might be and realized he didn't care for the noise they made.

Smith walked up to the counter and spotted his gear on a bottom shelf. He pointed at it. "That's mine."

The sergeant looked startled and said, "You have some identification, sir?"

Smith produced his ID card, which the sergeant examined carefully. "Your name attached to the bags?"

"Yes."

The sergeant turned, examined several of the bags and then pulled them from the rack. He turned and dropped them on the counter. He examined them again, finally found Smith's name stenciled on them and said, "There you go, sir."

"You don't want to check them for contraband?"

"No, sir. You're an officer and something of a VIP. We know that you wouldn't think of sneaking in something that you're not supposed to have. Besides, we're more concerned with what guys are shipping out."

"What would they be shipping out?"

"Mostly illegal weapons like AK-47s. We've even found hand grenades. You'd be surprised at what they try to send home."

Smith shrugged, grabbed his bags, and said, "Thanks."

He turned and the Spec Four was standing right behind him. "I'll escort you back to your vehicle."

The jet that had brought him from Washington to Saigon had been leased from an airline and Smith had a seat in the first-class section. To get to Nha Trang, he had been riding in the back of a C-123 that had red canvas seats that were stiffened by metal pipe. He was leaning back against the fuselage frame. On the ground, it was hot but as they climbed to altitude, it became cooler until it was downright cold. There was no beverage service and no stewardesses. Just a male crew chief who was short and stocky and in something of a foul mood. He didn't supply much in the way of a pre-flight safety briefing and seemed to be annoyed by the passengers. Smith said nothing to him during the flight.

As they neared Nha Trang, they didn't make a slow, steady approach. Instead, it was as if the bottom had dropped out as they engaged in a high-speed turn that forced him back against the fuselage. A moment later, they flared out and suddenly were on the ground, the engines roaring as the pilots worked to slow the aircraft.

They pulled up in front of the operations building and the engines suddenly went silent. The rear ramp dropped open, and the crew chief said, "We're here. Unass the aircraft and check in with operations unless you're heading back to your unit of assignment. Then that's where you go."

As Smith moved toward the ramp, the crew chief said, "Thank you for flying Interpaddy Airlines, your low cost means of travel to the garden spots of this tropical oasis." He grinned broadly.

Inside, the operations building had the same look as those Smith had seen in Saigon. Plywood floors, sandbags halfway up the walls and screens the rest of the way. There were ceiling fans spinning slowly above, and the flare parachutes hanging from the rafters, just above the fans. It was a standard decoration throughout Vietnam.

Smith introduced himself to the clerk behind the counter who said, "Yes, sir. You'll want to get over the Special Forces area. I'll call down there and see if I can scare up a ride for you. They're pretty good at getting people rides."

Thirty minutes later, Smith was at the Special Forces Headquarters in Nha Trang. He'd been traveling for nearly two days, had eaten little other than what had been provided by the commercial airline or a sandwich, an apple and box of milk provided by the military at the refueling stops. He was hungry, tired, dirty, and more than slightly irritated.

He found himself in a hootch with a cot, an empty wall locker and little else. There was an outhouse fifty feet away, electricity that failed frequently and the sound of artillery which was mostly outgoing but sometimes a round or two of incoming. He had been shown the officers' club, the shower and told he could draw a weapon in the morning. He was now in Vietnam and there was a war going on. He heard several officers use the excuse, "It's the only war we've got."

Unhappy with the rough living conditions, with the lousy food in the mess hall, and the warm beer, he wondered how the soldiers managed to survive an entire year in Vietnam. He decided that the combat pay and the tax break was not sufficient compensation. Rather than find a way to extend his tour into three months, he wanted to shrink it to just a couple of weeks. The first chance he would have to find out how to do that would come in the morning at the first briefing scheduled for nine.

The conference room was set up so that classified information could be discussed inside without fear of compromise. The plywood went all the way up the wall and there were sandbags outside to nine feet. The theory was that anyone who wanted to listen would have to climb to the top of the sandbag wall and would therefore be conspicuous to anyone who happened by. Of course, during a classified briefing, there were guards in position to ensure that anyone attempting to get close enough to listen was either chased away or shot.

Since the room was closed in and there was a tin roof over the whole building, temperature became a problem. To combat that, an air conditioner was built into the wall. It served two purposes. It cooled the room, and it created noise that made it difficult for anyone to listen from the outside. There were two fans on stands at opposite ends of the room to circulate the air. It could be quite comfortable in the heat of the afternoon.

Situated in the middle of the room was a long table surrounded by eight chairs. Six of the chairs looked as if they were part of a set but the other two seemed to be leftovers or stolen from other places. The table had been highly polished at one time but years of sitting in the room, with all sorts of briefings with all sorts of equipment and beverage containers sitting on it had marred the surface. It was a sturdy table that would never again be used in a VIP conference room but was reliable. There was a platter in the center holding pastries, a coffee pot, a water jug, and several mismatched cups.

Major Mack Gerber sat in one of the chairs at the end of the table and Sergeant Major Fetterman sat at the opposite end. Sergeant First Class Eric Mendes was standing behind one of the chairs as if waiting for permission to sit down. Mendes hated meetings because he thought of them as a waste of time, but then, a necessary part of what he did. Sometimes, the meetings were productive and short. That was a rarity.

"Is anyone else from your team coming?" Gerber asked.

Mendes shook his head. "No, sir. I'm stuck with being here. Morgan and Crockett are running a check on our equipment. We do that about once a week if we haven't used the stuff.

There was a knock at the door, which was made of plywood layers with a screen stapled over it. No one was sure what purpose the screen served. Since the door was solid, or as solid as a door made of layered plywood could be, there had been no reason for the screen.

One of the guards opened the door, slowly, and then stuck his head in. "I have Colonel Bates here."

"Let him in," said Gerber.

Bates, wearing tiger-striped jungle fatigues, which were prohibited for American soldiers with few exceptions entered. He was carrying a thick stack of folders that had a top-secret cover sheet on top. He was armed with both an M-16 and a Colt .45. He set the rifle on the table, which accounted for some of the scratches on the surface.

"Where's that guy from the Pentagon?" asked Bates.

"Not here yet," said Fetterman. "We believe that he was informed of the meeting and because he is an officer and a gentleman, figured he would be able to find his way here."

Bates shook his head and said, "But he's from the Pentagon. That should have told you something about him."

The door opened again, and the guard said, "There's a guy out here that says he's from the Pentagon and that he is supposed to be here."

"We have nothing going on at the moment that is classified so let him in," said Bates.

Smith, wearing bright green jungle fatigues that looked brand new, entered. There were no insignias on them and looked as if they belonged to Smith's bigger brother. As he entered, he said, "Sorry to keep you waiting, sir. I had some trouble getting a proper uniform."

Bates waved a hand to dismiss the comment and said, "Sergeant Mendes, lock the door please."

When the door was locked and everyone was sitting around the table, Bates said, "Though unnecessary, I remind you all that this briefing is classified top secret and will not be discussed with anyone not cleared to possess any of the details about it."

Bates noticed Mendes look toward Smith. "Captain Smith has the proper clearances and we have been asked, ordered actually, to allow him to sit in."

"Yes, sir."

"This is phase one of the operation, which I haven't given a code name yet. I'll have to check on that."

He then pulled the cover sheet from the stack of documents. "The initial phase of the operation is in your hands, Sergeant Mendes. This will be a HALO insertion into an allegedly neutral foreign country under the cover of darkness…"

"Foreign country, sir? As opposed to Vietnam?" asked Mendes.

"Laos, not to put too fine a point on it."

"We have authorization for this?" asked Gerber.

"I believe the mission is directed by the Pentagon," said Bates. He turned his attention to Smith.

"I am just here to observe HALO operations," Smith said. "I have no additional knowledge about your mission nor am I authorized to provide any additional information if I had it."

"Okay," said Bates, not fully understanding Smith's role. "Sergeant Mendes, I'll give you the grid coordinates later and I'll arrange for an aircraft for the drop. Are there any special needs?"

"We'll be jumping from around thirty thousand feet, sir. When you open the aircraft for our jump, that depressurizes the interior. Some of them have cockpits that can be sealed off from the rest of the aircraft. At any rate, once the ramp is down, the cargo area will depressurize and everyone in there will have to be on supplemental oxygen or they will be unconscious in about ten seconds. I guess it would be the same for the pilots."

"I'm sure that our Air Force people are aware of all that."

Gerber said, "I worry about compromise…"

"We're getting into the weeds already," said Bates. He then added, "But what do you mean?"

"Status of Forces Agreement requires Vietnamese on the base. A special aircraft will be noticed and probably will be reported to the enemy."

"I'm not sure that is a problem, Major," said Mendes. "There is nothing about the aircraft that would distinguish it from the others, at least from the outside. Our equipment will be in standardized containers. All that would be seen, if it is seen, is that we and a bunch of stuff were loaded on the aircraft. That happens all the time."

Bates said, "If I might continue?"

Mendes said, simply, "Yes, sir."

Bates dug through his folders and took out several aerial photographs. He passed them to Mendes. "This is the potential drop zone. It is a mile long on its long axis and nearly half a mile wide. Is that a sufficient DZ if we drop at night?"

Mendes pulled the picture close and examined it. He noticed, at the top of the picture, there was a stream or a river. The rest of the photograph was filled with trees except for the DZ.

"Providing that there is little wind, though in free fall we can gain great directional control. If we jump in the right area, then this should be sufficient."

"You hesitated there, Sergeant."

"Well, yes, sir. You said that we would be dropping in the dark but there is no provision to mark the DZ. At night, in most areas in Laos, there is not enough ambient light for us to see the DZ, especially as we jump without a moon. If the navigation is off, we'll land in the trees and could be miles from the proper DZ."

"How do we rectify that problem?" asked Bates.

"Jump at the time of the full moon on a cloudless night."

Gerber spoke up. "Doesn't that defeat the purpose of the HALO jump?"

"Depends on several factors, sir. If we're high enough, if the wind is blowing in the right direction, if the plane is blacked out, then we'll probably get away with it. We don't really need a C-130 because there are only four of us. A smaller plane with fewer engines increases our chances of getting away with it."

"Then you're agreeable to making the jump at night," said Bates.

"There are no technical problems. There are several other problems such as resupply and strategy."

Bates stopped shuffling his papers and said, "Resupply?"

"We're jumping from a long way up and we can't carry all that much. You toss resupply parachutes out with us at that altitude, and they could scatter all over Southeast Asia before they hit the ground, sir."

"Shit."

"We can jump with enough for three or four days. Water is the problem but there are alternative sources of it, including rainfall. Weapons and ammunition are also heavy."

"You are not to engage in combat," said Bates.

"Sometimes that decision is taken out of our hands, sir. We will engage for self-defense, but we won't initiate combat." He reached for a glass and the water pitcher. "How deep into Laos will we be?"

"Is that relevant?"

"If we're close to the border, or close enough, it'll make resupply easier."

Smith asked, "Why not use the DZ? Won't you be close?"

Mendes set his glass down carefully. "I thought you were just here as an observer." He didn't append "sir" to his comment.

"I'm just trying to learn as much as I can."

"We assume that the enemy will have discovered the DZ and will be watching. We don't use the same location more than once."

Bates said, "If we were close to the border, you could walk in. We thought a HALO operation would be the best way to infiltrate."

"Colonel," said Mendes, "what is the purpose of this?"

"I was about to get to that. This is a sneak-and-peek mission. Once you reach the location, you lay low and just watch. Extraction will be by helicopter. What I need to know is how long you can stay in the field."

"As I said, we can't take much in the way of supplies. We'll have to be resupplied if we're going to stay very long."

Bates flipped through the folders and extracted a sheet of paper. "We want additional observation of an enemy camp and possible training facility for the locals. Numbers of people there, national origin if you can determine it, and anything else that you might consider relevant. We just want to gather intelligence about this operation and nothing more."

Gerber asked, "Colonel, what is the importance of this mission?"

Bates shot him a look and then said, "We believe that this is a training camp, and we want to verify the nature of it."

"But it's in Laos and from what you say, not all the close to the border of Vietnam, what is our interest?" Gerber asked again.

"You mean ours, here in Nha Trang, or those at the Puzzle Palace East?" Bates laughed at his own joke. "What makes you think that I would be interested in this if the word had not come down from on high?"

Mendes asked, "Do you have a list of essential elements of intelligence for me?"

"That'll be in the briefing package. Right now, I just want you to think about how you want to run this mission."

Gerber said, "Okay, we get what Mendes is going to be doing, but I don't understand what Sergeant Major Fetterman and I have to do with this."

"That'll come later. I first want to see what Sergeant Mendes comes up with. If he's out, then we need a backup plan. Part of that will be your responsibility, Major."

"Yes, sir."

As they left the briefing room, Fetterman said, "Well, there's a good ninety minutes that I'll never get back."

"Hey, we were sitting in air-conditioned comfort, there was water, coffee and pastries, which, I noticed, you didn't touch."

"Poison, Major. I don't know who put the pastries in there."

"Were you really worried about poison?"

"No, sir. I just hoped you would accept that answer and we could move on from there."

"Well," said Gerber, "if you want to change the subject, what do you think our role in this is going to be? Bates hasn't told me anything about it other than we might be responsible for a backup plan."

"If I were to guess," said Fetterman, "I think that Bates wants to destroy that training base. Keep the Laotians out of the war. Or maybe I should say, Washington wants to destroy it and Bates has the job."

Gerber raised a hand to shade his eyes. He saw a flight of helicopters maneuvering on the airfield. He wasn't sure what they were doing but they looked to be empty. To Fetterman, he said, "Do you think that they, and by they I mean those in the Pentagon, will authorize a mission into Laos?"

"We've run clandestine raids into Laos and North Vietnam, not to mention Cambodia, in the past. The only good thing is that the press hasn't found out about those yet. Besides, it seems that the mission is already authorized. Now it's just a question of who goes and how."

Fetterman thought for a moment and then said, "The press has been publishing speculations and some wild tales told by company clerks who returned to the World who wanted to expand on their duty or claim expanded duty. Look what a brave soldier I was." He laughed. "Almost anyone with half a brain will know that those stories are bull."

They reached their office. Gerber hesitated at the door, almost as if he was afraid to enter. Standing there, in the bright sunlight, he said, "I don't think we're going in on this. I think they're going to use some of the local indigenous soldiers so they can claim a South Vietnamese Army operation. Plausible deniability."

Fetterman pulled open the door and said, "I think you're right. I'm surprised that Bates didn't say anything to us about it."

"He might be waiting for clarification from Washington or from MACV before he brings us too deeply into it."

"Before we get too deep into this," said Fetterman, "I think I'll stroll over to the hospital and visit with a nurse."

"She got a friend?"

"Yes, sir, she sure does, but I don't think they'd be interested in an old man like you. They like the young warrior types and sometimes even like Marines."

"At some point, Sergeant Major, I'm going to want to meet this nurse who fascinates you."

"Certainly, sir. What are you doing for dinner?"

"I thought about eating it, but you have a better idea?"

"Yes, sir. Come and meet the nurse. I'm having dinner with her tonight."

"Why, thank you, Sergeant Major, I would be delighted."

CHAPTER 8

The training of the local, indigenous personnel was not progressing as fast as Major Leonid Semenov had hoped. The recruits were frightened of all the Soviet soldiers after one of their fellows had been executed. It didn't matter that he had accidentally shot a fellow soldier, who had not survived the mistake. It was also the training schedule that had them working harder than they did in the field. There, they set the schedule and the activities, but here, in this camp, they were forced into a training regimen that taxed them physically and mentally and required them to gain skills for which they had no need.

Semenov thought that he suffered from the same rigors as the recruits. He was living in a hootch that was infested with some sort of vermin. He wasn't sure what was crawling around in the thatch of the roof or on the mud walls. He could hear them in the night and wondered what they were doing and if they were a danger to him.

And, while it was nearly oppressively hot during the day, in the night it was worse. He expected a cooling so that he might sleep but the temperature and the humidity remained high, making it difficult to sleep. If they dared to set up generators for electricity, they would call attention to themselves. Someone would see the lights or hear the generator running.

It also set up a resupply problem. The generator would require fuel to run. The logistics of getting the fuel to them would point an arrow at them. The mission was clandestine, and anything done to bring a little comfort to the Soviets would also indicate that something strange was going on. That was a bad thing.

Now he had a reluctant army, afraid of their instructors, afraid of the weapons and worn out by the training they didn't understand. The Soviet soldiers were slowly wearing out as well. They were far from home, in a foreign country that had little to offer them. The only good thing was that they could provide the benefits of communism to the locals. Of course, the locals would have to wait many years to receive any of those benefits.

Kapitan Aleksei Petrov entered the hootch and pulled a handkerchief from his pocket to mop his face. He looked as if someone had dumped a bucket of water over his head moments earlier. He saluted and asked, "You wanted to see me, sir?"

Semenov returned the salute and pointed at the only other chair. "Have a seat and tell me how training is going."

"We have learned that the recruits are unfamiliar with firearms, afraid of them and that they have a reluctance to become proficient. We have been drilling them on small unit tactics, but they can't seem to grasp any of the concepts. They don't seem to understand the thinking and that they must adapt to the changing situation rather than waiting for someone to tell them what to do. They exhibit no initiative."

Semenov sat back in his chair, causing it to squeak. "You're not suggesting that the recruits should be engaging strategic thinking?"

"No, sir. I thought it important for them to understand the basics so that they would be more alert. I realize that these recruits will never be able to lead, but we wanted them to be aware of the situation around them. They would need to respond to the commands quickly and if they can anticipate those commands, on a limited basis, well, it might be the difference in a fight."

"What is the next step?"

"I'm a little hesitant to end the rifle instruction until they can hit the target with some consistency. Wanting them to hit the bullseye is something of a dream right now."

"We must progress," said Semenov.

"Of course, Major. We're planning a patrol with an ambush. They think of a patrol as a stroll in the jungle that gets them out of some of the other work. We'll set up a mock ambush to test them."

"When does this take place?"

Now Petrov smiled. "Sergeant Volkov is going to lead the patrol and he's staging it right now. Lieutenant Fedorov and Sergeant Sidorov left about thirty minutes ago. They have the route of the patrol and they're going to set up an ambush at some point to see how the patrol reacts. Scare them enough so that they'll be more responsive to instruction."

"Isn't that somewhat dangerous?"

"No, Major. There is no live ammunition, just blank rounds, and artillery simulators for grenades. No one will get hurt." He thought about that and then said, "No one will get shot."

"Are you going to participate in this?"

"No, sir. I'm leaving most of it in the hands of the NCOs. They're very good at this sort of thing."

Although it was a violation of good small unit tactics, the plan was for the patrol to follow an animal trail into the jungle. After about a mile, it jogged to the left, near a shallow stream. On one side was a high bank and thick jungle. It provided cover for the ambushers. Using signs and hand signals that had been taught to the recruits, Sidorov positioned the recruits in an L-shaped ambush. One recruit was sent down the trail about one hundred yards. When he heard the approaching patrol, and Sidorov was sure he would hear them because their noise discipline was non-existent, he would run back.

Fedorov watched as the recruits took up their positions. He stationed himself at the rear of the long axis of the ambush where he would have a better view of the fight. For a while he stood there, near a large tree with gnarled bark and a strange odor. Eventually, tired, he knelt on one knee like a player taking instructions from a coach.

The plan had been for the patrol to follow in thirty minutes, but it was nearly an hour before the recruit came running back. He shouted that they were near, but neither Sidorov nor Fedorov understood the words. They knew what they meant. The patrol was near, but Fedorov wished the recruit would shut up.

The patrol was heard long before it could be seen. They weren't practicing noise discipline as Fedorov had expected. They were chatting with one another and Volkov wasn't doing anything to correct them. His philosophy seemed to be that he'd allow them to learn from their mistakes. He knew about where the ambush would be sprung. He had coordinated the ambush with the other Soviet soldiers the night before.

They reached the bend in the stream. After the front had passed, the ambushers opened fire using blanks. The sound wasn't all that different from what would be heard in a real ambush.

Some of the patrol fell to the ground, their hands over their ears. Others turned to flee the way they had come, and a few jumped into the steam, scrambling up the bank opposite of the ambushers.

Volkov began yelling, "Cease fire." He spoke in both Russian and Laotian.

Fedorov, who had been behind the ambush, watched for a moment and then tried to enforce the cease fire. He was also watching the patrol. No one there was making any defensive move. They had been told, ordered, to charge the ambush to break it up. That had been during the instruction at the camp, and in the briefing conducted by Volkov before they moved out.

Volkov ran into the middle of the ambush. He kicked at the soldiers lying on the ground. He screamed at them. He ordered them to fire back. He told them this was a rehearsal. They had nothing to fear.

Fedorov, who had seen some of the patrol run into the jungle, ordered Volkov to chase them down and bring them back. He pointed in the direction they had run. But Volkov was trying to organize a response to the ambush. He thought that was the most important lesson.

Sidorov grabbed at the men next to him. He pushed them into the jungle and then waved for them to follow him. He ran through the thick growth, ignoring the thorns and stickers. He pushed aside the branches blocking his path with the barrel of his weapon. When he looked back, he saw that he was alone. That didn't matter. He wanted to catch those who had run.

Volkov joined Fedorov and said, "This was one fucked up exercise."

"Round up everyone. Get a head count and then head back to the camp. We'll have a debriefing there."

"Yes, sir. You know that some of the recruits ran as if it was a real ambush."

"I saw that. Sergeant Sidorov is in pursuit. He'll bring them back."

"He'll be outnumbered."

"Do you really think that is going to make a difference. Once he catches them, they'll stop running."

"I'm not so sure, sir."

Fedorov turned his attention directly to Volkov, staring into his eyes. "What does that mean?"

"It means that the recruits don't believe that I'm fluent in their language. I've kind of cultivated the belief by not responding to some of the insults they throw around. I think those who ran into the jungle were deserting."

"Is Sidorov in any danger?"

"The recruits are unarmed, well, they have no live ammunition. Sidorov's rifle is loaded with live ammo, and he has his pistol. The recruits won't try to ambush him and if they turn to attack, he can take them."

Fedorov looked back over his shoulder, and wondered if that was true. They were farmers and peasants, but they had now had several weeks of military training. They might have learned enough to use some of those lessons against Sidorov.

He said, "Get the recruits out of here. I'll go after the others."

"Yes, sir."

Fedorov dropped the magazine holding the blanks from his weapon and shoved in one with live rounds. He forded the stream, climbed the bank, and followed the trail. The recruits had not attempted to disguise their path. Even though he was not a skilled tracker, he was able to follow the path easily.

He picked up the pace, aware that he was breathing heavily, though he wasn't running. The jungle was tough. The heat was oppressive. He wished he was back in the Soviet Union, in one of the northern cities where the weather was tolerable even if it was cold.

He came to a place where it looked as if the recruits had split up. That worried him. It suggested planning on their part. He hadn't thought much of the recruits, believing them to be of low intelligence. They responded slowly to training. They failed to grasp the simplest of concepts and were poor marksmen. They were poor soldiers doing only enough to avoid punishment.

He stood there for a moment, looking at the various directions he could take, worried about a real ambush. Finally deciding on a direction, he pushed forward, but his pace had slowed. He was looking for that ambush.

Then, to his right, he heard an AK firing on full auto. That had to be a recruit. Fedorov knew that Sidorov was not shooting. Fedorov pushed through the jungle, not using a path but trying to take a direct direction to the firing.

As he got closer, he heard the single shots that would be Sidorov. Then he was there, looking at the back of a recruit aiming at Sidorov. Without hesitating, Fedorov raised his own weapon and fired. The recruit fell, looking as if the bones had suddenly melted.

There was return fire, but it was poorly aimed. Fedorov dropped to a knee, searching for the source. He saw a recruit standing up, looking around. Fedorov aimed at the man's head and fired. The recruit disappeared into the foliage around him.

"Who's there?" asked Sidorov.

"Fedorov. Are you engaged?"

"No. I think the guy only had blanks. Wasn't smart enough to pick up any live ammo."

"Are they all accounted for?"

"Not yet. How many have you seen?"

"I dropped two of them."

"Then there is one more out there somewhere."

Fedorov thought that over and then said, "Retrieve the weapons. Leave the bodies to rot where they fell. We'll get a head count at the camp and figure out who is missing. Then we'll go retrieve them."

"Yes, sir."

Semenov was waiting for the return of the patrol and the ambushers. He had been in radio communication with Fedorov and knew that the exercise hadn't just failed, it had turned deadly. He knew that some of the recruits had fled the area with their weapons.

Volkov led the recruits into the compound. He nodded toward Semenov but didn't salute him. He halted the patrol and turned around, facing them. "Take your weapons to the armory and stay there with them. Do not empty your pockets or remove anything from your rucksacks."

When they started to move, Volkov yelled, "Do not move until I tell you to go!" Now he looked back at the major and said, "Sir, I need to have the rest of the team at the armory."

Confused by the request, Semenov said, "They'll be there in a few minutes." He then headed to the Russian hootches.

When Volkov saw his fellow soldiers walking to the armory, he said, "In single file, let's march to the armory."

Lined up under the tent, at the tables that had been used during marksmanship training, were the Russian soldiers. They were all wearing American-made jungle fatigues, boonie hats and pistol belt holding a Colt 1911A1 pistol. Major Semenov was standing behind them, watching everything carefully.

Volkov ordered, "Line up behind the tables and wait for instructions." Figuring that they wouldn't understand the orders, he pushed them into lines, so each Soviet soldier had several recruits in front of him.

"Release the magazine from your weapon, set the magazine and the weapon on the table in front of you. When the soldier tells you, empty your pockets and empty your ruck."

The first few recruits had nothing extraordinary in their possession. Volkov was surprised at some of the things they had carried into the field. Although this was an exercise, they had been told to take nothing with them of a personal nature. Carry only military issue. Everything else was contraband and would be confiscated if found.

It was in the second round of the inspection that the first personal item was spotted. It was an old knife with a handle wrapped in some kind of cord. The blade was chipped and the knives that were issued to the recruits were harder steel and held a sharper edge.

Volkov walked to the table, slapped the recruit on the side of the head and picked up the knife. He held it in the air and said, "You were told not to take a personal item with you. This is now mine."

The recruit stared at him but said nothing. He didn't look ashamed. He looked angry because he had thought of the knife as a weapon of war.

Just as Fedorov and Sidorov returned, carrying the weapons recovered from the recruits, Volkov saw the first live round. It wasn't clear if he had intended to reveal it or had accidentally grabbed it, but he dropped it on the table.

Semenov jumped forward and snatched it from the table. In Russian, he screamed, "What in the hell are you doing with live ammunition?"

The recruit didn't understand the question. He stood there, mute, his eyes large and frightened.

Volkov, in a voice filled with anger, asked, "What are you doing with that?"

The recruit looked down at the ground, and shrugged. He didn't answer the question.

Volkov bent down and began pawing through the recruit's ruck. In the bottom, he found more live ammo. There had been none in the magazine he had surrendered, but then, there were no blank rounds in it either. That meant he had planned to replace the blanks with live rounds at some point.

Volkov held up the ammunition. "Where did you get this?" The answer was obvious. Someone had stolen it during the marksmanship training. Volkov didn't know how widespread the theft had been. He knew that the Russians had been lax in counting the ammo. That would have to be changed.

Semenov finally said, "Place the recruit under arrest and confine him to one of the huts with a guard on the door."

Before the order could be carried out, Fedorov threw three AK-47s on the table. Next, he tossed the magazines on it. He said, "They were loaded with live ammo."

"What did they expect?"

"I believe, Major, it was a plan to escape our training here. It failed because the ambush was such a failure. Rather than shooting us, they fled into the jungle. I guess they thought we wouldn't notice."

"What happened to them."

Fedorov wiped his face with his bare hand, rubbed the sweat onto his jungle jacket and said, "We caught them and killed them. Rather we killed three of them, but there were others involved. One, maybe two, outran everyone. I thought it more important to report back here."

Semenov nodded. "Yes, of course. Do we know who they are?"

"I thought we'd muster the recruits and work it out from there. Once we know who, we should be able to find them."

"How would we do that?"

"Simple, Major. These are not sophisticated recruits. They'll head home."

Semenov took a deep breath and said, "They were sophisticated enough to gather ammunition without our detecting it. They were sophisticated enough to switch the blank ammunition with live rounds without our detecting it."

Now Volkov said, "We have caught one of the conspirators alive." He was standing with one hand on the shoulder of the man they had caught. "We can learn something from him."

Semenov said, "That's right. And there might be more here. Continue with the inspection. Separate those caught with live ammo from the rest of the recruits. I want the guilty interrogated immediately."

He thought for a moment and then said, "Collect all the weapons now. We have serial numbers so that we know which weapon belongs to which recruit. I want the hootches searched for other contraband and I want an inventory of the armory. I want to know if there is anything missing such as grenades."

"Yes, sir."

"Petrov, set up a guardhouse in one of the vacant hootches. I want a Russian guard on the door, and I want another Russian guard at the rear in case some wise guy figures to escape out the back. If someone tries that, kill him."

"Yes, sir."

"When you have that arranged, we'll put those we find there, starting with the one we have caught. All right, let's continue the search."

Kapitan Aleksei Petrov listened to the report on the patrol and what the ambushers had seen. He listened to both Fedorov and Volkov, learning what they had seen and done. He knew the general direction that the recruits had taken, and he now knew their names based on a head count.

There wasn't much to do to plan the new patrol. Petrov, Fedorov and Volkov would be leading it. Only five recruits would go with them. These were the best of the recruits who had grasped some of the finer points of sneaking through the jungle. Petrov suspected they had been hunters. Stealth was an important skill for hunting. The closer the hunter could get to the prey, they better the chance for a kill.

Petrov wanted to move out as quickly as possible. They would need little in the way of supplies, just some rations, water, and two spare magazines. They would move through the jungle directly toward the little hamlets where the deserters were probably holed up. The time frame for the patrol was scheduled for less than forty-eight hours.

Petrov wasn't thrilled with taking any of the recruits with them. There was some animosity between the Laotians and the Soviets. In any military organization, the lower ranking soldiers often believe they are being oppressed by the more senior members. They just didn't realize that the senior members were once in the same position and had the same attitudes. The senior members worked their way up, but when a soldier is on the bottom, everything seems oppressive.

As they formed on the southern side of the camp, Petrov asked Volkov, "Can we trust these recruits?"

Volkov grinned. "Of course. They're the brown noses. They work hard, they understand the lessons, and they are the best of the marksmen."

"When we find the deserters, are they going to side with their countrymen?"

"I believe, Kapitan, that they wish to come to the Soviet Union when all this is over. I have cultivated that idea, that we'll take those who perform well back to Moscow when we leave here."

"You stay with me to translate my orders." He turned his attention to Fedorov. "You act as a rear guard, only you'll be watching our recruits. I accept Sergeant Volkov's assessment, but I don't fully trust them when we open fire."

"Yes, sir."

With the sun directly overhead, they moved toward the trees. They didn't follow a regular path because they didn't want to create an indication of activity in the area. They wanted it to look as if it was just a collection of huts that weren't occupied, or at least, not used often.

Volkov, who had taken the first compass reading, found a point to enter the jungle and then, directly in front of them, a tall tree that had been hit by lightning that made it stand out. When they reached it, he used the compass again, finding another landmark some distance away, and walked toward it.

They weren't in enemy territory. There would be no Americans around, no South Vietnamese, and given what he had been told, there would be no members of the Laotian Army. The Laotians were their allies. There was nothing to fear from them.

After only two or three hours, they came to a ridgeline that was some fifty feet above the jungle floor. Volkov climbed it carefully, crouching as he neared the crest. Although there was thick jungle at the top, he wasn't sure what was on the other side.

At the top, off to the right, he noticed that the jungle was much brighter, suggesting an opening. Crouching slightly, he moved in that direction. The jungle thinned and spread out; in a slight valley was an open area that held rice paddies. It wasn't a large area but one that was being cultivated. Volkov took a knee in the soft, wet vegetation and waited for Petrov and the rest of the patrol to catch up.

He saw Petrov coming and waved him down. Petrov crouched, worked his way around a fallen tree and a large bush covered with thorns. He said, quietly, "What we got?"

"This is the first hamlet. I would think that if I was running away, I'd want to put more distance between me and our soldiers."

"You think they're here?"

"I don't know, sir. But there is smoke coming from one of those huts. Someone has built a fire in there."

"Why would the recruits do that?"

"Because they don't know better and because they're hungry and they're cooking their food just as they would if they hadn't been recruited by us."

"Okay," said Petrov. "We'll take up a position here. I'll have Fedorov take two recruits with him around to the right where he can watch that side of the hamlet. We'll wait until we're sure that they're here."

"If they're not, we're just giving them a chance to get farther away."

Before they could execute the plan, one of the recruits came out of a hut, held a hand to his forehead to shield his eyes against the sun. He turned slowly, as if fearing that someone might be nearby. When he saw nothing, he returned to the hut.

"They're here," said Volkov unnecessarily.

"I see that."

Fedorov crawled up and said, "Did you see?"

"Yes."

"What are we going to do?"

Petrov grinned. "Approach carefully, call them out and when they appear, kill them."

"Without explanation? Without a hearing of some sort?"

"They're deserters. They deserve nothing from us."

"We have other recruits with us," said Fedorov.

"Yes, and they'll tell the others what happens to deserters who steal and attempt to kill us."

Fedorov shrugged. "How are we going to do this?"

"We'll take up positions with a good view of that hut where there is smoke and call them out. When they don't surrender, we will fire what we will call warning shots."

Volkov gave instructions to the Laotians. Three of them moved out with Fedorov, staying just inside the trees. When he was in position, Volkov walked out into the open and shouted. There was no response. He moved closer and ordered, "Come out with your hands up."

There was a single shot that came nowhere near him. He stood his ground and ordered, "Throw out your weapon. Come out with your hands up." He didn't wait for another shot but hurried back to the trees.

Petrov aimed at the door of the hut and fired a three-round burst into it. Nothing happened. He fired again and this time there was return fire, but it was wide to the left. There was another burst, but Petrov didn't see either the muzzle flash or any movement.

Fedorov ran from the jungle, toward the hut, crouching low as if to avoid a strong wind. A man appeared in the door. Volkov took aim and fired. The man fell back, into the shadows.

Now Petrov was up and moving. Using the cover of the other huts, he ran down the slope and skidded to a stop with his back to one of the mud walls. There was more shooting and Petrov looked around the corner.

Fedorov was kneeling with his weapon to his shoulder. He fired several single shots into the hut. He then stood up and shouted, "I got him!"

Petrov left his cover and as he did, he saw movement to his right. He spun and saw another recruit taking aim at Fedorov. He opened fire on full automatic. It was a long burst and caught the recruit by surprise before he could pull the trigger. The man dropped to the ground and didn't move.

Fedorov laughed and yelled, "Thanks!"

"You should have known better." He turned and waved at Volkov, telling him to search the other huts. They found nothing in any of them. The recruits had fled into the jungle with almost nothing other than their weapons. They had been found, the weapons recovered and the deserters dead. They would leave the bodies where they fell. There was nothing more to do.

CHAPTER 9

Sergeant First Class Eric Mendes had called for the briefing in one of the corners of the Tactical Operations Center. It was a heavily sandbagged building, partially sunken into the ground, making it a more difficult target for enemy mortars and rockets. Although it was underground, which helped to keep it cool, there were two air conditioners blowing cold air and there were both floor fans and table fans circulating that air.

Sitting in a variety of chairs were the rest of his team, dressed in the same fashion. There was no table there, but Mendes had an easel set up that held a partial map of southern Laos alongside several aerial photographs of the drop zone.

Staff Sergeant Ian Morgan held a can of Pepsi in one hand and was still wearing his sunglasses, though their corner of the TOC was in semi-darkness. Across from him was Sergeant Bruce Hendrick. Staff Sergeant Thomas Crockett leaned back in his chair, the back of his head against the plywood wall. It looked as if he was about to fall asleep.

Mendes, his voice quiet, said, "We go tonight. We'll have enough moonlight for the jump. We'll go out at thirty thousand feet and free fall to two thousand feet. I know that you know that, but we have to be careful with a night jump. The perspectives are different and our margin for error is tiny. Of course, you can pop your chute at a higher altitude if you need the extra time to adjust your landing."

Mendes turned and tapped one of the pictures. This is the DZ. It's shaped like a rhombus…"

"What in the hell is a rhombus?"

"It's my word for the day," said Mendes. "Think of it as a parallelogram with strange sides."

"That's not helpful."

"It's a misshapen square for crying out loud," said Morgan. "Is this relevant?"

"Thank you, Ian," said Mendez. "You'll note that there is a large stream about a klick from the DZ. That'll help you orient yourself. It should be easy to see in the moonlight."

Mendes turned his attention to Hendrick, the youngest member of the team. "Bruce, you'll be responsible for the radio. If you lose all your equipment, you had better hang onto the radio."

Hendrick said, "I'm not stupid."

Mendes ignored the comment. He said, "We've been over this several times. It seems that I should be making some sort of speech about the importance of the mission and how we all know our jobs, but I don't know what it would be."

Crockett said, "How about keep your head down and keep your powder dry?"

"That's not helpful," said Mendes. "I will only stress that we need to get into position before morning beginning twilight. If we can't make the target area, we'll have to hole up for the day. I don't want to spend any more time out there than I have to. We have a long way to go in the dark of a jungle, but we should be able to make it."

Mendes was about to end the meeting when he had a thought. "I want to go over the SAFE areas. If something happens and we get separated on the infiltration, then we are supposed to make our way to the objective. We can rally there. On exfiltration, we will head to areas to the south and east. There are two designated PZs. If we find enemy soldiers in one, then we go to the other."

He stopped talking and pointed to an area on the map. "You can see the landmarks here for PZ one. It is bordered by that road running down the west side of it. There is supposed to be a stream on the east side, and we are not to cross it. The second PZ is here. The landmarks are not as evident. We need to stay inside the confines of these areas. If we are separated on exfiltration, then there are selected areas for evasion. They're farther away but closer to the South Vietnamese border. Any questions?"

"Chow?"

"I understand that there will be steak and eggs for us later. I want everyone to rest this afternoon. Get some sleep. It'll be a long night."

As they stood up, Mendes said, "Remember, no smoking in the hour before we take off. No drinking tonight. I don't want someone half in the bag when we climb on the aircraft."

"You don't have to tell us that," said Crockett. "We know the rules."

"But as a top-notch NCO, it is my duty to make redundant comments. Keeps you people on your toes."

About two hours before sunset, Mendes made his way to the staging area, which was a secured location in the rear of one of the hangars. It was a large room with a single door and no windows. There were chairs, tables and little else. An air conditioner was built into the wall to keep the temperature tolerable in the room.

For hours, their equipment had quietly been moved into the room so that it didn't seem that a mission was being staged there. Mendes worked his way through the equipment, ensuring that it was in good condition.

Crockett arrived next carrying a Pepsi in one hand and his rifle in the other. He was dressed in tiger-striped fatigues and wore a rucksack. As he entered, he said, "I'm here, Eric. What do you want me to do?"

"Run a check on the equipment over there. Make sure that it is in operating condition and then separate it into loads for the others."

Crockett set his weapon on one of the tables, took a long pull at the Pepsi and then tossed the empty can at a waste basket. He missed but didn't bother to pick it up.

Morgan and Hendrick arrived about twenty minutes later. They found Mendes and Crockett relaxing. They were playing gin rummy with an old, worn deck of cards. Mendes knew that the deck was missing the ten of hearts, but it seemed that Crockett had not caught on.

Mendes looked at his watch and said, "You're about five minutes late."

"Traffic," said Morgan.

Mendes put his cards on the table and said, "Let's get suited up. The smoking lamp is out now."

"We've got an hour before we board the aircraft and then a long flight," said Hendrick.

"Don't care," said Mendes.

Hendrick dropped his equipment on the floor and then sat down. He picked up one of the cards and then dropped it back on the table.

Mendes said, "Do we need to go over the mission profile again?"

"We have it, Sergeant," said Morgan.

After they were ready, Mendes said, "I think there will be a truck pulling up close and we can ride out to the aircraft. I don't really think anyone would see us walking out there or think anything about it, but a little security never hurts. Anyone have any issues?"

"How do I get out of this chicken outfit?" asked Hendrick.

"Just refuse to jump."

Now Hendrick smiled and said, "But I'd end up with a leg company humping the boonies. No thank you."

"So, you don't really want out?"

"Why should I get out? I get jump pay and combat pay and given our status, we're pretty much left alone."

Crockett stopped the discussion. "Truck's ready for us."

Mendes said, "This is the point where I'm supposed supply some sort of pep talk but I have nothing to say that you haven't heard a hundred times. Let's go." That was almost his standard speech.

There was a knock on the door and someone, mimicking Mendes, shouted, "Let's go."

Crockett shouldered his gear and then opened the door. Sitting five feet away was a deuce and a half with the tailgate down and the screening canvas flipped back. He walked to the truck, tossed his ruck into the back, and climbed in. The rest of the team followed with Mendes entering last.

Once concealed inside, Mendes said, "When we're about thirty minutes from the jump, we go on oxygen."

"We know that," said Hendrick.

"Of course you do. I just like hearing the sound of my own voice. Besides, it's going to be loud in the airplane. When I go on oxygen, you all do the same."

"Yes, Drill Sergeant," said Hendrick using the term that recruits in basic training used.

About a minute after the C-130 took off with Mendes and his team, the first of the enemy rockets hit the base with a loud flat bang that distinguished the detonation from that of a mortar. Fetterman, who was standing near the door, didn't flinch when the rocket hit. He said, "I think that was south of here. Not all that close."

Gerber, who had been sitting and reading, looked up from the book and asked, "That it?"

"Don't know. They usually fire a barrage."

There was another bang, just a little closer, but both knew that rockets were difficult to aim. Gerber closed the book and stood up. "Should we head for a bunker?"

"I think it will be over before we can get there. I see a fire burning close to the hospital."

There were several crumps. "Mortars now," said Gerber.

"Nowhere near us. We best stay put."

"What if they hit the hospital?" asked Gerber.

"Carmen wasn't working tonight," said Fetterman.

Gerber grabbed his weapon and asked, "Should we head over there? Might be able to help."

Fetterman turned and picked up his M-16. "I'm ready when you are."

They listened but heard nothing more. There had been half a dozen rockets and then a dozen or so mortars. They heard one of the helicopter gun teams winding up the aircraft for countermortar. It was a flight of two gunships that scrambled after the first rocket had hit. They were supposed to suppress the enemy artillery, but the rocket and mortar attack was more harassment than the prelude to a ground assault. The enemy knew the procedure and they would be long gone before the helicopters got off the ground.

They ran across an open field, crouching slightly, though it wasn't necessary. They reached an area of hootches that belonged to an infantry company, ran through it. The fires were now brighter. Gerber thought that they might have hit one of the POL fields and it was the jet fuel burning. He wasn't sure.

They rounded a building and saw that it wasn't the hospital on fire but one of the supply buildings. Fetterman said, "I think they hit the nurse's billets." He diverted to the right.

When they arrived, there were several nurses sitting outside while others worked on them. Fetterman yelled, "Carmen? Are you here?"

Fetterman grabbed the arm of one of the nurses and asked, "Carmen…"

"Over there. Shrapnel wound to the left leg. Nothing bad. Didn't hit the artery. She'll be fine."

Fetterman said, "I'll go talk to her."

"Right behind you, Tony."

Carmen was sitting in a ragged lawn chair. There was blood on her leg but there wasn't much. She saw Fetterman and grinned. "Purple Heart."

Fetterman laughed. "You going to accept the Purple Heart for that scratch?"

"Damned right. I earned it. I have shed blood in the defense of my country. Why shouldn't I accept it?"

"No reason," said Fetterman. "Anyone hurt badly?"

"No, just some scratchers here and there. Minor wounds, though one of the doctors had a piece of shrapnel lodged in this left arm near the shoulder. They took him to the hospital. That wasn't hit."

Fetterman knelt beside Carmen and took her hand. "You going to tell your parents?"

"I signed the form that said I didn't want them told in the event of a minor wound. No reason to scare them. I might try to get through to them on the MARS radio in a couple of days to tell them. Then I can tell them that it had happened a couple of days ago."

"It is minor?"

"Yeah. I bandaged it myself. No stitches and probably a small scar that won't even be noticeable."

"Is that a good idea? Treating yourself?"

Carmen hesitated for a moment and then said, "It was minor, more of a small cut. There were those who were hurt worse than me." Then she grinned. "You've heard the proverb 'physician, heal thyself.'"

Gerber, who had been in the background, said, "You must know that infection is a major concern."

"Yes, sir. I'll meet with a doctor and make sure that we watch for infection."

Gerber turned to Fetterman. "Tony, we're good here?"

"Yes, sir."

"I'm going back to make sure that the team got off safely. I doubt the attack was directed at them, but I want to make sure the aircraft was gone before the first rocket hit."

"I'll catch up in a few minutes."

Mendes was always uncomfortable in the rear of the C-130s. He found the canvas seating on the metal tubing didn't seem to be designed for humans. He knew it was designed the way it was to accommodate the highest number of soldiers that it could. The aircraft was built by the lowest bidder and the comfort of the soldiers was not a major concern. True, there were what were known as "comfort pallets," but those were used for the big brass. The comfort pallet could be loaded and strapped down just as other cargo. They contained comfortable seats and other amenities, that made up for having to ride in the rear of a noisy C-130. Mendes thought they could have provided a comfort pallet because he and his team were the only passengers and given the nature of the mission, it would have been nice for them to ride in comfort. No reason not to.

Thirty minutes away from the DZ, they went on the supplemental oxygen. The lights turned red and dimmed to enhance their night vision. Mendes first looked at his team. They all seemed to be relaxed, which sometimes startled him. They were about to jump into enemy territory, they were hours from help if things turned to shit, and the stress level was going to be high because jumping from thirty thousand feet was not a normal parachute infiltration. There were so many things that could go wrong and yet it looked as if Crockett and Hendrick were asleep though he knew they must be awake. Morgan was sitting there, staring at the floor. Mendes thought about saying something to him, but he didn't want to shout over the noise of the engine.

The crew chief, who now had a supplemental oxygen bottle strapped to his chest, knelt in front of Mendes. He flashed ten fingers and then five, telling Mendes they were fifteen minutes from the DZ. Mendes nodded his understanding and slapped Morgan on the shoulder, alerting him. Both Crockett and Hendrick had seen the crew chief's sign.

Mendes unbuckled his seat belt and stood up. He gathered his personal equipment, and the team equipment he was supposed to carry. Around him the rest of the team did the same thing.

The crew chief walked to the rear of the aircraft, tethered to one side so that he wouldn't fall out. He dimmed the lights so that there was just a ghostly red glow to everything. Just before the ramp was lowered the lights would go out so that there was no chance of anyone on the ground seeing anything. Mendes thought little of the precaution because there was a bright moon, and they were thirty thousand feet in the air.

There was the ringing of a bell and when that happened, Mendes and the others moved closer to the ramp. The crew chief lowered it, and the interior of the aircraft was plunged into freezing cold. All those in the cargo area were wearing warm clothes.

The crew chief held up one finger and Mendes moved out, onto the ramp. A moment later, the crew chief pointed to him, and Mendes stepped into space. The others followed immediately. Mendes looked down but couldn't see much of anything. There were clouds in the way, and he thought that was a good thing. No one would have seen them tumble out of the aircraft. As soon as they were out, the C-130 turned to the southeast, heading back into the relatively friendly skies of South Vietnam.

Mendes broke through the cloud deck and saw the black of the jungle under him. He finally spotted the stream that he had seen on the map. It was a silver ribbon looking more like a highway than a stream. Finally, he saw a break in the trees that was the right shape that he had studied on the aerial photographs. He adjusted his free fall, aiming for that area. The other team members were doing the same thing.

He watched the lightly glowing numbers on the altimeter reel off as he plummeted toward the ground. He passed through five thousand feet and when he was sure he would land on the DZ, he pulled the ripcord. He heard the rasping of the nylon being pulled free and was suddenly jolted as the parachute canopy filled.

He hit the ground, rolled over and hit the quick release. He was down, uninjured. An instant later the others were there with them. Mendes crouched on one knee, searching the jungle, and listening to the sounds around him. There were no indications that they had been spotted.

He stood and said, quietly, "Let's get this stuff hidden, and get going. We have a long way to go before dawn."

There was no verbal response. Although it seemed they were alone, they didn't want to alert any enemy around them by talking. Hendrick pulled at his chute, and then gathered that used by Morgan. Crockett did the same and moved to the northwest side of the DZ.

Mendes, who had been freezing minutes before was now covered with sweat. The night was humid, which was no surprise. He stripped off the special suit he had been wearing and then collected the suits from the others. They would go into the same hole as the parachutes.

He reached the edge of the tree line and dropped the clothes next to the chutes. Morgan said, "It's almost impossible to dig here. Too many tree roots."

Mendes studied the ground around them. There were several fallen trees with bushes growing near them. There was a large space under the trunks of one of the trees. Mendes snapped his fingers and pointed. Quietly, little above a whisper, he said, "Shove everything under here and pile the dirt and other debris up to hide the opening."

"Someone is going to find this," said Morgan.

"Probably not soon and maybe not ever. Doesn't matter. We only need a few days until we're out of here and we aren't all that close to the target."

Crockett pushed one of the chute canopies under the log and then said, "There's a lot of room under here."

It only took ten minutes to hide the rest of the equipment. That put them ahead of schedule. The plan had called for a longer period for hiding the chutes and other gear. Mendez checked his watch and then the compass, looking at the faintly glowing numbers. "I'll take the point. We need to keep each other in sight and if it gets too dark, we'll need to stay in physical contact."

He stepped off the DZ and into the jungle. For a minute or two, he was able to see the stars and to orient himself by the constellations. They were bright in a night sky that wasn't ruined by light pollution or hidden by clouds. In a big city, all the lights would obscure the stars.

But once they moved deeper in the jungle, away from the DZ, the overhead canopy hid the stars and he had to rely on the moon and the compass. Mendes didn't believe there would be any enemy forces out until they got closer to the enemy camp. He had been told that it was a suspected training facility which meant there could be night patrols, but they would stay close to home. They wouldn't expect an American force nearby. But that didn't mean that Mendes could ignore his training.

After about an hour, Mendez halted. They were deep in jungle with only animal trails around them. In Vietnam, he would have avoided them, worried about boobytraps, but in Laos, there wouldn't be any such traps. The only people who would see them were civilian farmers and other members of the local population.

They set up back-to-back so that all sides were covered. Mendes slipped out his canteen and took a drink. He sloshed the water around in his mouth and then swallowed. At this point he wished it was a cold beer rather than tepid water that tasted slightly of plastic.

Ten minutes later, he tapped Morgan on the shoulder, who tapped Crockett, who tapped Hendrick. They moved out again, pushing through thicker jungle and moving slower. Mendes didn't pick up the pace. They were still ahead of schedule as far as he could tell.

They crossed a shallow stream that hadn't been on any of the maps they had and was not on any of the aerial photographs. Given the canopy and the size of the stream, Mendes wasn't surprised. He believed they were still on course. They had carefully plotted the route long before they left Vietnam.

They began a slight climb which, according to the intelligence, was about a klick from the training camp. Mendes slowed the pace, now worried about noise. The team was moving through the jungle carefully, but Mendes knew that one man could sneak through it without making a sound, but as you added people the problem of compromise by noise grew. He couldn't fault the team because he heard only the occasional sound from them. He was sure that the jungle around him masked the sound.

He halted just below what he thought of as the military crest of a ridge, knelt and surveyed the area around him. He crept forward slowly until he could see down, into the slight valley. His first thought was why they would build in a depression, surrendering the high ground to an attacking force. He then realized they probably had taken a site that already had the necessary structures so that they wouldn't have to construct anything and give away their presence.

Mendes stretched out on his stomach. There was no movement below and no sign of guards. That didn't mean there weren't any guards, only that he couldn't see them. There was no sign of electricity, but he knew there were generators down there. At the moment they were shut down. Even as far away as he was, had the generators been operating, he would have heard them.

He felt the rest of the team spread out around him. The camp was a collection of mud and thatch hootches arranged in no real pattern. There were no vehicles visible, but then a truck or jeep would give away the nature of the camp. They were working hard to ensure that the footprint in the aerial photographs would not reflect the military nature of the camp. Although Mendes didn't know the number of men below, he did know there were about a dozen men assumed to be Soviets or other Europeans and probably a hundred men recruited from the local populations.

Without having to give the order, the men moved into positions. They tried to keep each other in sight but spread out enough that if one was discovered, it might not give away the others. They would have a good view of the camp, given the ridgeline they were on and the layout below them.

Mendes found himself getting sleepy. It had been a long day and would be even longer. He dozed for a moment, jerked awake but only a few minutes had passed. He took a small pill from a packet he carried, put it in his mouth and then swallowed a mouthful of water. By the time the sun came up, he knew he would be wide awake and ready to watch the camp until sunset. A long day lay ahead, but he knew he would be awake for it.

CHAPTER 10

When Kapitan Aleksei Petrov walked out of his hootch about thirty minutes after dawn, he sensed that something had changed. He looked out into the jungle surrounding the camp but saw nothing out of place. There were the common sounds of the jungle coming alive as the sun rose. There were areas of mist, the result of high humidity and the cool of the morning.

He heard someone walking up behind him and said to Sergeant Volkov, "You're up early this morning."

"Couldn't sleep. Too hot. I was sweating like a pig and decided that I should just get up."

Petrov said, "Same with me. Just looking at the jungle. Doesn't seem to be quite right this morning."

"I don't see anything, sir."

"Just a feeling. There is something different out there, but I don't know what it is."

"You know, sir, we have the recruits. I could take a patrol out to look around. See if I can find anything."

Petrov considered that for a moment and then said, "Might make for an interesting training exercise. Have them on the lookout for anything out of place. Circle the camp that way. See if they can find anything strange."

"Do you know what is bothering you, sir?"

"That's just it, I don't. I can't tell you where to look. It just seemed to me that something changed in the night. It's probably nothing. One of those hunches that goes nowhere."

Volkov stretched, reaching up as high as he could. He turned slowly, studying the jungle around them. "Don't see anything different, sir."

"I don't either. Let's go find some breakfast. The cooks should have something ready for us."

They walked toward the hootch used as a kitchen and mess hall but found it deserted. No cooks and no recruits on KP. Petrov wondered what was going on because this didn't seem right but as he was about to send Volkov to wake up some of the recruits, Sergeant Popov, who had been designated as the Mess Sergeant arrived.

"Good morning, sir. May I help you?"

"Aren't you getting a late start this morning, Sergeant?"

"No, sir. Right on time. Recruits will be here momentarily to light the cooking fires. Hot breakfast will be ready in thirty minutes or so. You can have a cold breakfast now. Got some fruit, some of that dry cereal so popular in the West, but we don't have any milk made. I can get that done in five minutes."

Petrov said, "Well, I'm not all that hungry, just bored. I'll wait for the hot breakfast."

"Scrambled eggs and toast. I think we still have some orange juice, and coffee, of course."

"I'll wait here," said Petrov. He pulled a chair away from the table. It wasn't a comfortable chair, and the table was as sturdy as it could have been. He sat down and wished he had a morning newspaper to read. Had this been a Soviet camp anywhere else, there would be overnight messages which could be as entertaining as a newspaper. Here they were maintaining radio silence. Listening didn't pose a threat, but the major only wanted the radio monitored during duty hours, and, of course, when the generator was shut down, there was battery backup. But the major didn't want them draining the batteries, so there was no overnight radio traffic to entertain him.

Now he sat there, his legs crossed, smoking one of the last cigarettes that he had. He hadn't packed enough of them, had smoked too many too fast. Now he had to ration them or run out completely.

The recruits assigned to kitchen duty straggled in. One got the cooking fires going while others prepared the cold food. Popov dropped into a chair opposite him. "We'll have some eggs ready in a few minutes, sir."

"You seem to have this well-organized."

"Just followed the manual, sir. It outlines everything for me. And some of the other sergeants have been helpful."

Petrov coughed once and then said, "You notice anything strange this morning?"

"Strange? No, sir. Everything seems to be fine. Why?"

"Just wondering."

More of the Soviet team was arriving for breakfast. Major Semenov sat down and said, "How's it going?"

"Fine, sir. Going to have a training patrol go out this morning. An exercise in getting the patrol going out with little notice. Test the recruits. Then small unit tactics this afternoon."

"Again? They aren't taking to the training?"

"It's all new to them. They have nothing in their background to prepare them. Takes more time to teach them. They learn, but it is slow. Repetition is the key to success."

"Will you be going out with the patrol?"

"I don't think so, sir. Volkov will act as advisor, but I'll tell him to just observe unless they do something really stupid. Best way for them to learn is to let them make mistakes."

Popov showed up and asked, "Something I can get you, Major?"

"I'll just have what the Kapitan is having."

"Yes, sir."

Petrov took a deep breath and then asked, "How much longer are we going to be here?"

"Training schedule is set up for another six weeks. You know that."

"Yes, sir. But that doesn't tell me when we rotate home."

"There is another team scheduled in here at the end of the current syllabus. Once they're established, we can get out of this hellhole."

Petrov chuckled. "I thought you liked it here."

"I worry about my career, Petrov. This is not an assignment that leads to promotion. Who is here to see what we do? Unless something interesting happens to draw the attention of the brass, this will be seen as some sort of a second-rate assignment."

Popov arrived with a plate of scrambled eggs. He set it down in front of the major and then glanced at Petrov, who nodded just slightly. While Semenov's superior was somewhere else, Semenov was Petrov's superior. Petrov wanted to keep him happy so that he received a good rating when they finally returned to the Soviet Union.

Mendes was wide awake when those in the camp began to stir. At first, there was a single man walking around. Mendes thought he was taller and more robust than the average Laotian. He was wearing what looked to be American jungle fatigues and appeared to have lighter skin. Mendes didn't believe he was an American, only that he was wearing an American uniform.

The man stood there, looking up into the jungle around him. He didn't move for several minutes. He just stared at the jungle as if there was something strange to be seen. Mendes knew there was no way for him to know that he and his team were there, but it was unnerving. Mendes didn't believe in telepathy, but sometimes he'd had feelings that turned out to be true. It was a gut-level intuition that he had learned to respect. It wasn't always right, but there was no reason to ignore it. He wondered if that man down there had some sort of intuition that told him there was something wrong in the jungle. Finally, that man turned and walked back into the center of the camp.

Not long after that, the camp came awake. There were more men, all heading to one of the hootches in the middle of the camp. Smoke began to rise from one side of the building which was longer and narrower than the others. Mendes thought it might be an operation hootch but decided that it was probably used as a mess hall. Information that was mildly interesting but not very important in a tactical sense.

Others appeared, dressed in either black pajamas or in American tiger-striped fatigues. These were smaller men, thin, looking like civilians put into uniforms. They too moved toward the long building.

Mendes glanced to his right. He thought that Crockett was there but had camouflaged himself so well that he was nearly impossible to see. If Mendes hadn't known he was there, he would never have been able to spot him. Beyond Crockett was Hendrick. No matter how hard he looked, he couldn't spot him, and he was no more than forty feet away. The team had found good places to hide.

He turned his attention back to the camp below them. Somehow it didn't look like a military facility. Maybe it was the way the men meandered toward the mess hall. None were armed, expect for the Caucasian men and they were only carrying side arms. That gave it a somewhat military flavor, but it was not like anything in the Special Forces camps in Vietnam.

Slowly, Mendes removed his canteen from the cover, opened it and swallowed some water. Then he set the canteen near his right hand so that he wouldn't have to make much of a movement if he wanted more water. The key was to remain as motionless as possible.

For more than an hour, it looked more like a small village of civilians beginning their day without much coordination. Had it not been for the men in American-made uniforms, Mendes might have thought they had the wrong place. But then, as breakfast ended, there was shouting, and the men fell into formation. They kept the formation close to the buildings, trying to hide them from aerial observation.

Weapons were handed out. To Mendes it didn't seem the weapons had been assigned to a specific man. They were just handed out and he wondered if they worried about zero. The AK-47 was an automatic weapon and in the jungle environment such a weapon, putting out a lot of rounds rapidly rather than as aimed fire, might make the difference in a close fight or an ambush. In the jungle environment pinpoint accuracy wasn't nearly as important as suppressive fire.

A group of about thirty men formed at the perimeter of the camp, all armed, all dressed in American fatigues, with canteens and chest pouches holding additional magazines. It was a patrol that was going into the jungle for several hours but not for a long-range patrol.

They moved rapidly across the open ground between the edge of the camp and the beginning of the jungle. They entered it about a klick from where Mendes and his team hid. Mendes had to wonder if he had made some mistake that had been observed from the camp.

Once the patrol was in the jungle, Mendes lost sight of them. But then, he heard them. They had no noise discipline. They were coming towards Mendes and the team, reinforcing the idea that someone had spotted them. Mendes didn't know how it would have been possible. He just couldn't believe the mission had been compromised so quickly. Slowly he moved his hand along the side of his weapon and moved the selector from safe to full auto. And then he froze. Movement, however slight, could be the kiss of death.

He never saw the patrol once it had entered the jungle. He listened to them as they walked by his position, ten or twenty yards to the rear. There didn't seem to be flankers out, which meant that no one would be stumbling over him or the others. Although he wanted to watch the patrol, he didn't dare move. The slightest movement could catch the attention of the patrol, especially the trained soldiers in it. By remaining completely motionless, he had a better chance of avoiding detection.

After what seemed like an eternity, the noise faded in the distance. The patrol had passed them without finding them. Mendes breathed easier. His team was well trained and knew what they were doing.

Colonel Alan Bates entered the office of Major Mack Gerber without knocking. It was one of the benefits of being a colonel. He didn't have to knock on many doors before entering. Gerber was sitting at the desk, his feet propped up on it, holding a can of Pepsi in one hand and a sheet of paper in the other.

Without preamble, Bates said, "Team is down, and we assume in place. No communication from them."

Gerber dropped his feet to the floor and began to stand, but Bates waved him down. "As you were."

"Can I offer you a soft drink, sir? It's not exactly cold but it'll do until something better comes along or we get later in the day."

"Where's the Sergeant Major?"

"Checking on his nurse friend. She was wounded last night." Gerber held up a hand and said, "The very definition of a flesh wound, more of a scratch than anything else."

"Nurse friend?"

"Nothing like that, Colonel. She's the daughter of an old friend of his. He wanted to check up on her so that he could send a note to the family."

Bates finally said, "We need to talk about phase two of this operation. We have the HALO guys on the ground. Once they return, what are you going to do?"

Gerber said, "We've been to Song Be and talked to Martin and we were going to see Bromhead at his camp. Put together a strike force of the best of the Vietnamese soldiers, give what they need and send them in to take care of that camp."

"Just Vietnamese?"

"We thought about that," said Gerber. "There are a number, four or five, Special Forces soldiers fluent in Vietnamese who are of Asia descent. We thought they should go in as well."

"Anyone else?"

Gerber raised an eyebrow in question. "You have something in mind, Colonel?"

"I'm a bit concerned about command and control here. I'm sure the Special Forces soldiers are capable of handling the operation. Don't we have any officers qualified?"

Gerber laughed. "Every Special Forces officer is qualified. They are disqualified by their physical appearance. They're bigger, more robust, taller and are not as fluent in Vietnamese as they could be. Why do you want an officer to go in with them?"

"Political concerns —"

Gerber interrupted. "I would think sending in an American officer would be of great political concern if the mission goes south."

Bates nodded but said, "I'm a little worried about sending a force of South Vietnamese soldiers into Laos without a stronger command and control structure. I don't know why I'm bothered by this but I'm am."

"Do you have an officer in mind or are you looking for recommendations?"

"Recommendations."

Gerber rocked back in his chair, tented his fingers under his chin and looked up, as if seeking divine inspiration. "Well," he said, "I really hate to do this to him, but I think Bromhead would be good at it." He grinned. "After all, I trained him."

"Anyone else?"

"Martin at Song Be has a good relationship with his strikers. They are well trained and didn't panic under fire."

"No," said Bates. "Too new in-country and this is his first tour."

"You know, Fetterman would be perfect except he's not an officer. He doesn't stand out from the Vietnamese by very much. He's a little more robust than the average ARVN soldier, but he would fool them until you get up close. He speaks Vietnamese."

"As you say, he's not an officer."

"Next thing to it. I mean, I bet we could get him a warrant with no trouble."

"Paperwork would take too long," said Bates. "And I don't think he'd want to lose the prestige of being a sergeant major to become a wobbly one."

Fetterman entered the office and asked, "What are the two of you plotting?"

"How would you like to be a warrant officer?"

Fetterman looked from Bates to Gerber and back. "Why would I want to be a warrant officer? There are teenagers who are warrant officers. There are no teenagers who are sergeant majors. It takes time and talent to earn your way to sergeant major but only takes normal intelligence and reflexes to become a warrant officer. Few months in flight school and there you are."

"Don't worry about it, Tony. How is Carmen?"

"She's fine. More worried about what her parents will think. It really wasn't much of a wound."

"Colonel Bates was in here with his thoughts on phase two, or rather he was asking about my thoughts on it."

"Actually," said Bates, "I wanted to get both of you involved in this. The team is on the ground and gathering the intelligence."

"So, now we're talking about the strikers. Forming the company and getting them into position," said Fetterman.

"Exactly. How long will that take?"

Fetterman started to answer but Gerber cut him off. "Ten days from the point that the intel reaches us. That is, if we have the logistics figured out and the intel doesn't turn up something unexpected."

Fetterman added, "We should get Bromhead and Martin here to talk about this so that they can begin their planning."

Bates stood up. "I'll put out the call and they should be here by this afternoon, unless one or the other is out on patrol."

"We'll be here," said Gerber.

"Of course you will," said Bates as he left the office.

"Well, that was nice of him to drop by," said Fetterman. "Is the Pepsi cold?"

"What do you think?"

"I think not."

"You wouldn't be interested in an appointment to warrant officer?" asked Gerber.

"Really, sir? Can you see me as an officer?"

"Actually, Tony, I think you'd make a fine officer. Not a warrant officer, but a commissioned officer."

"Yeah, but this would cost me money, too. It's just not a good deal for me. I'm too old to be a wobbly one."

"Just wanted to make sure that it wasn't something you'd consider."

"Shouldn't we begin thinking about phase two?"

"Not until after lunch."

The feeling of unease had not deserted Petrov. He had not gone into the jungle with the recruits because he didn't trust them. He saw the way they looked at him and the other officers. It was with hatred. They blamed him and the other officers for their recruitment and their confinement to the camp. They weren't allowed to go home to see their families. They were watched, and if they disobeyed, the punishment was harsh. They'd already seen several of the other recruits killed.

The problem, though, was not the recruits. He just felt that something had changed, and he wanted to know what the patrol had found. He paced around the small hootch that had been assigned to him. His quarters, and that of the major, were the only quarters that were single occupant. Petrov wasn't sure that was an advantage, but it wasn't a privilege that he planned to surrender.

He had headed to watch one of the training sessions. The recruits were seated on the ground, listening to the lecture that was in Russian and translated by Sergeant Igor Smirnov. Smirnov's Laotian wasn't as good at that of Volkov. He spoke slowly and hesitantly, as if thinking about what he wanted to say in Russian and then translating into Laotian. Petrov knew that it wasn't the best way to speak a foreign language and Smirnoff had to repeat himself frequently.

Petrov didn't have much to do with Smirnoff. It was just the way the assignments worked out. He knew that Smirnoff had grown up in a small town in Siberia. He had joined the Army to get out of town and that might have been inspired by some sort of conflict with the police. Petrov didn't know the details and frankly, he didn't want to know them.

That was the trouble with the military. Sometimes men were accepted, or even drafted into service that shouldn't be soldiers. Smirnoff seemed to be one of those. He had a shady background. He looked overweight but that turned out not to be true. He didn't seem to be all that bright, yet he spoke four languages. Not all fluently, but well enough to be understood and to understand what was being said.

The biggest black mark against him was that he had political influence. Had it not been for that influence, Smirnoff probably would have found himself in a rifle company or in a tank battalion attached to a motorized rifle division. Not a bad assignment, but not as prestigious as serving in the Spetsnaz which could lead to better things after discharge. Petrov didn't like these politically connected soldiers but knew enough not to make enemies of them.

As Smirnoff shouted at one of the recruits, a flash to the right caught Petrov's attention. The patrol was returning. Petrov waited for the outcome of the shouting match before leaving. Smirnoff smacked the recruit on the side of the head, knocking off the recruit's hat.

If nothing else, Smirnoff was a tough disciplinarian. Petrov suspected he was more than a little sadistic, but sometimes, in training, a sergeant had to be a little sadistic to make the point. It gave the recruits the incentive to perform at their highest level. It sometimes made the difference between an adequate soldier and a good one.

Trying to suppress a smile, Petrov left the training area, heading toward the patrol. Volkov was giving them instructions in Laotian. They stood there for a moment and then dispersed. Volkov saw Petrov. He started to raise his hand in salute and then remembered there was to be no saluting.

"I was just telling them to clean their weapons and then turn them in to the armorer. I thought they should get some lunch after that."

"You weren't out very long."

"Didn't take long to circle the camp, even in the jungle. We went around twice but we didn't find anything."

Petrov didn't feel relieved. He still felt there was something wrong. "You made a good circuit? Searched carefully?"

Volkov glanced at Petrov and then asked, "Just what did you see?"

Petrov shrugged. "I didn't see anything specific. It was just that the jungle seemed wrong this morning."

"Any particular place?"

Petrov waved an arm, indicating the jungle to the south of them. "Something there. Something about it. I can't explain it."

Volkov removed his hat, rubbed a hand over his head and then put the hat back on. "Well, the patrol wasn't exactly the best example of military discipline. Had we been in a combat environment, the enemy would have heard us coming from a long way off. I let them go because I thought letting them get used to working as a unit was more important than noise discipline."

Petrov thought about that for a moment and couldn't think of a reason that it made a difference. Instead, he said, "You let them get away with it?"

"Yes, sir. This was more of a walk in the jungle than a military patrol. Sometimes you just have to let things go."

Petrov shook his head. "No, Sergeant. We must maintain the highest standards, teaching them to be good soldiers all the time. It must become second nature to them."

"Yes, sir. But we're still in the training environment. Given this was a last-minute training change, I was a little more lenient than I would normally be."

The discussion was sliding off in the wrong direction. Petrov waved a hand as if to clear the air. "Was the patrol adequate? If there was something wrong, would you have found it?"

Volkov considered the questions. "We found nothing out of the ordinary. I saw nothing in the jungle that didn't belong there. We were making noise, but I don't believe that caused any trouble for us. Just what are you after, sir?"

"I don't know, Sergeant. It was just a gut feeling that something was wrong."

"I could take out another patrol this afternoon. Training schedule today is flexible enough to do that. I could make it a full-scale tactical patrol with enforced noise discipline, a point man, flankers, and a rear guard. Maybe forty recruits. I can do it right."

"You didn't do it right this morning?"

"Sir, if there had been anything out of the ordinary, I think we would have found it unless the trouble was deeper in the jungle. Do you want us to go back out there?"

Petrov shook his head. "No. I don't think that will do any good."

"Is there anything else, sir?"

"No. Go get something to eat."

Petrov watched as Volkov walked away, toward his hootch. He turned and looked into the jungle again but the feeling that something was wrong would not go away. There *was* something wrong, he could feel it, but there was nothing more to be done.

CHAPTER 11

Major Mack Gerber was early. The meeting was scheduled for 1400 hours, but Gerber found himself in that limbo between when the meeting was to start, and the little time left before he needed to be there. There wasn't enough time to get anything done, other than walk to the conference room. He thought he might as well wait there as anywhere else. The conference room had air-conditioning while many of the offices and other facilities were just hot.

Gerber sat at the table, reading a newspaper that someone had left in the room. There was a beverage service on the table, but it contained no beverages. He wondered who had forgotten to fill it, and then wondered what he would want in it. Probably just water considering the time of day.

The door opened and Colonel Bates entered. "Comfortable?" he asked.

Gerber started to rise but Bates waved him down. "You're a bit early."

"Yes, sir. But, at least, I'm here."

Bates pulled out the chair at the end of the table, sat down and then set a stack of folders with a "Secret" cover sheet on them in front of him. "I see you have no notes."

"Don't need them. This is a planning session where we're going to be throwing around ideas based on what you tell us today. Bromhead and Martin will be the stars of this show. And Fetterman will have a notepad and pen with him in case we need to write down anything."

Bates grinned and said, "Shouldn't you be out painting rocks white or something useful instead of reading a newspaper."

"To make it worse, the paper is twelve days old. It not so much news as it is now history."

"Mack, is this a good idea?"

Gerber was surprised at the question. "I'm not sure what you mean, Colonel."

Bates tapped the folders in front of him. "There is nothing illegal about that camp in Laos. Or rather, we have no authority to do anything about it. The Soviets are there by invitation. At least I believe they were invited in."

"What is the ultimate purpose?"

"Here we run into a bit of a problem. That earlier recon didn't tell us much but from the little information I have, they are training the locals in the same way we do here. I don't know if they plan to engage in combat here in an attempt to establish a camp like those we have done. I don't know if they are looking to operate here or just in Laos. Our best course of action might be to withdraw our team and pretend that they are not there."

"I think we would overrun such a camp easily," said Gerber, unsure of what was bothering Bates.

"The VC and NVA haven't had much luck in overrunning our camps. They succeeded at Lang Vei because the Marine QRF was tied down at Khe Sanh and the camp was close enough to the border that the NVA brought in tanks."

"True," said Gerber, "but we control the air and ground here. Such a camp would be overwhelmed because we could cut the lines of communication. We wouldn't even have to attack. Just wait them out."

Bates was silent for a moment and then said, "But that doesn't really answer the question about us attacking that camp in Laos."

"Plausible deniability, Colonel. It won't be us. It'll be the South Vietnamese who did it."

"You think the world will buy that?"

"Our allies will fall in line behind us. The Laotians might complain but the Soviets won't make much of a stink because they're involved, and the communists in other parts of the world will protest, not to mention the college students."

Before Bates could respond, the door opened and both Bromhead and Martin entered, followed by Fetterman, who carried a case of beer and a six pack of Pepsi.

Bates asked, "You plan for a long meeting, Sergeant Major?"

"I was in here earlier and saw that there was a lack of liquid refreshment. I rectified that situation and caught up with the captains at the door. Beer is cold at the moment. The Pepsi, not so much."

Bates looked at his watch. It was now two minutes after the hour but about three hours before it was the cocktail hour.

"Gentlemen," said Bates, "I believe regulations prohibit our partaking in the beer at this early hour." He hesitated. "But as there's no one here but us, who would know." He pulled the beer close and attacked the cardboard case with his Ka-bar combat knife.

Sergeant First Class Eric Mendes was hot, tired, and his right leg was beginning to cramp. He had counted ten Caucasian men in the camp below him. They were all dressed in American jungle fatigues and carried American-made weapons with a single exception. Mendes knew that many Americans carried AK-47s captured after a battle or found in a weapons cache. He'd seen so many AK-47s, SKS rifles, and RPGs that he sometimes wondered if the enemy was supplying weapons to the Americans and the South Vietnamese.

He slowly stretched his leg, trying to work out the cramp. He drank more of his water and that seemed to help. What he wanted to do was stand up and massage his leg. To walk off the cramp, but it was about the middle of the afternoon. There was no one around him other than other members of the team. The enemy below probably wouldn't see him. Mendes knew it was a violation of the rules. Stay hidden. Don't move and observe. Do nothing to call attention to yourself.

There was more movement in the camp. He couldn't get an accurate count of the locals in training. Too much movement and nothing distinctive about them. He did count twenty wearing American fatigues that looked as if they belonged to an older brother who was taller and stockier. The rest were dressed in black pajamas, just as the VC wore in South Vietnam.

Mendes watched what he thought of as a class in hand-to-hand combat. The moves being taught were basic and the students didn't seem to understand what they were shown. Their efforts were half-hearted. They were going through the motions to avoid the wrath of the Caucasian men in the American uniforms.

Mendes realized that he was thinking of them as Caucasian men in American uniforms as opposed to Americans. There was something about them; the way they moved, the way they interacted with the Laotians, the way they carried their weapons and equipment, all suggested they weren't Americans.

There was nothing to tell him who they were or where they came from. He was too far away to hear anything that was being said. Given the briefings he had received, he believed they were Soviet soldiers, but there was nothing to actually prove that.

The only way to gather additional information was to move closer to the camp. Mendes could see no reason to do that. He had confirmed the Caucasian men training the locals in tactics, marksmanship, unit discipline and other military subjects. He was studying the layout of the camp, and he was forming opinions about the value of the training, which was what he was supposed to be doing. He thought it might be time to pull out and initiate the retrieval operation. There wasn't much more to be learned.

Captain Martin, who didn't know the others in the room as well as he might, hesitated, even with Bates opening a beer. Gerber grabbed a Pepsi and said, "Just what I need, another shot of caffeine. Only had three today."

Fetterman chuckled and grabbed a beer.

Bates held up an unopened can, looking at Martin. He said, "Well, if you insist, sir. How can I refuse?"

Bates was tempted to toss it to him but suppressed the urge. Instead, he just handed it to Martin.

Bromhead followed Gerber's lead and took one of the Pepsis. He said, "I haven't seen one of these in about two weeks."

"Disadvantage of being at the end of the supply line. Those in Saigon pick over everything so that by the time the supplies reach us, the really good stuff is long gone."

Bates took a long pull at the beer and said, "Hey, that's pretty cold. How'd you manage that, Sergeant Major?"

"When you're a sergeant major, you have to know these things."

"Okay," said Bates, "we need to get this started. This is a preliminary planning section. Captain Martin and Captain Bromhead, you are here because we're going to be drawing manpower from your commands. Major Gerber along with Sergeant Major Fetterman will have overall command."

Bates waited, saw the acknowledgements, and then said, "We have a HALO team in place, in Laos, gathering intelligence. They'll withdraw sometime in the next seventy-two hours to update us on the situation."

Martin interrupted. "The situation?"

"We'll get onto that. Our immediate concern is to create a pocket battalion, meaning a unit somewhat larger than a company but smaller than a battalion to deal with a unit being created in Laos. The soldiers for this will be drawn from your camp, Martin, and from yours, Bromhead."

"Yes, sir," said Martin.

"You don't seem to be enthusiastic, Captain," said Bates.

"I was wondering how you selected our camps," said Martin.

"Location, state of training and experience. Captain Bromhead has been here before and understands these clandestine operations. While you haven't been in-country all that long, Captain, your strikers have engaged in combat operations in the past. Makes them qualified for this sort of mission."

Bates held up a hand. "Before you ask any more questions, Captain, let me finish. I won't go into the history of this, other than to say that it does have the interest of those in Washington and has been endorsed by General Abrams."

Martin merely nodded and sipped his beer. Bates turned his attention to the others. "Mack, Tony, I know you are fairly aware of this, but I'm bringing the captains up to speed."

"Not a problem, sir."

"What we want," said Bates, "is to create a force capable of standing up to the force being created in Laos. I fear there will be a cross-border favor to this. If they begin to move toward

Vietnam, I want them, which is to say, the Pentagon wants them intercepted and annihilated, preferably in Laos."

"Why not bomb the camp?" asked Martin. "That would take care of the problem."

"You are advocating an act of war against a neutral country. We can't do that."

Martin snorted. "Imaginary lines on the ground."

"Imaginary or not, we are obligated to pay attention to them. If you feel this mission is somehow offensive, then maybe you should think about another line of work." Bates was unaware of the irony of calling the mission offensive.

"We will establish this provisional battalion at Martin's camp. They will undergo enhanced training. I believe, Captain, that you've had some trouble with mortar and rocket attacks recently."

"Yes, sir. Minimal damage and a couple of strikers with minor wounds. Major Gerber and Sergeant Major Fetterman provided some guidance that has reduced that problem."

"Yes, well, I think that we can put that to an end with this new unit. Give them a real-world mission without tipping our hand about the real purpose of this training."

Bromhead asked, "Who's in charge of this?"

"I thought I had made that clear — Major Gerber is in charge."

"My strike force is not at full strength," said Bromhead, "and there are rumblings about an attack on us in the near future."

"I have that intelligence here. You've got two fire support bases close by and I can give you a company of infantry, if you think that will help."

"I'm not set up for a company of American infantry," said Bromhead, "assuming you were referring to an American unit."

"I was."

"How about a platoon and fighters on call for us in case things get hairy?"

"That can be arranged, though the on-call aircraft might be Army gunships with the fighters available."

"That'll work, sir."

"I'd like to see this unit formed and in place in the next seventy-two hours. I want your best."

"Do I supply NCOs?" asked Bromhead.

"I will assume from your question that you're asking about American NCOs."

"Exactly, sir."

Gerber took the question. "Let me have a run at that, John. Let's get the names and qualifications from this ad-hoc unit and then decide who would be most beneficial to the mission."

Bromhead looked at him and then said, "Of course, sir."

Bates opened one of the folders and took out several sheets. He passed them around. "This is a non-classified assessment of what we're going to need. Major Gerber suggested that we cloak it in an operation to take out that mortar, or mortar teams that have been harassing you, Captain."

"Yes, sir."

Bates looked at his watch, drained his beer and asked, "Any questions?"

Bromhead, grinning, asked, "When does that seventy-two-hour clock start running?"

"Ten minutes ago."

Petrov had spent an hour with high-powered binoculars, scanning the jungle around the camp. He moved around to gain a different perspective. He knew that he was becoming obsessive, but he just couldn't shake the feeling that something was wrong. Something was different. He was unable to spot anything that had changed, but the feeling just wouldn't go away.

Once he finished another circuit, he went to find Major Semenov. Semenov was in his quarters, lying on his cot with a wet cloth over his eyes. He didn't move when Petrov knocked on the wooden post and when Semenov didn't acknowledge the knock, Petrov said, "Major?"

Semenov said, "What do you want?"

"I need a minute of your time, sir."

Semenov finally stirred, pulled the cloth off his eyes, and sat up. "I have a headache and I'm tired."

"Yes, sir. I would like to take out a patrol. I want to make sure that no one is near us."

"Why?"

"That's the problem, sir. I don't know why, but I just want to make sure our perimeter is secure."

"You have some evidence that something is wrong?"

"No, sir. But I want to be sure that the perimeter is secure. It will be a good training exercise."

"You don't need my permission to order a training exercise. You can order any training exercise that you believe necessary. Why bother me?"

"I thought I'd alert you in case something happened."

"You believe something is going to happen?"

"I hope not, sir, but thought I would mention it."

"Be back by nightfall," said Semenov.

"Yes, sir."

Semenov twisted around, put his feet up and laid back down. He put the cloth back over his eyes.

Petrov watched for a moment and then left. He spotted Volkov near the mess hall. He caught up with him and said, "I think we should send out another patrol. I want to walk along the perimeter of the jungle. If I was out there spying on us, that's where I would be."

"You mean now, sir?"

"You have something better to do?"

Volkov grinned and said, "I was going to teach some hand-to-hand. That's more fun than wandering around in the jungle."

"I want twenty-five recruits, armed, at the northern end of the camp in fifteen minutes. They are to carry enough water to keep them hydrated for two hours and a basic load of ammunition. They are required to have their web gear with them including a first-aid kit and a combat knife."

For a moment Volkov didn't move. He seemed to be rooted to the ground and unable to understand his orders. He then said, "Yes, sir."

"I'll meet you there."

As Volkov headed toward his hut, Petrov went to his. He put on his web gear, took his pistol from his holster, and checked it. He shook his canteen, and it was filled. He then picked up his rifle.

He waited ten minutes and then headed to the north side of the camp where Volkov waited with the patrol. He walked to the front to take the point and turned to Volkov. "Have them follow me. I want flankers out and I want four recruits bringing up the rear. You stay with them. Just tell the recruits to do what they have been taught."

"Yes, sir."

Mendes was surprised by the sudden activity in the camp. The men were running around as if there had been some sort of an alert. Mendes thought that it was more training, but he didn't like the way they were forming up on one side of the camp. It was clearly another patrol.

He alerted the rest of his team. He indicated the patrol. He was sure they had seen it too. From the movement in the camp, it looked like they would be entering the jungle about a klick from where Mendes and his team were concealed. He waited to see what they did.

They turned toward him, and Mendes knew that if they stayed where they were, they'd be found. The patrol was just inside the tree line and Mendes had spread his team out in that location. He caught the attention of the man on his right and signaled him to withdraw.

Mendes, staying low, pushed himself to the rear carefully, slowly, trying not to expose himself to anyone who, in the camp, might be looking for them. The team assembled around twenty-five feet deeper in the jungle. Mendes leaned close and whispered. "I don't know what's going on, but it seems they have spotted us."

Crockett said, "Then why didn't they come straight at us?"

"This is not the time for a discussion of their tactics. We have to get out of here. Follow me."

Mendes took a quick compass reading and then headed off on an angle away from the enemy patrol. He didn't move quickly but kept the pace steady. They were moving without noise or discussion. They were just moving away from the enemy.

They reached a dry stream bed, crossed it, and stopped in the bushes on the other side. Mendes watched the jungle and listened carefully but didn't hear anything. The patrol had not spotted them yet, and he thought they had gotten away clean.

Without a word, he turned, changed his course slightly, toward the extraction point. It would take them hours to get there, but he had no choice. The mission was compromised, though he didn't know what happened. To him, it was clear that the patrol was looking for them. He just didn't know why.

Petrov was moving quickly. He knew about noise discipline but didn't believe it mattered here. If there was anyone hiding in the jungle, they would be more interested in hiding than in engaging in a firefight. Petrov believed in sneak-and-peek missions and understood the concept. It was to spy but not fight. If there was anyone watching, they would already know there was a patrol. There was no need to be quiet. It was speed that was necessary.

He led the patrol along the edge of the jungle, with a flanker deeper in the trees and another out in the open on the slope that led down to the camp. Petrov could see the whole camp spread out and could see some of the training going on below him. They were coming to a spot that would have provided the best view of the camp.

He walked just inside the trees. He suddenly caught a whiff of something that smelled bad. He recognized the stench and held up a balled fist, stopping the patrol. He looked right and left and sniffed the air. He crouched for a moment but found nothing. He stood, took a step, and looked at his feet. The vegetation was crushed into a man-sized spot.

He raised his eyes and about ten feet away spotted another crushed area. He stepped to it and found a crushed can that was OD green and with black lettering that appeared to be English. Suddenly, he realized that his intuition had been accurate. Something in the jungle had changed in the night and he had known it. He had just taken too much time to act on it. Volkov's morning patrol had walked by this area and seen nothing.

Silence meant nothing now. "Sergeant Volkov, I need you up here."

Volkov appeared with his weapon ready. Petrov said nothing. He just pointed at the ground. Volkov didn't know what to think until he realized that the vegetation had been disturbed.

"How long?" asked Petrov.

"How long, what?"

"How long ago did they leave?"

There was no clue in the vegetation because Volkov didn't know how long it would take to recover. But he had an inspiration. "Thirty minutes or less. They watched us leave the camp."

"That's what I thought. Can we find their trail?"

Volkov was not a tracker and none of the other Soviet soldiers were. He thought that some of the Laotians might be able to follow a trail, given their lifestyle. He turned, and in Laotian ordered, "Everyone forward."

When they had gathered around, he asked, "How many of you have experience tracking animals through the jungle?"

No one responded until Petrov said, "Tell them that there is a reward for helping us track those who left here."

Volkov thought for a moment and then repeated the statement. He added, "This is a real mission now. Those who supply additional assistance will be rewarded by the major."

Two of the recruits stepped forward. One said, "I can track animals."

The other said, "I have experience in the jungle around here."

Petrov pointed to the crushed vegetation and said, "This is the starting point. Find the trail that leads away from here."

Volkov translated and one of the recruits walked around the area. Petrov said, "They will be moving deeper into the jungle, not toward the camp."

The recruit stepped into the center of the area, crouched, and then pointed into the jungle, towards a path that was angled away from the camp.

"Tell them to follow me, flankers out, looking for signs of broken branches and stepped-on vegetation. We will now enforce noise discipline. Anyone breaking it will be severely punished."

They came to a dry stream bed and the signs that someone had crossed it were evident. Petrov saw a footprint in the dry sand. He couldn't tell how long ago it had been made, but he knew it was human.

On the other side, he couldn't see where the enemy had gone but the recruit didn't hesitate. He pushed off, deeper into the jungle until Petrov caught him with a hand to his shoulder.

"Ask him what he sees."

Volkov asked the question and then said, "Three, four men pass here, a short time ago."

"Ask him how long?"

Volkov translated. "He doesn't really understand what you want. He can only say that it was a short time ago."

"Let's speed up," said Petrov.

But the recruit didn't move faster. He was examining the ground, turning right and left, as if he had lost the trail. Then, just as Petrov was going to say something, the recruit moved forward several steps. He pointed and mumbled a few words that Petrov were sure was, "This way."

Mendes, who rarely got excited, especially in the field, found his heart racing. He believed that the enemy patrol was getting closer. He knew that they would find where his team had been laying. He was sure they would be able to figure out the direction they took, but he also believed there would be no one in that patrol who would be able to track them through the jungle. They weren't Apache. They were Laotian farmers.

He picked up the pace again, wondering if he should worry about noise discipline. At this point, it was more important to get away. He knew that he couldn't allow the team to be captured. He was confident if it came to a fight, the team could defeat the patrol, but he didn't know how many others would be following that patrol. They hadn't seen anyone else form a patrol and were unsure how many people were in the village or camp, but he was sure that he was badly outnumbered.

The closest PZ was more than twenty klicks away. He just didn't know if they could get there, and if they did, could they defend it until the helicopters arrived to extract them.

The mission, he thought, had gone to shit pretty fast.

CHAPTER 12

In the Army it was very easy to become a subject matter expert. The wrong word in the wrong place could identify a soldier as the subject matter expert. In this case, Warrant Officer One, known as a Wobbly One, Gary Russell, was suddenly the subject matter expert.

He was summoned to the company commander's office, but the CO wasn't there. The first sergeant told him that the CO was in the officers' club. Russell could find him there.

Russell entered the club and blinked, having moved from the bright light of the afternoon sun into the subdued darkness of the club. There were fans blowing but the club was air conditioned. At first it looked deserted, though the jukebox was playing. Behind the bar was one of the pilots acting as a bartender.

Then he saw the CO sitting at a table in the corner with a single, bright light overhead. He was studying a folder and had a beer sitting in front of him. Russell was surprised by the beer in the middle of the day. He walked over and asked, "You wanted to see me?" It wasn't exactly military protocol, but then reporting to the CO in the officers' club wasn't exactly military protocol either.

The CO looked up and with the pencil in his hand, pointed to one of the other chairs. "Have a seat? Want a beer?"

"Thank you, sir, but no. I'd take a Seven Up if we have any."

The CO raised his voice and said, "Skip. Seven Up?"

"No, sir. Pepsi, Coke and some kind of local thing that I've never heard of and am afraid to taste."

"Coke," said Russell.

Once he had the Coke, and was settled, he looked at the CO and said, "You wanted to see me?"

"Yeah. Got tasked with a single ship mission out of Song Be. You're familiar with the area, been there several times and thought it would be a good choice to send you."

Russell took a drink and then asked, "What exactly is this?"

The CO closed the folder and pushed it aside. He leaned closer and said, quietly, "It's an on-call extraction of a special team. They don't know exactly when they will call for extraction, but we must be ready to go. Song Be is the best place for you to stage."

"Okay," said Russell, slowly, and then added, "sir."

"Here's the thing. The PZ will probably be in Laos. Not all that far from the border because we don't have the range. There are several PZs that they might want to use. I have the map here," he tapped the folder.

"We're going into Laos? That seems a bit extreme, sir."

"Priority came down from on high."

"Aren't there other companies closer and are familiar with the AO?"

"It is in our area of operations. I'm not sure why we have the tasking, but we do, and I thought you would be the best man for the job. You can take whoever you want as the Peter Pilot."

"Gaines was with me the last time I was in there."

"Gaines it is. Your assigned aircraft is in for its hundred-hour maintenance. You can take whichever one you want."

"Doesn't matter, sir."

"Okay. I'll have operations make the call and alert the crew. You can get with Gaines and if he has any questions, he can see me. You'll need to take enough for a couple, three days. Mission won't last any longer than that. Questions?"

Russell sat there for a moment, thinking. He wondered about this cross-border operation into Laos and what would happen if they were shot down on the wrong side. He asked, "Back up?"

"One of the other companies has been alerted that they might be required for a mission, but this is single ship. In and out. Shouldn't be a problem. You just pick up the team and take them to Song Be."

"This seems a little, I don't know, haphazard?"

"Simple single ship mission. Get in, pick up the team and get out."

"Gun team?"

"On call but probably twenty minutes away. They won't cross the border unless you call for them. They'll launch when you do, but they'll stay on the Vietnamese side of the border."

"What about refueling? We're going to burn off thirty minutes or so flying up to Song Be."

"Someone was thinking ahead. Fuel truck with JP4 is on station at Song Be. You can refuel there."

Suddenly Russell grinned. "Is this a volunteer mission?"

"Nope. I made a decision based on experience in-country. You won based on your flying into Song Be recently. You need to be off in about an hour or so."

Russell drained his Coke, pushed his chair back. "Then I better get going."

"Yes, you had better. Give operations a call when you get off and then when you land at Song Be."

"Yes, sir." Russell left the club and headed to his room to pick up his weapon, helmet, and shaving kit.

Sergeant First Class Mendes had slowed down and was listening. He figured that the enemy had probably discovered where they had established their observation post. He didn't know if they would be able to track them through the jungle. He didn't know if the team was leaving a path that could be tracked. He did know that he had to stay far enough in front of them so the helicopter could get in and then get out.

He halted and the team spread out, watching the jungle around them. Mendes pulled out his radio and keyed it twice. He didn't say anything. He waited one minute and did it again. And a minute later, a third time. That was the emergency extraction signal.

Then, in a whisper, he said, "Let's go."

Again, he took the point, leading the team toward one of the extraction points. He shot a compass heading as he moved. He slowed, searched the jungle, and found a good reference point in front and headed toward it.

He wanted to get to the closest PZ because it was the closest. He had seen photographs that showed it to him. A helicopter could be there, pick them up and get out in just seconds. If they could get there far enough in front of anyone chasing them.

Then, from behind them, there was a single shot. It was barely perceptible in the jungle over the other noise of the animals and the wind and the rattling of the leaves. He thought that it might be a mile away, maybe more. That suggested the enemy was twenty to thirty minutes behind him.

They came to another stream. He knew that the evasion experts suggested they stay away from streams unless they were being tracked by dogs. He didn't think there were dogs, but if they had a soldier who could read the signs, the water might be the best way to avoid getting caught.

Again, they stopped. Mendes took out his map. There was another designated PZ to the southwest. The stream was flowing in that general direction. If they stayed in the water long enough, it could throw off the pursuit.

Mendes waded into the water and began to follow the stream. The team followed him. The water was warm but not all that clear. Any silt they stirred up would be settled before the enemy found the stream. Mendes thought it would buy them more time. Surely the tracker would have a difficult time finding where they had exited if they were careful.

Crockett caught up to him and asked, "Are you sure we are being pursued?"

Mendes shook his head. "I just want to get out of here."

"What about a mechanical ambush?"

"Negative. We don't know who's back there or if anyone is. We don't want to set something up that will be tripped by the farmers in a week or a month. Our strength is our speed and our knowledge of our destination."

"Can they get a helicopter there?"

"Promised they would."

"And you believed them?"

Mendes didn't answer. He kept up the pace. They'd be on the run for hours. The second PZ was farther away, but closer to South Vietnam.

The shot had come from the rear of the patrol. Petrov halted them and walked back. He saw Volkov and nearly shouted, "Who fired his weapon?"

Volkov pointed at a recruit who was standing at attention, holding his weapon above his head. Petrov grabbed it and then hit the recruit in the mouth with the butt, knocking him to the ground. He flipped it around and pointed it at the recruit who covered his face with his hands.

"Sergeant, I want this man sent back. Two others will escort him. If they fail to arrive at the camp, we will find them all. It is a matter of two choices. Take the recruit to the camp or try to evade us. You tell them that."

"Yes, sir." He pointed at two of the recruits. Volkov believed they were trustworthy. In Laotian, he repeated Petrov's orders and then asked, "Do you understand? Fail in the mission and you will be in more trouble than this recruit."

One recruit nodded and the other said, "Yes, Sergeant."

Petrov jerked the recruit to his feet and pushed him toward the other two. "Take him away now."

As they moved out, Volkov said, "Do you think they can find the camp?"

"They live here. Why should they get lost? We must get moving again. We have time to make up."

"Yes, sir."

"Get that tracker out, now."

Volkov ran forward and the recruit began moving forward slowly. He was swinging his head back and forth. He crouched once, picked up a broken branch and then tossed it aside. He stood up and turned in a full circle, as if lost.

Petrov watched impatiently, wanting the recruit to get moving, but he knew little about tracking anything through the jungle. He wanted to shout but that would have been counterproductive, so he just stood there, glaring at the recruit's back.

Finally, the recruit began to walk forward but at a slow pace. Petrov wondered if he had lost the trail but kept his position. Volkov was at the rear of the patrol, where Petrov wanted him.

Eventually, they came to a stream. Even Petrov could see the evidence that someone had climbed down the bank. Following the recruit, he crossed to the opposite bank, but the recruit had stopped. There was no sign that anyone had climbed out of the water. They had entered but not exited.

Petrov retreated and found Volkov. "I need to know what is happening. You need to ask the recruit."

Volkov asked the question and then told Petrov. "He said they didn't leave the water. He doesn't know which way they went, though he suspects it was downstream."

"Why?"

"He thinks that there would be evidence in the water if they had gone upstream, there would be silt and debris drifting down. We'd see some sign of it. If they went downstream, then the water here would be clear."

Petrov was surprised by the analysis. He had little to no respect for the recruits, but this made sense to him. He looked at his compass and realized the stream was flowing to the southeast. Those he was chasing would be seeking sanctuary in South Vietnam.

"Tell him to head downstream. They are trying to conceal their movements with the water."

The patrol splashed down into the water. The tracker led the way, now walking faster, but looking right and left searching for the point where the enemy would have climbed up on the bank.

Mendes had been worried about leaving traces of their passing in the stream bed. True, it was muddy, and the flowing water filled their footprints with silt rapidly, but he was still worried. He knew his team was watching their steps. The last thing they wanted was to make tracking them simple, if there was someone following them.

Mendes kept his eye on the compass. The stream was meandering, increasing the distance to the PZ. If the enemy figured out what they had done and had a good map of the area, they might be able to anticipate where they were going. He didn't think they could do that, but it worried him.

They came to a point where the stream widened and there were shallow banks leading down into the water. Mendes held up a hand, stopping them, and studied the bank. If they were careful, they might be able to exit without leaving a trace. He realized that was unlikely to work, but they might be able to extract themselves without leaving a big enough trace for the enemy to find this place.

The team joined him, and Mendes said, "Let's get up on dry land. Step carefully, try to leave no clue that we're out of the water."

They nodded. Mendes pointed right and left, spreading them out, thinking they would be less likely to leave any sign behind them. He wondered if they should follow one behind the other, narrowing the path, but decided against it. They would spread out and do their best to avoid leaving any trace of their movement.

Mendes climbed out of the stream and reentered the jungle. When he looked back, he could see nothing to indicate that he had left the stream. The rest of the team joined him. Mendes took another compass reading and then pointed to the southeast. "This way," he said.

They started off again, with Mendes in the lead. He figured that he was about thirty klicks from the PZ. He picked up the pace because stealth was no longer a consideration. Mendes realized that they had to get out of Laos as quickly as possible, even if there was no pursuit.

He found an animal trail and decided they could make better time on the trail. There was no chance there would be any booby traps on the trail. The most important factor was to get to the PZ.

After an hour, he halted them. He took a drink from his canteen. He wiped the sweat from his face. He finally said, "We need to get to the PZ prior to sunset. Overwise we'll be here overnight."

"Then let's get going," said Hendrick, then added, "I need a beer."

Russell spotted the Song Be Special Forces Camp and began the slow descent for landing. There was a long runway near the camp that was paved with gravel and Russell made his approach toward the center of it. As he hovered forward and touched down, a jeep raced out of the camp. It stopped near the helicopter just as Russell shut down the engine and the rotor slowed. The jeep passenger jumped out and then stepped up on the helicopter's skid, leaning into the cockpit window.

"We have an emergency recall from the team in the field," he shouted. "You need to get out to pick them up."

Russell said, "I need to refuel, and I need to know where the PZ is. I need to know which one they'll be at."

"I'll get that information from my Ops guy. Have that information in a few minutes for you."

The fuel truck drove out the gate but didn't approach until the rotor blades had slowed and stopped. The driver pulled up on the right side of the aircraft. The crew chief leaped from his position in the well of the aircraft, took the fuel hose from the rear of the truck, and pulled it close to the helicopter. He began to refuel.

Russell got out of the cockpit. Captain Martin, the senior officer at the camp, spread a map out on the hood of his jeep. "Are you familiar with the Laos locations?"

"I looked at the maps in our Ops and got the compass headings from here to the identified PZs. Not much in the way of landmarks and I don't have good winds aloft information."

"The latest intel we have here is that they're heading to this PZ. Not the closest to their target but probably the best for extraction. I suspect they might have been discovered and are getting the hell out while the getting out is good."

"We have enough daylight to get in there. Don't really need that much to get back. If they're not in the PZ, we can't hang around long."

"You afraid of being shot at?" asked Martin.

"No," said Russell, more than a little annoyed. "We are at about our flight range. We stay there too long; we won't have the fuel to get back. You'll then have to raise a rescue mission for us."

"I can send an NCO with you if you have the space. He's familiar with the area and can work as a navigator. Might make it a bit easier to find the PZ."

"He close by? He know you're volunteering him for this?"

"He actually suggested it to me."

"I'm picking up four guys and what equipment they might have with them. I can't see where taking him along will be a problem and it might be helpful."

Martin nodded. "How long before you can take off?"

Russell looked back and saw that the crew chief was giving the hose back to the truck driver. The aircraft had been refueled. He said, "As soon as I can take a piss and get a drink of water."

"Okay."

"Where's the gun team?"

"They haven't launched yet. I can get them in the air whenever we need them."

Russell realized that they were giving him a great deal of authority and sending him on a mission that could have international complications if he screwed it up. Of course, if the HALO team was in the PZ and if there were no enemy around, the extraction would be simple enough. Russell didn't think their exposure in the PZ or in the area around the PZ would be more than ten or twelve minutes. Then it was just a case of getting back across the border as fast as possible before anyone realized that they had violated Laotian airspace.

"Launch them in about thirty minutes and have them orbit here." Russell pointed at the map near the border. "I'll cross about here and come back to the point, or near this point if I need some help from them."

"Is there anything else you need from me, here?"

"Can't think of a thing other than get that guy out here," said Russell. He saw that the crew chief was back in his well in the helicopter. Neither the door gunner nor Gaines had moved from their positions. Both were strapped in and ready to go. For some reason, Russell wondered if they had taken a bathroom break. They wouldn't have the opportunity to do so for the next couple of hours.

"Good luck," said Martin, holding out his hand.

"Thanks, sir," said Russell, grinning. "We'll be back as quick as we can."

Russell walked to the rear of the helicopter and relieved himself. It wasn't the first time that he'd done something like that. In fact, pissing on the skids was something of a tradition. As he turned around, he saw another jeep coming from the camp. It stopped and a small, thin man leaped out. He carried an M-16 and web gear that held only a canteen and a holster with a .45 in it.

"I'm Costner."

Russell shook his hand and said, "Climb aboard. Once we cross the border have the door gunner loan you his helmet so that we can communicate."

"I've got headphones, sir. I can just plug into the system myself."

"Great."

Russell climbed back into the cockpit and strapped on his helmet. "You guys ready to go?"

Gaines nodded. Russell waited and got confirmation from both the crew chief and the door gunner on the intercom. Costner sat on the troop seat, his headphones on, and held up a thumb.

As he finished strapping himself in, Russell said, "Then let's light the fire."

Petrov was getting frustrated. He was knee-deep in the stream and could see no sign of the trail. He knew they were pursuing spies. There was no other explanation for the evidence he had seen. He didn't know how they had gotten to the camp or how long they had been there. All he knew was that he became worried about them that morning. No evidence of anything unusual, just a feeling that something was wrong.

Finally, he called to Volkov. "Stop."

Volkov relayed the order, and the patrol froze in place. Volkov came forward. Petrov said, "They must have gotten out of this stream. We missed it."

"How do you know?"

"I just know. Tell the tracker to backtrack from this point and to examine the bank carefully. He missed it."

"Yes, sir." Volkov relayed the instructions to the tracker. He looked surprised and said that he had missed nothing. Volkov said, "I don't care. We are to backtrack from this point."

The patrol turned. This time they moved slower. The tracker stopped frequently, examining the banks of the stream. He found an area where there was evidence the vegetation had been bent. There were no footprints and nothing other than a few broken blades of grass.

The recruit called out, "Here."

Volkov came up and Petrov tried to see what the recruit had seen. The recruit spoke to Volkov, who translated. "He thinks they might have left the stream here, but he's not sure."

"Let's sweep the area around here and see if he can pick up the trail."

The patrol climbed out of the stream as the recruit searched the ground. He found what he thought was the trail. He pointed it out to Volkov, who in turn pointed it out to Petrov.

"Does he know where they've gone?"

Volkov asked the recruit. "He's not sure. He thinks they might have left the stream at this place. He thought it happened two or three hours ago, but that is just a guess."

"So, we've lost three hours."

Volkov didn't know what to say to that. He asked, "Should we follow the trail?"

"Yes. Of course. Let's go."

Eventually, they came to a game trail. The recruit pointed to it and told Volkov that he thought the enemy had taken it. Volkov repeated to Petrov what he had learned. Petrov said, "Go. Hurry!"

They picked up the pace. Petrov was right behind the recruit who was following the trail, bent at the waist, his head down. He didn't want to miss any sign. Petrov knew if the enemy, whoever they were, was using the trail, they would be moving at a faster clip.

Mendes held up a hand and stopped. He knelt, used his compass, and pointed to the left. Quietly, he said, "We need to head in that direction. We're getting close."

He started out again, looking for the landmarks. They were subtle. The bend in a stream. A slight hill, a collection of hootches or a break in the jungle. Little things that were often easy to miss if he moved too fast.

Now they pushed into the jungle itself. After half an hour they came to a clearing that was two or three hundred yards long and fifty to sixty yards wide. Mendes crouched, studied his map, and said, "This is it."

"Now what?" asked Crockett.

"I make a coded call and we wait for extraction."

"And if anyone shows up?"

Mendes looked up at Crockett and said, "We either evade or engage, depending on the circumstances. Our best bet is to stay here. Spread out and lay low. Helicopter should be inbound."

"How long?"

Mendes shook his head. "I don't know. Shouldn't be more than an hour or two. Depends."

Hendrick said, "I hope that pilot can find us. This is out in the middle of nowhere."

"It's what they're paid to do," said Mendes, sounding more confident than he felt. "They'll get here."

"I hope you're right."

"Yeah," said Mendes. "Me too."

CHAPTER 13

Captain George Smith was confused. He had been sent to Vietnam to study HALO operations. But he didn't know exactly what had happened to the subject matter experts. They had been deployed on a mission and while he knew something about it, he didn't know much. He walked into the headquarters building, down the hall and came to a closed door. He knocked on it using his knuckles and when there was no answer, he used his fist, nearly rattling the door and its frame.

"Whoever is out there, stop knocking. If you have business with me then enter but if you're wasting my time, go away."

Slowly, carefully, Smith opened the door and peeked in. Major Mack Gerber was sitting at his desk fanning himself with a manila folder that had a "Secret" cover sheet on it.

"Do you have a minute, Major?"

Gerber waved a hand and said, "Enter at your own peril."

Smith opened the door wider and stepped inside. He saw Sergeant Major Anthony Fetterman sitting in a chair pushed close to the air conditioner. Gerber said, "The sergeant major is sucking up all the cold air and I am stuck fanning myself with classified documents."

Smith wasn't sure of the protocol here. He wanted to talk with Gerber, but Gerber outranked him. In the regular Army, or maybe just in rank-conscious Washington, he would have moved to the desk and saluted, requesting permission to speak. But this was Vietnam and some of the stateside protocols were simply ignored.

Finally, he walked toward the desk, stopping about three feet away and said, "Request permission to speak."

Gerber looked up at him and grinned. He decided to play along. "Granted."

"I noticed that Sergeant Mendes is missing."

"Not missing," said Fetterman from his corner. "We know where he is and what he's doing."

"Am I missing something?" asked Smith.

"You mean like a need to know?" asked Gerber.

"I was sent here to observe; for the last day or two there has been nothing for me to observe."

"Mendes and his team are in the field at the moment," said Gerber. "You knew that was going to happen."

"I thought there would be briefings or something. I thought I'd be kept in the loop about the mission."

Fetterman said to Gerber, "Well, he doesn't look like a VC spy."

"No, he doesn't, and I doubt he would know what to do with the information if he was. What do you want to know?"

"They have been deployed into the field?"

"That is correct. They are on an assignment, and you were at some of the briefings about that. The first phase of a longer mission."

"What happens next?"

Gerber put the folder on the desk. "I'm not sure what that has to do with HALO operations. You have the information you need."

"My orders say —"

"Nothing about compromising combat operations," finished Gerber.

"Sir, I just want to gather complete information."

Gerber leaned back in his chair. "Just what *is* your mission here?"

"I told you. Learn about HALO operations."

Fetterman joined the discussion. "That doesn't make a whole lot of sense to us. You could learn about HALO at Camp Mackall. There must be experts at the Pentagon. You didn't need to come here to get an accurate picture unless you just wanted to draw combat pay."

Smith looked at Fetterman. "There is nothing nefarious about my mission, Sergeant Major. I'm just trying to learn about HALO in the combat environment. I'd be much happier back in the World."

"What confuses me," said Gerber, "is that you were at the initial briefing, you heard what both Colonel Bates and Sergeant Mendes had to say."

"But I wasn't aware that they had deployed," said Smith.

"I'm not sure how that is relevant," said Gerber. "Did you plan to go with them and watch them exit the aircraft?"

"No, sir."

"You didn't think that relevant?"

"I don't see how, sir."

Gerber grinned and said, "One of the best ways to learn something is to watch it executed."

"I understand about the high altitudes."

"But do you understand about the cold? About the need for supplemental oxygen and the rules for smoking prior to the mission? Have you observed all the little details that make HALO a bit more difficult? We can talk about it, but had you flown off on that plane, you would see the subtleties that are sometimes not mentioned but important. Seems to me that you bungled your mission."

Smith didn't know what to say to that. Gerber was taking his, Smith's job, more seriously than he was. He said, "I didn't think about that."

"Well, I'll tell you. We don't run all that many HALO operations. There are too few men trained in them, and here, in Vietnam, there isn't much need for them. You missed a great opportunity."

"Yes, sir."

"You have any questions?"

"When will Sergeant Mendes and his team return?"

"They're scheduled back here in two days, subject to change based on mission requirements. Anything else?"

Smith came to attention. "No, sir. Thank you, sir." He did an about-face and retreated.

When he was gone, Fetterman, who was smiling broadly, said, "Was that really necessary?"

"Nah. I just felt like jerking his chain. Made me feel a little better."

"When is Mendes due back?"

Gerber made a show of looking at his watch and then said, "Just as I said. Sometime in the next two days unless something goes wrong or there is a change in the mission requirements."

Although they had reached the PZ and Mendes had sent the coded message for an emergency extraction, he knew they still weren't safe yet. They really wouldn't be safe until they were back in the World, but they'd be somewhat safer on the helicopter and a little safer when they crossed the border back into South Vietnam. And, of course, things would improve at the base camp where they could shower, have a good meal and sleep on a cot that was a little more comfortable than the floor of the jungle.

The team stayed in the trees, hidden from those who might be in the area. Mendes could see nothing to suggest that there was anyone around. He thought about it for a moment and then decided that they should take positions on the opposite side of the clearing. That could provide a little more warning of an approaching enemy.

"Let's move to the southern side of this area," he whispered. "We can wait there until the airlift arrives."

It didn't take long to reach that point. There was good cover for the team. Once they were undercover, Mendes used his radio again, confirming that they were now in position for retrieval. Mendes crouched on one knee and searched the jungle they had left. He could see nothing to suggest that anyone was close to them.

This was the closest he had ever come to being caught by his target. Usually, they had no knowledge that he and his team were around watching them. The enemy went about his business, oblivious, while Mendes gathered all the intelligence he could. Had the enemy not left their camp where they did and had they not turned toward them so that it seemed they were coming for him, Mendes would have stayed put. But the actions of the enemy officer could only be interpreted in one way. They had been discovered. If that was true, then Mendes had to abandon the mission.

He didn't know if the enemy was able to follow him once they had reached the stream. If they had, Mendez didn't know how long it would take them to arrive at this PZ. With some luck, the helicopter would be here and gone. They would be on their way home before the enemy arrived.

Crockett knelt near him, his lips just inches from Mendes' ear. "We in the clear?"

"I think so, but I just don't know. I can't figure out how we were spotted."

"You sure we were?"

Mendes shrugged. "It sure looked like it. We got out of there in time. I don't think we made any noise but if they were doing their jobs, they found where we had been. And I didn't like that rifle shot."

"Could be meaningless," said Crockett. "Could be an accidental discharge."

"You want to stake your life on that?"

"Sure don't. Did we get what we need?"

"We know that Caucasian men were running that camp. They certainly weren't either Laotian or North Vietnamese. Didn't seem to be Chinese. That leaves the Soviets. They didn't seem to be Americans. We saw their operation, the training, and have an idea of the size of the unit."

"Then we got it?"

"Yeah, I think we did. All we have to do is get the hell out of here. Now, let's spread out."

Crockett nodded and slipped off to the right.

As they approached the border, Russell put his hand on the controls and said, "I've got it."

Gaines released the controls and said, "You've got it."

Russell pushed the collective down, descending toward the ground. Over the intercom, he said, "I'm going to be nap-of-the-earth. If you look at the maps, you'll see the border marked as showing triple A up to eleven thousand feet. Means they're using .51 cal or something even larger. We stay low enough; we'll be safer than at fifteen hundred feet."

Russell was flying no more than ten, twelve feet above the ground at eighty knots. He swerved right and left to avoid trees, structures, and other obstacles on the ground. Flying low level was more fun than flying straight and level at altitude. At least he felt like he was actually controlling the aircraft that way.

Over the intercom, Costner said, "I think we need to bear right, sir."

"You sure?"

"Pretty sure, sir."

"If we miss the PZ, it'll be on your head."

"Yes, sir."

Russell turned to the right and kept going for another five or ten klicks and then popped up to fifteen hundred feet — he was out of small arms range and that triple A on the border was no longer an issue. Fifteen hundred feet was the altitude that slicks used in Vietnam.

"See the bend in that river, sir," said Costner.

"Got it. Should be a bridge … ah, there it is. We're on course."

"We should be about twenty minutes from the PZ," said Costner.

Russell began a climb to seventeen hundred feet. He was more comfortable at altitude because he could see more of the landscape and more of the landmarks, though they were not as common as they were in South Vietnam.

Russell said, "You've got it."

Gaines put his hands on the controls and said, "I've got it."

Russell pulled out his map and checked the landmarks on it. He found the river with the bridge and the highway that led to it. The next landmark was three hills in a triangular formation. They were to pass south of them, but Russell believed they wouldn't be able see them. If they flew over them, then they were too far north.

There was a small village ahead of them and Russell found it marked on the map. They would have to fly over the top of it, but there was little chance that anyone living there would be inclined to shoot at them and certainly couldn't alert anyone that they had flown over. They probably didn't have a radio or the electricity to operate it.

Once they flew over the village, Russell said, "Change course to three ten degrees."

Gaines altered the course. "I don't see the next landmark."

"Coming up in a few minutes. Nope, there it is. We're on course."

Costner said, "We're getting close. You need to alert the team on the ground."

Russell wanted them to pop smoke, which would help locate the exact location of the team, but it would also alert anyone chasing them. The jungle below them was becoming thinner. There were several open areas that would take a helicopter. It was the reason this area had been selected.

Russell checked the map again, checked the landmarks around the main open area. They flew over the clearing and continued for several klicks before turning around.

They had left the animal trail and turned to the southeast. Although Petrov feared they had lost the enemy, Volkov assured him that the tracker was reading the signs properly. He had slowed down as the vegetation became thicker and the ground darker. It was hard pushing through the thick foliage and keeping a watch for evidence.

In the distance, Petrov heard rotor blades. He knew that the Laotians would not be flying any helicopters in the area at any time. He wasn't even sure that they had helicopters. He looked up, looking for a hole in the jungle canopy, but it was almost as solid as the roof of a house. He couldn't see the sun, though he knew where it should be.

He pushed by the tracker, moving toward a shaft of sunlight. He reached it but didn't see any aircraft. He turned slowly, following the sound. It had flown over, but Petrov hadn't got to the open area fast enough.

He raised his voice and yelled, "Follow me!"

Volkov translated the instruction. "Follow Kapitan Petrov. Hurry forward!"

He crashed through the foliage, pushing aside a bush that held four-inch-long, needle-sharp thorns. They tore at his clothes and exposed skin, but Petrov ignored them. He was in a hurry. He was sure the enemy was just ahead of him. His gut had been right. There had been spies watching them.

He halted and turned. "Spread out in a line. Move forward on my command. Weapons ready."

Petrov then pushed forward, through the trees. The jungle thinned and Petrov saw the open field. He stopped. Around him the recruits did the same thing. Petrov couldn't see anyone else on the field. He could see no sign that anyone had been in the area recently.

Mendes had looked up when he heard the helicopter but didn't see it. Over the radio he said quietly, "You've flown over."

Russell clicked the mic switch twice, telling those on the ground that he had heard them.

He said, over the intercom, "I've got it."

Gaines released the controls and said, "You've got it."

He banked around and then said, over the radio, "Say location."

"South side of the PZ."

"On approach."

Russell descended to treetop level, watching as the jungle flashed under him. As he came over the edge of the PZ, he flared to slow the aircraft. At the same time, he pulled pitch, loading the rotors so that he slowed more. It was what he thought of as a gravity stop.

As he levelled the skids to touch down, he saw the team leave the protection of the jungle and he hovered forward. As he touched down, the northern edge of the jungle erupted in small arms fire. The crew chief returned the fire, raking the trees where he had seen the muzzle flashes.

Four men seemed to rise from the jungle. They sprinted toward the aircraft. One of them dived into the cargo compartment. He scrambled to his knees and yelled, "Go! Go!"

Unnecessarily, Gaines yelled, "Hurry up!"

Russell felt a round hit the armored seat. He ducked instinctively. Another round ripped through the windshield. He glanced into the cargo compartment and saw the team sprawled on the deck. Costner was pulling the last of them clear of the cargo door.

From the rear, some again shouted, "Go! Go!"

Russell pulled the collective, dumped the nose and pushed forward on the cyclic to gain airspeed. They raced toward the trees at the far end of the clearing. Russell felt more rounds hitting the aircraft. The firing increased as he pulled back on the cyclic and popped up, over the trees. Clear of them, he pushed the cyclic forward again to gain air speed and keep the helicopter from climbing back into view.

"We're clear!" yelled the crew chief. Then, more calmly, he repeated, "We're clear."

"Anybody hit?"

There was a moment's hesitation and then the crew chief said, "We've got one wounded."

"How bad?"

"Don't know. They're trying to bandage the wound."

"Let me know."

Russell kept flying at a low level. He didn't know where the enemy might be or how many there might be. Low level reduced his exposure to them. It was the best thing he could think of at the moment. They were clear of the enemy, clear of the trees, and he wanted to keep it that way as they raced for South Vietnam.

Petrov was surprised at the sudden appearance of an American UH-1H Huey helicopter. There were not supposed to be any American helicopters operating in Laos. He aimed at the helicopter and shouted, "Open fire!" It had to be three hundred, three hundred and fifty yards away.

He wished he had tracers loaded in the weapon. He wasn't sure where the rounds were going. He thought he was hitting the helicopter, but he couldn't be sure. He stopped firing on automatic and switched to single, aimed shot.

Around him the recruits were burning through their ammunition. They didn't have much and would be out in a minute or two. Petrov wanted to shout at the recruits, but it was too late. They had just pointed in the general direction but weren't using the training they had received.

Petrov lowered his weapon for a moment. He watched as men left the jungle, scrambled on board. The aircraft lifted off the ground and the nose dropped, looking as if they wanted to fly into the ground. Instead, it flew across the open area, and began a rapid climb near the trees.

Petrov switched back to full auto and pulled the trigger. He held it down until his weapon was empty, but the aircraft reached the trees and popped up over them. Instantly, it was gone and around him the recruits stopped shooting. He didn't know if it was because the target was out of sight, or they were out of ammunition.

He didn't call for a cease fire. There was no reason to do so. The recruits could see that the target was gone. He looked for Volkov and yelled, "Sergeant. Where are you?" There was no longer a reason for stealth.

Volkov appeared next to him. "Yes, sir."

"I think the chase is over. That was an American helicopter. It took those men out of here."

"That was my impression, sir." He confirmed, "It was an American helicopter."

Petrov knelt. He was aware that his knee was getting wet, but he didn't care. "Let's take twenty minutes. See how much ammunition is left. I want to know if anyone was smart enough not to burn through it all."

"Yes, sir."

"Then we'll head back."

"You don't want to search the area for evidence?"

"What do you expect to find? There are probably enemy 7.62 cartridges but that doesn't really prove much. I think we just need to return to camp as quickly as possible without endangering ourselves."

"Yes, sir."

"You have a comment, Sergeant?"

"I just thought it would be a good idea for us to teach the recruits something about checking the area where we have engaged the enemy."

"Not much of an engagement."

"We're in a training environment, for the most part. I just thought it would make a good training opportunity," Volkov said.

"We're going to lose the daylight soon. I thought the trek back to the camp would be easier with a little bit of daylight."

Volkov nodded. "Yes, sir. I hadn't thought of it that way."

"If there was anything of value that they might have left, I'd say let's go look, but the truth is, anything they dropped probably isn't worth the effort to recover it. Or, rather, recover it tonight. We can always return tomorrow."

"Yes, sir. I'll get the weapons count." He grinned and asked, "How much ammo do you have?"

"I have a fully charged magazine. I did empty one at the helicopter but only because they were lifting off."

Russell had turned due east, heading for the closest point on the Laotian-Vietnamese border. He didn't think anything vital had been hit, there was no indication that they were losing fuel, and all the instruments were still in the green.

The one thing he didn't do was climb to fifteen hundred feet. He was low and fast, but flying high enough to avoid small arms fire and he didn't have to worry about slamming into anything on the ground. All he had to do was avoid the hills.

Over the intercom, Russell asked, "Who's hit?"

"One of the passengers."

"How bad?"

"I think we've got the bleeding stopped but we need to get to an aid station or medevac hospital."

"You've got it." When Gaines took control, Russell twisted around to look at the wounded man. He could see blood on the cargo compartment deck. There looked to be a lot of it. He saw that one of the passengers had pulled the first-aid kit from its position of the bulkhead behind his seat. Parts of it were strewn around. They were covered in blood and Russell wondered if the man was going to die from blood loss.

"We've got maybe forty minutes before we can reach anywhere there might be a doctor. He going to last that long?"

"I don't know," said the crew chief. He leaned close to one of the men and asked a question. He then said, "As long as there is no internal bleeding, he should make it. That is, if we hurry."

To Gaines, Russell said, "Roll over to a hundred knots."

Gaines didn't respond. He just increased the air speed.

They crossed the border into South Vietnam. Russell said, "Come up on zero forty-five degrees." He reached down and used the Fox Mike to alert the closest evac hospital they were on the way with a wounded man.

"Where is he hit?" asked a voice from the hospital.

Russell switched to the intercom and asked, "Where's he hit?"

"Right side, below the ribcage. I think the bullet has gone all the way through."

"Think?"

"We pressed a bandage against his back when we stopped the bleeding."

Russell relayed the information to the hospital. They asked, "How far out are you?"

"I make it ten to fifteen minutes," said Russell. "We're trying to get there as fast as possible."

"Roger that. We'll have a doctor on the helipad. Call us three minutes out."

Russell than put his hands on the controls and said, "I've got it."

As soon as Gaines removed his hands, Russell altered the course by ten degrees and pushed the helicopter to one hundred and twenty knots. That was the redline for that model, but Russell knew that he could safely exceed that by another ten to twenty knots. The Army built a safety factor in for just such emergencies.

Gaines was scanning the ground that was beginning to darken as the sun set. He saw some lights come on and pointed at them. "There."

"Got it," said Russell. He pointed the nose of the aircraft at the lights but didn't slow down. He called the tower and said, "This is Crusader Seven Seven One. I have wounded on board and need a straight in to the evac hospital."

"Seven Seven One, you are number one. No traffic in the pattern. You can land on the evac hospital helipad."

"Roger. Is it lighted?"

"It will be."

"Roger." He switched back to the intercom and said, "Tell the guys that we'll be on the ground in less than five minutes."

Russell was scanning the darkened area to the right of the runway when he saw the lights come on at the helipad. He keyed the mic and said, "I have the helipad in sight."

"You are cleared to land."

Russell entered the traffic pattern and slowed to sixty knots. Once over the runway threshold, he veered to the right, aiming at the lighted square. He could see a half dozen people waiting. He continued the descent, slowing, coming to a three-foot hover in the center of the pad. As he set the skids on the ground, two men climbed into the cargo compart as another two pushed a gurney close to the aircraft.

They lifted the wounded man onto the gurney and began pushing it rapidly toward the hospital doors. One of the team jumped out to follow. Russell wasn't sure what to do. His orders were to get the team to Song Be as quickly as he could. He glanced into the cargo compartment. There was quite a bit of blood on the deck. He could smell the coppery odor of fresh blood.

He then rolled off the throttle and began the shutdown procedure. Gaines said, "We need to get to Song Be."

"I know that. But I need some information from the team leader. Let's see what we can do to wash the blood out of the aircraft and see if we can scare up something cold to drink."

"I think I have to insist," said Gaines.

"Well, as the aircraft commander, I have decided what we're going to do, given the situation. You're just going to have to live with it. There is nothing that we know that can't wait an hour or two. Besides, that'll give us time to check on the wounded man."

CHAPTER 14

They had to bring extra chairs into the briefing room. Sitting on the table were soft drinks, water, coffee and even some orange juice. Major Mack Gerber sat in one of the chairs at the end of the table and Colonel Alan Bates sat the opposite end. Sergeant Major Anthony Fetterman sat near Gerber and reached over for one of the soft drinks. Sitting next to him was Captain George Smith, who was more interested in the juice than who was sitting at the table or what the topic of discussion might be.

Sitting across from him was Sergeant First Class Eric Mendes. He had on a clean uniform that was devoid of any insignia. Finally, sitting next to him was Warrant Officer Russell, who was there to talk about the extraction. In the extra chairs, pushed back against the wall, were Staff Sergeant Ian Morgan and Sergeant Bruce Hendrick. Staff Sergeant Thomas Crockett, who had been wounded during the extraction, was on his way to a hospital in Japan.

In one of the chairs, pushed into a corner and next to one of the large fans, was a captain who held a document with a "Secret" cover sheet. He looked as if he had been awake all night and was uncomfortable being in the room with all these men.

On the other side of the fan were Captains Martin and Bromhead. They had been invited because the strike force was to be created from their units. While they would not be leading the strike force, they would select the strikers and pick the leadership for it.

Bates looked at the door and the sergeant who had been standing next to it and nodded. The sergeant stepped out and closed the door behind him. Bates said, "Okay. Let's get started here. We are going to be entering what I think of as phase two of the operation which is classified as top secret. Sergeant Mendes will begin the briefing."

Mendes looked confused and Bates said, "Just tell us what you observed."

"Yes, sir. We jumped into Laos on —"

Bates interrupted. "We know the details of the HALO operation. Just tell us what you observed once you were in position near that camp."

"Yes, sir. We took up positions on the south side of a small complex of buildings, well, hootches really. There were twenty of them, clustered around a long building in the center that I suspect was a sort of mess hall. I noticed that everyone in the camp made their way to that building early in the morning."

"How many soldiers?" asked Bates.

"That's a tricky question, Colonel. There was a group of Caucasian men that I thought of as soldiers and fifty or sixty locals that acted more like trainees than they did as soldiers. Total in the camp might have been about a hundred. They were armed, though they didn't always carry their arms, other than the Caucasian men. They were always armed."

"Carry on."

"We watched as they engaged in some training. A group sat around while one of the Caucasian men was lecturing them. It appeared that the man was speaking to them in their own language. I thought of the way our Special Forces train the locals."

Gerber snorted. "You're telling me that they have taken a page from our playbook?"

Mendes shrugged. "That was my impression, sir." He waited and then said, "One thing that caught my attention was a patrol that went out in the morning. We had no frame of reference, so I didn't know if this was normal, part of their training, or they were looking for something. I guess I would say they were providing security, though they weren't very disciplined."

Bates interrupted. "Why do you say that?"

"Their formation was sloppy and they had no noise discipline. We could hear them from a long way off. They swung by us but had no flankers who would have stumbled over us. They were going through the motions. They were like men who guard something for a long time and nothing ever happens. They relax the standards."

The captain sitting away from the table asked, "Who do you think the Caucasian men were?"

Mendes looked uncomfortably at Smith. "We'd heard rumors that there were Soviets operating in the area. I believe they were Soviets."

"Did you see anything to corroborate that conclusion?"

"Well, sir, most of the Caucasian men were in American jungle fatigues. But there was one man, and if I remember the Soviet rank structure correctly, he was a major, who wore a khaki uniform. I believe the rank insignia was that of a major, though we were pretty far away, and I can't be sure. He did seem to be in charge. He was the only one I saw in khakis and only for a short time."

"Why do you think that?"

Bates said, "We're getting into the weeds here, Captain. You can question Sergeant Mendes further when we conclude our business here."

"Yes, sir. Sorry, sir."

"The patrol, which, as I said, was maybe some kind of security, moved around the camp. They passed behind us by a good fifty yards. We just remained chilly, and they never came very close to us."

He reached out and grabbed a Coke. He popped the top and took a deep drink. He looked at Bates and said, "Sorry, sir. My throat was dry."

Bates waved a hand and said, "Never mind."

"There were two of the Caucasian men —"

"Oh, hell," interrupted Smith. "Call them Soviets and be done with it."

Bates started to speak, stopped, and then said, "I was going to advise against jumping to that conclusion, but I think it's a fair assumption given the earlier intelligence we had."

Smith said, "That is our information too, sir. I have some of the documentation here."

"Save that for later."

"Yes, sir."

"Let's skip ahead," said Bates. "Why did you issue the recall?"

"There was this one guy," said Mendes, "A big guy, wearing American fatigues, who seemed to have seen something. I don't know what, but he kept looking up into the jungle around the camp. He'd been on the patrol, too. He was sort of leading it. When they got back, after making two circuits, he was still bothered about something. He walked around the perimeter, staring up and I thought, at one point, he had seen us."

Mendes looked at Morgan and asked, "Did you notice that?"

Morgan shrugged. "I was too busy trying not to be seen."

"Why did you say that?"

"I don't know, sir. It just seemed that the guy knew we were out there somewhere but not exactly where we were."

"What about the other Soviets?"

Now Mendes shrugged. "They were just going about their regular duties. They weren't studying the jungle. They were just going through their training."

Mendes waited and when no one said anything, he continued. "Anyway, after lunch, he led another patrol into the jungle. This one was different, more professional. And they started out just inside the jungle. Had they turned toward us, they would have found us in about ten minutes. He turned the wrong way, and it took him longer. I knew we had to get out. I initiated the recall and told the team we had to leave."

"But they saw you," accused Smith.

"No, sir, they did not. We got out of there clean. If they looked closely, they'd find where we had been, but they didn't see us then. Once we were clear of the area, we began to move rapidly. I followed the escape and evasion rules, though we did follow an animal trail for a while. I figured that the animal tracks would disguise our footprints unless they had someone who knew about tracking."

"That would seem obvious," said Smith. "You didn't get away clean."

"No, sir. They didn't see us as we pulled out. They didn't see us in the jungle. Someone on their patrol fired a shot. Not at us — I think it was an accident. From the sound, I could tell they were about an hour behind us. They had someone who knew what he was doing."

"Did you think about doing something to slow them down?"

"I didn't want to use a mechanical ambush because there was no guarantee they would trip it and I didn't want to leave someone behind to engage them because there was a good chance he would be killed or captured. I thought the best thing to do was move rapidly to the extraction point."

"I thought you guys were never captured?" said Smith.

"That is correct," said Morgan. "We are not captured." He glared at Smith. "We used a stream to hide our path and I think that slowed them down a little more. We gained a couple of hours on them. We got to the PZ and set up on the south side of it."

"Did you broadcast a signal for the helicopter?"

Russell, who had been sitting quietly, shook his head. "No. We were able to navigate to the proper location without a signal from them. I had seen aerial photos and there were good landmarks around the PZ. I'm sure that is why it was selected."

Bates said, "That is precisely why it was selected."

"Anyway," said Mendes, "we set up just inside the trees so that we wouldn't be easy targets if the enemy arrived before the helicopter. They all got there about the same time. The chopper flew over once, turned, and came back. As the skids touched the ground, we scrambled into the aircraft."

"That's when Crockett got hit," said Morgan. "There was a hell of a lot of shooting, but they weren't hitting much."

Russell said, "We were down and out in about thirty seconds. We took some hits in the aircraft, but they hit nothing important. Just sheet metal damage."

"Okay. Questions?" asked Bates.

Gerber interrupted and said, "We've been at this for a while and it's getting close to lunch."

Bates looked at his watch and nodded. "That's right. Let's reconvene after lunch in about an hour. Captain Smith, I don't believe that your presence will be necessary since we will not be discussing HALO operations."

He stopped for a moment and turned his attention to Russell. "Mister Russell, is there anything you need to bring up?"

"No, sir. We had good intel on the various PZs. I saw nothing that would add to our knowledge, though I will say that we were engaged by small arms. Just M-16s, as far as I could tell. They were poorly aimed. If you're not planning another venture into Laos, I'd just as soon head back to the company."

"You are excused, Mister Russell, and thank you for your professionalism pulling off the extraction."

Bates now turned toward the captain who had been sitting quietly. "Is there anything you need?"

"I'd like to talk with both Mendes and Russell at some point, but it's nothing of interest to the group."

"Okay. After lunch. Back here." Bates pushed his chair back, and everyone stood up. The meeting had ended.

Kapitan Aleksei Petrov sat in the dim hootch that Major Leonid Semenov used as his office and personal quarters. Semenov was sipping coffee but had not offered any to Petrov. Semenov was not in a good mood but was attempting to hide his true feelings as he questioned Petrov about what had happened the day before.

Semenov put the coffee down and asked, "Why did you organize the patrol yesterday?"

Petrov sat there thinking. Finally, as the silence grew uncomfortable, he said, "There was something different about the jungle."

"What would that be?"

"I don't know, sir. It just didn't look right or feel right. I wanted to find out what was going on."

"So, you took twenty, thirty recruits out on the patrol?"

"It could be viewed as a training exercise. In fact, there are elements of the training syllabus that require them to learn how to properly patrol in the jungle environment. I just moved part of that training to yesterday."

"There are two dead and one wounded."

"Yes, sir. We found evidence that the Americans had discovered our camp and had been observing it."

"How do you know it was the Americans?"

"They were pulled out of the field in an American Huey helicopter."

"Tell me what happened?" said Semenov.

Petrov took a deep breath. "We went out on patrol and found a site with a good view of the camp. It appeared we were under surveillance by four enemy soldiers. We were able to find a trail that suggested they had just fled the area. I ordered a pursuit."

"And were you successful?"

"A complex question, Comrade Major."

"Explain."

"We were able to follow the trail into the jungle. I believe we were not far behind them. We did catch them just before they were extracted by helicopter. Although we took the aircraft under intense fire, they were able to escape."

"Why were you so slow in finding them?"

"Tracking this enemy through the jungle was a difficult task. They used many tricks to slow us down. They used a stream to disguise their movements. They were very good at what they were doing."

Semenov leaned back and rubbed a hand through his hair. "I am wondering why they were able to get away from you."

"They had a head start on us and they knew where they were going. We had to find signs of their movement while they were trying to disguise it. We did not have them in sight until the last moment."

Petrov didn't know what more to say about that. He had explained the situation. He had discovered someone spying on them and had almost caught them. Had there been Soviet soldiers available, he probably could have caught them and either captured or killed them. Instead, he had to rely on recruits who were still learning soldier skills.

He then said, "Given the circumstances, we nearly caught them. We do need additional weapons training. You can't just hand a weapon to a farmer who has never fired a rifle and expect him to be an expert marksman. That takes some practice."

Semenov took a deep breath and said, "We seem to be behind schedule here. The recruits are not progressing as rapidly as I had hoped."

Petrov said, "They came to us without the sort of skills that someone raised in a society that uses much of our modern equipment has. Recruits in the Soviet Union have a knowledge of automobiles and radios and even firearms. The skills these recruits have are more aquarian than urban."

"Sounds like an excuse for your failure."

"I am just talking about the reality of the situation."

Semenov waved a hand and said, "Never mind that. I want the training to be intensified. We have a timeline that we must meet."

Petrov didn't understand the pressure to train the recruits. They were working hard but it was difficult when they spoke a different language, and everything had to be translated. But he understood that this was the end of the meeting. He stood up and said, "Yes, Comrade. We'll revise the training schedule."

For this meeting, everyone had a seat at the table. Colonel Bates, naturally, had the seat at the head of the table. Gerber was opposite him. Bromhead and Martin were on one side and Smith and Fetterman on the other. Bates surveyed the situation and then said, "Captain Smith, I don't believe we'll need anything from you. You are excused."

Smith looked annoyed but he was outranked. He said, "I have orders from the Pentagon."

"Yes, and they are impressive orders. But this has nothing to do with HALO operations and since you have no need to know, you are excused."

It looked, for a moment, as if Smith was going to protest further but then he pushed back his chair and said, "By your leave then, sir." It was his attempt to save some dignity.

With everyone seated and paying attention, Bates said, "Now that we have the complete debrief from that team brought in, we can begin to plan the next phase."

"Which is?" asked Fetterman.

Bates shot Fetterman a look and said, "You're normally a tad more patient than that, Sergeant Major."

"Would you believe that I have a date tonight?"

"No, I don't think so." Bates waited for a moment for a laugh and then said, "We know that someone has set up a camp in Laos and we believe it to be under the direction of the Soviets. The question is if we have an obligation to eliminate it. Is it a threat to us here, in Vietnam?"

Gerber said, "It could be that they are thinking in terms of controlling the Laotian government."

Bates ignored that and said, "Let's create a contingency plan if we learn that they begin to move toward the border and deploy into Vietnam. Major Gerber?"

"Sergeant Major Fetterman and I have been studying this problem since that camp was discovered. While they are inside Laos, they pose no real threat to our operations in Vietnam. However, if we learn they are going to deploy, then we must stop them. We can't allow the Soviets to widen the war using a proxy from Laos."

He stopped for a moment and then said, "To that end, and as we have hinted, we want to draw a company-sized unit created from both your camps. They need to train together and be prepared to deploy if necessary."

Bromhead asked, "Two companies or a single company made from our camps?"

"One unit of about two hundred men for a pocket battalion. They should be among the best of your strikers. They will be led by their own officers and NCOs. We'll want to train at Song Be and we'll have aviation support as we need it."

"The point," said Fetterman, "is to create a team. Once the training is complete, the strikers will be returned to their parent units. From that point, there will be combined training periodically."

"That training," said Gerber, "will include weapons practice, patrolling and small unit tactics. We'll need a list of strikers for the company and Captain Martin, you'll be responsible for billeting the strikers. Both you and Captain Bromhead should coordinate the training syllabus."

Gerber left the conference room as soon as the meeting broke up. He stopped and turned. Fetterman caught up with him and asked, "What are we waiting for?"

Gerber pointed at Captain Jonathan Bromhead. "Him."

"May I ask why, sir?"

"I thought we should chat with him about this upcoming cluster fuck."

Fetterman raised his eyebrows in question, but Gerber didn't elaborate. Bromhead was carrying an M-16 with a magazine in the well, looking as if he expected the enemy to storm the wire at any moment.

"John," called Gerber. "A moment."

Bromhead detoured and joined them. "Yes, sir?"

"I thought we might chat for a moment about this operation. I've got Pepsi in the office, though I don't think it's very cold. We could swing by the club for a beer, but it isn't quite as secure as my office."

"My time is yours," said Bromhead. "Well, at least until about sixteen hundred. Chopper is scheduled to take me back to my camp."

Gerber led the way, opened the door, and stepped into the office. He pointed to the bucket with Pepsi in it. The ice had melted but the water was still cold. Gerber thought about drinking that instead.

Once the drinks were handed out and everyone had found a chair, Gerber said, "This is going to be a little dicey."

"Sir?" said Bromhead.

"This could turn into an unauthorized cross-border operation. If we have Soviets training the Laotians the way we train the locals, they're creating a force to do their dirty work. I mean, the Soviets could deploy that force into Vietnam and not get their hands dirty."

"Yes, sir. I wondered about that." He took a sip of Pepsi and then made a face. "What's wrong with this?"

Fetterman laughed. "Those particular bottles were brewed locally. The formula is slightly different than that you're used to."

"I have told the sergeant major that I don't think it is the formula. I think it has more to do with the cleanliness of the bottling plant. The PX was out of the good stuff, and we had to settle for this."

"Tastes like there is pepper in it," said Bromhead.

"Not to change the subject," said Gerber, "but Tony and I thought we might warn you about some of the dangers of this mission. We don't want anyone who looks like an American soldier to deploy with that ad hoc battalion, if time comes to deploy it."

"Who's going to lead?"

"Vietnamese officers with the services of a couple of our NCOs who don't look particularly like Americans. Those who speak the language with great fluency would be at the top of the list."

Bromhead set his Pepsi on the floor near his chair. It looked as if he wasn't interested in drinking any more of it. "Plausible deniability?"

"More or less. We know that Soviet pilots, and maybe some Chinese, have been flying missions against our bombers in the North. I think they've recorded some air-to-air chatter that was in Russian. Nobody wants to talk about it. Fear of expanding the war is the reason."

"And that's sort of the problem we face here," added Fetterman. "We don't want any Americans to get into a firefight with the Soviets. It might, just might, irritate the Soviets."

"So, we train the strikers and send them out."

"They need to be well-versed in small unit tactics. They must know to charge an ambush, how to disengage and when to attack. They must learn the things that we, meaning you, me, Fetterman and the other American NCOs already know. They must take on the mission as, well, you might say our proxies to fight their proxies."

"And leave nothing behind that can be identified as American," said Bromhead.

"That's another interesting take. We can certainly arm them with AKs, but according to the intel that Mendes brought us, the Soviet unit is dressing in American uniforms and carrying American weapons. The irony is that our guys will probably be dressed more like the VC and carrying Soviet weapons."

Fetterman laughed out loud. "That seems to defeat the purpose of a sterile operation with both sides using the other sides' weapons."

"Then why not just take our own? Let the world think that we ambushed an American unit by mistake."

"An interesting thought," said Gerber. "But no, I think we're better off using the enemy's equipment as much as possible. Of course, there are two possibilities that would render all this moot. First, they never move out of Laos and that operation has another purpose which is, basically, no concern of ours."

Gerber hesitated and then added, "Or they simply disband the unit, send the locals home and exfiltrate the Soviets."

"To what purpose?"

"Serve as a cadre if the Soviets, or the North Vietnamese for that matter, decide that they want to cause disruption or an insurrection in Laos. Then the communists, again either the North Vietnamese or the Soviets, can move in to topple the government."

"And in the meantime," said Bromhead, "I train my soldiers to use the AK-47 and the RPG."

"Exactly. We're not having this discussion with Captain Martin," said Gerber, "because he doesn't really have to know about this deep analysis that the sergeant major and I have engaged in. You just need to direct some of the training to these other considerations."

"That begs the question, Major, who is in overall command?"

"Who's senior?" asked Gerber, though he already knew the answer.

"I am, by a good deal, not to mention that I have more experience in-country than he has."

"Then you have overall command, but I really don't want this to descend into a pissing contest about command. I'm sure you'll handle this with great diplomacy, even though the training will take place at his camp."

"Of course."

"Sergeant Major Fetterman and I will be on hand to assist and to advise. We'll have the latest intel for you and Martin."

"How long is this going to go on?"

"That's the real question. We don't know because we don't know the overall purpose of what the Soviets are doing. It'll be a couple of weeks to six months."

Bromhead snorted. "In six months, I'll have rotated out of here. I'm getting short."

"Most of us will, but that simply means that we'll have to educate our replacements." Gerber hesitated and then added, "We'll be at Song Be in two or three days. We'll let you know. We can organize there."

"Yes, sir."

"You have any questions?"

Bromhead shook his head.

"Then let's go get something to eat."

CHAPTER 15

Captain George Smith left the meeting in a rage. He could not believe that he had been kicked out by some backwater colonel who did not seem to understand what Smith was supposed to be doing and the authority that he held to do it. He didn't believe he could complete his assignment when he was limited to what these Special Forces officers thought. They didn't understand that no one at the Pentagon appreciated the way they operated or their turning traditional military service into some sort of adolescent game. They would not get away with it.

He returned to his room which was not exactly VIP quarters. It was a single room with wooden-paneled walls halfway up and then a screen the rest of the way to the ceiling. It was designed to create air flow and cooling, but it didn't work all that well, which was something else that annoyed him.

There was a cot, not a bed with a mattress but a cot that had a poncho liner for a blanket, one sheet and a pillow that looked as if it had been crushed, flattening it to about an inch in thickness. There was a small table, a chair and an overhead light that did little to illuminate the room at night. Smith, as a representative of the Pentagon, had expected something a little more luxurious. He'd felt slighted by his treatment ever since he had arrived. This latest room was only slightly better than the one he had originally been assigned.

Smith pulled the chair around and sat down at the table. He took out his pen and a pad and began writing a long letter for transmission to the Pentagon. He'd show these clowns just what he thought of them by bringing the force of the Pentagon down on them.

For an hour, he wrote, ignoring all that was going on around him. He filled sheet after sheet and when he finally slowed down, he thought it was good. He began to read what he had written, but didn't care for the tone. It was too combative and had a whining quality to it. He was being maligned by the Special Forces officers. They were being mean to him and didn't recognize his importance or the importance of his mission.

He tore the pages from the pad and then tore them into small pieces. He sat thinking about what he wanted to say and what outcome he desired. The letter he started was not going to do it. They'd tell him to suck it up because there was a war on, and sacrifices had to be made.

And then inspiration hit. He was interested in revenge. He wanted to see the officers punished for not taking him seriously. For thinking of him as a chairborne ranger or a Friday night commando. But they had engaged in one illegal, cross-border operation and it seemed they were about to do so again. They didn't have the authority to drop American soldiers into Laos, supposedly a neutral country. It really didn't matter if the government of Laos was freely elected, a monarchy or communist, it was a neutral country. That was the wedge that he needed in his complaint.

He remembered Mendes as the leader of the HALO team, and he remembered that Bates and Gerber had been in on planning that mission. The HALO team jumped into Laos, spied on the camp, and then had to be extracted under heavy automatic weapons fire. One of the men was badly wounded. The evacuation had been another illegal cross-border operation. He didn't know if it was luck or the skill of the pilots that got the team and aircraft out of Laos with only minor damage and the one man wounded.

Smith read the letter over and decided it needed to be tweaked. He changed some of the wording, so it wasn't quite as critical, thinking of it as more of an after-action report rather than an accusation of illegal operations. He rewrote it twice, until he was happy with the wording. He tore the earlier versions of the report into tiny pieces and then realized that the information was classified. To be safe he should burn those earlier drafts and several of the pages of his notepad underneath, so that he could be sure that no one would be able to read anything from the impressions made by his pen.

He dropped all that into the waste basket and set it on fire. He watched it burn, not worried about the smoke, which was blowing out through one of the screened walls. When the fire was out, he stirred the ashes. No one would be able to read even a single word that he had written in those earlier drafts.

The next question was how to get it transmitted the fastest. He could mail it, but that could take ten or twelve days and he didn't want to wait that long. He could use the MARS system to make a telephone call, but there were too many people involved, from those operating the radios here in Vietnam and in the States, not to mention the employees of the telephone company and then whoever answered the telephone at the Pentagon. Just too many ears in a world that was listening for anything bad to say about the military and who might be looking to move up in the world.

There was a communications center for official message traffic, that could transmit classified information. A message addressed to the proper agency would get there with little outside scrutiny. Smith had orders that would allow him to use that communications center to send information to the

Pentagon. This seemed to be the best solution. In a matter of minutes, his message could be read in Washington, and he could expect some sort of response in less than a day, with a little luck.

He had some trouble convincing the NCOIC that he was authorized entry to the commo center. He showed his orders, but the man just shook his head. He was a large man with a receding hairline but who looked as if he knew what the rules were and was going to adhere to them regardless of the paperwork handed him by an officer he didn't recognize. His name tag said that his last name was Napier.

"You can read that I am authorized communication with the Pentagon can't you, Sergeant Napier?"

"Yes, sir. I see that. But I don't see anything here that means you are authorized to use the specific communication network that we use."

"You're splitting a hair, Sergeant. Call the officer in charge."

Napier shrugged and said, "He's going to tell you the same thing that I have."

"Let's just see what he has to say."

"It'll be just a minute."

It was closer to ten minutes. Napier returned with a tall, thin man wearing glasses. He was also wearing the golden oak leaves of a major. He studied Smith for a moment and said, "Your orders do not cover the use of our communications facility here. I would guess that it was meant for the facility at Tan Son Nhut or the MACV compound in Saigon."

"I'm sure that there will be no trouble with my communication, sir," said Smith. "It's not as if it is a personal message."

The major thought about that and said, "Let me see it?"

"Sir, it is classified."

You know we can't send anything that we are not allowed to read?"

Smith didn't move, thinking about it. He realized that those transmitting the message would have to read it to transmit it, but unlike the other systems, they were all cleared for classified information. He had reached a stalemate.

"Come on, Captain. I don't have all day."

Reluctantly, Smith handed over the message. The major read it over and said, "This is not on the proper form. I'll need to have it retyped and then you'll have to proofread it. Take us about an hour or so. You could come back then for the final approval."

"Yes, sir. About three, then?"

"Three or a little after."

"Yes, sir. Thank you." Smith left the communications center grinning to himself. In two or three hours, depending on the volume of traffic, his message would be in the hands of those in the Pentagon and the situation would change.

Major Richard Karstairs watched as Smith walked down the corridor, toward the exit in the communications center. He thought that there was something about Smith he didn't like. Maybe it was the air of superiority that Smith had because he worked in the Pentagon and he was here, in Vietnam, on TDY orders. Maybe it was the way that Smith expected him to bend the rules for him because he worked in the Pentagon.

As soon as Smith was out of the building, Karstairs returned to his office and sat down. He read through the message again and immediately understood the ramifications of the accusations included in it.

Karstairs yelled, "Napier?"

Napier appeared at his door. "You bellowed, sir?"

"I most certainly did. I'm going over to the Green Beret compound for a while. I don't know when I'll be back."

"I thought you might be taking a trip after that nonsense about a proper form and whatnot."

"Keep this to yourself."

"I understand, sir. Are we going to transmit it?"

"I doubt it. I'll be finding out for sure from Colonel Bates. It's his ass on the line with this."

Karstairs left the center and looked at his jeep. Someone had parked it so that the driver's seat was in the sun, and they hadn't leaned the seat forward to protect it. Now he wished he had a towel or something to cover it.

He drove over to the Special Forces compound, parked in front, looped the chain through the steering wheel and locked it.

Inside, he was stopped by an NCO manning a desk in much the way a receptionist would. He said that he needed to speak with Colonel Bates. The NCO suggested he come back later but Karstairs said, "That won't do. I need to see him now and he's not going to be happy when he learns that you turned me away."

"Just a moment, sir, and I'll check."

The man returned and said, "The colonel will see you now."

Karstairs entered the office, walked to within three feet of the front of Bates' desk and said, "Major Karstairs requests permission to speak with the colonel."

"What do you want, Karstairs?"

Without preamble, Karstairs handed Bates the papers he had carried in. Bates took them, scanned them, stopped, and turned back to the first page.

He read the whole thing carefully and then asked, "Where in the hell did you get this?"

"A Captain Smith gave those to me for transmission to the Pentagon. I told him that it would take an hour or more to prepare them and that we would need him to proofread the final copy before I would transmit it."

Bates shuffled the pages until he had the first page on top. "He actually wants you to send this?"

"Yes, sir."

"What are the rules for this sort of thing? This a personal message or an official document?"

"Given the way he presented it, I believe it is more of a personal message rather than an official after-action report. It does not fit into any Army style."

"May I keep this?"

Karstairs hesitated but then said, "Yes, sir. I suspect it should be a classified document. You'll need to either destroy it or safeguard it."

"Okay. That I can do. Thank you for bringing this to my attention, Major. If I need anything more, I'll reach out for you."

Karstairs saluted and left the office. He heard Bates shout, "I want to see Major Gerber, Sergeant Mendes and Captain Smith in here as quickly as possible."

"Yes, sir. Do you want MPs?"

"Do you really think I need an MP to deal with Smith?" He stopped and then asked, "How do you know that I might want MPs?"

"An inspired guess, sir."

"Keep you inspired guessed to yourself." He hesitated, then asked, "Do you think I need MPs?"

"No, sir. I just thought you might want them to escort Smith back to his quarters when you're finished with him. Keep him under your thumb. Sir."

"Thank you, Sergeant. Just get those people in here."

As soon as Gerber entered the office, Bates handed him the document. He read it through and frowned. "Who in the hell wrote this? Where'd you get it?"

"Let's wait until the others get here," said Bates.

Fetterman appeared at the door and asked, "Should I be here, sir?"

"Come on in, Sergeant Major, this concerns you too."

Just then, Mendes knocked on the door and waited to be invited in. Bates waved him in and right behind him was Captain Smith.

Smith looked around and asked, "You asked for me, Colonel?"

"Come on in. Pull a chair over here. Everyone, take a seat."

Bates waited for everyone to sit down before he began. "We have a problem here and I want to take care of it before it grows into something that is out of control."

Bates then picked up the pages as if to show them around. Smith suddenly sat up straighter. "Those are mine, Colonel. That is a classified message directed to the Pentagon."

"No," said Bates. "This document has not been properly classified, but even if it was, everyone in this room has a security clearance and is aware of the contents. There is nothing in this document that would disqualify them from access to it because they know all the pertinent facts in it."

"Sir, that was my personal message."

Bates handed the papers to Fetterman. "Take a moment to read this, Sergeant Major."

Fetterman read the first few lines, and said, "I can't believe anyone put this on paper."

Smith shot him a look and said, "You can put that down right now, Fetterman."

Fetterman looked at him, grinned, and flipped to the next page.

Bates said, "You wrote this document and you wished that it be transmitted to the Pentagon?"

"That's right." Smith was livid. He dropped the military protocol which required him to address Bates in a proper manner.

Fetterman asked, "What makes you think that the mission was illegal or that we were somehow exceeding our authority." He stopped for a moment and then asked, "And what is your authority to make such a report, or should I say, raise such an allegation?"

"You dropped a team into Laos."

Fetterman shook his head and said, "I didn't drop the team into Laos." Having finished reading the document, he passed it to Gerber. "I say let him transmit it. Let him hang himself."

"I had that thought," said Bates, "but I also worry about that document getting into the wrong hands. There are too many people who must handle it before it reaches the addressee. We can't have that."

"Because it exposes the illegal nature of your operation in Laos."

Bates slammed a hand onto his desk. "No," he said. "Because it would expose a classified operation that has been authorized by an authority much higher than some low-ranking Pentagon official who, I suspect, is about to see the end of his military career."

The color drained from Smith's face.

"Before I summoned you all here," said Bates, "Sergeant Branigan out there asked if I wanted him to summon the MPs to escort you to your quarters. You were about to compromise a classified operation by providing details to those not cleared to know about it. I don't know your motivation, Captain Smith, but unless you are careful in what you say in the next few minutes, you'll find yourself under arrest."

Smith seem to deflate. He said lamely, "Are all those in this office cleared for mission?"

"Everyone here has the proper need to know. We were a little generous in allowing you in on some of this because of your orders and your desire to learn more about HALO operations."

Gerber said, "If he withdrew that document, meaning that he would not require it to be transmitted —"

Smith interrupted. "That commo guy, that major, he shouldn't have shown that to you. He is as guilty as I am."

Bates laughed. "Major Karstairs was doing his duty. He realized that you were about to compromise a mission and took the proper action by alerting me to the possible leak. I'm thinking of awarding him an Army Commendation Medal for his service to this organization."

Smith suddenly realized there was a way to save his career. "Colonel, since the message was not transmitted, there has been no compromise. The compromise stopped with the major…"

"And the NCO you talked to first," said Bates.

"Yes, sir," said Smith, recovering slightly. "But if it wasn't sent, then I showed bad judgement when I wrote the document." Smith was thinking that if the problem was contained, in Vietnam, there was no reason for his rating officers for his Office Efficiency Report to know what he had done. It would be as if this never happened. Once he was back in Washington, he could ask a few discreet questions. He might be able to get himself out of trouble and those here into it.

Feeling better, Smith said, "Why don't we just burn that document."

Gerber said, "No. Colonel, we can't let him get away with this."

Bates said, "I can see no benefit in pursuing this any further. Captain Smith destroys his document and then keeps his opinion about our operations — about which he knows next to nothing — to himself and everything returns to the way it was at noon today."

Gerber shook his head in disgust.

"If you let me have that, Colonel," said Smith, reaching for the papers, "I'll burn it now."

Bates said, "I'll take care of it. I want to be sure we do this right." What he didn't say was that he wanted it as evidence if he ever needed it.

To the group, he asked, "We all good here?"

Mendes, who wasn't sure why he had been invited, said, "Yes, sir."

Gerber and Fetterman nodded. Smith said, "Yes, sir. Thank you, sir."

Captain Jonathan Bromhead, U.S. Army Special Forces, was standing at the bar in the officers' club. Like so much else in Vietnam, the bar was made from plywood, stained by a blowtorch to bring out the grain, and then varnished to a high gloss. It was an impressive bar.

Behind it, on a series of shelves, were the intoxicating spirits that included bourbon, Scotch, gin, vodka, and a smattering of other such beverages. Beer, not on tap, but in cans, was also available for those who didn't want to get roaring drunk quickly.

Bromhead, who wasn't all that big a fan of intoxicating beverages, had opted for a Seven Up. He liked that better than Coke or Pepsi or even Dr Pepper. He was amused by the loyalty that some showed for Mountain Dew, but those were mainly officers who had grown up in the south.

Captain Martin appeared beside him and said, "What are you drinking?"

"Seven Up. I'm not in the mood for anything stronger."

When the bartender came over, Martin said, "Give me a straight shot of bourbon, no ice."

Once he had his drink, Martin said, "You called this meeting."

"At the suggestion of Major Gerber. He thought that we should begin our end of the operation as quickly as possible. He wondered if we couldn't get everything done tomorrow." He held up his hand to stop the protest. "Yes, it's late in the day and I'm thinking the day after tomorrow would be possible."

"I don't have the facilities for fifty or more strikers showing up at Song Be. It'll take days to get these things arranged."

"I was thinking about that and thought that we switch the strikers around. You send fifty of your strikers to my camp. We have the facilities for them and that opens fifty spaces for my strikers arriving at your camp. Doesn't change the logistics or the strength of either camp."

Martin finished his drink in one gulp and signaled for another one. When it arrived, Martin left it sitting on the bar. "We can do that, though I don't like the idea of sending any of my strikers off to your camp. Breaks up my team."

"It's only temporary. As I understand it, once we finish the training, the strikers will be returned to their original camp."

Martin said, "I'm not a fan of this. I don't like breaking up my team, even if it is temporary."

"I understand that, but we have our orders."

"That we do. How is this transfer going to be made?"

"Colonel Bates has arranged for airlift. We can spread the strikers over nine aircraft. They can bring their equipment with them. Aircraft won't be overloaded."

Martin finally picked up his drink, sipped and then downed it, slamming the glass to the bar. "I suppose if we get the strikers chosen today and get airlift today, we could conceivably begin training tomorrow."

"I'm just not that convinced we need to move that fast. Certainly, by the next day we can get it done. Might take the men a day to get settled, used to the new environment and meet the other team."

"I was thinking marksmanship training first. Wouldn't take all that long to coordinate and while we're running them through the range, we can plan for the rest of it."

Bromhead nodded. "I'm thinking we need some team-building exercises and we need to break up the units so that they are made up of strikers from each camp. We have a short time to teach them to trust one another."

Now Martin grinned. "Patrolling. Set up an ambush here and there. Get them working together. We'll need to keep changing the assignments so that everyone gets to work with everyone else. Let them see how good the others are."

"You have any idea of the NCOs you're going to assign to this?"

"I've three who would work. Two are Puerto Rican and one is of Mexican descent. From a distance, they can pass for

Vietnamese. Get up close and it is going to be obvious they're not."

"I've got two in mind," said Bromhead. "We'll need to get the five of them together, so they understand what is going on here."

"The one thing I don't know for sure is if these NCOs will be accompanying this unit when, and if, it goes into the field."

"I think we can play that by ear. See what the situation is, if there even *is* a situation."

"I was going to say that I don't like this," said Martin. "But then I realized that this is just the sort of thing that we're supposed to be doing. We're responding to a threat from the enemy in the best way possible."

"The next few weeks are going to be a mess. I'm thinking that we should have dinner and get back to our camps. We can get some of this arranged today."

"I've talked to my exec," said Martin. "I told him I wanted him to pick the men for this assignment and have them ready when I get back to camp."

"Then you're one step ahead of me," said Bromhead. "I just told mine that I would be back this afternoon and that we had some work to do."

"Well, this is going to be interesting," said Martin.

"Yeah," said Bromhead, "I don't like this pulling strings when I'm not out in the field with the strikers. Too much can go wrong."

"Let's grab a table, order a steak and a beer, and then see about getting back to our camps."

"I'll buy the beer if you buy the steaks."

Martin laughed. "Already trying to put one over on me. The steaks are more expensive than the beer."

"True, but I haven't limited it to a single beer."

CHAPTER 16

Fifty strikers stood in the bright sunlight waiting while both Captain Bromhead and Captain Martin gave them orders. They were standing at attention, their weapons at their sides. All were dressed in tiger-striped jungle fatigues. They wore American-style helmets and web gear and looked as if they were ready to deploy into the jungle.

In fact, they were the quick reaction force. The inspection was to ensure that they were ready if a patrol of twenty-five, that had left earlier, ran into trouble. The various activities, from patrolling to QRF to guarding the approaches to the camp were rotated among the strikers.

The QRF was made up of two twenty-five-man units. One was detailed to go out if the patrol got into trouble. The second unit would accompany the first if there was a need for it, otherwise it would remain in reserve.

Martin had just turned away, heading back to the team house when they heard firing in the distance. He broke into a run, heading for the commo bunker to see what had happened. Bromhead remained where he was, cocking his head from side to side, trying to pinpoint the firing.

"Sergeant Trang, is your force ready to go?"

Trang turned and studied the strikers. In Vietnamese, he ordered them to check their weapons, insert a magazine but not to chamber a round. He told them they would need their spare ammunition, their canteens and first-aid kits. If they had a combat knife, it would be a good weapon to carry with them.

Once he had given his instructions, he said, "We are ready to go, Captain."

"Let's move to the gate."

Martin appeared and said, "Looks like the patrol ran into something of an ambush."

"What happened?"

Martin couldn't help grinning. "We've been using the same areas for training and patrolling, and I guess some wiseass VC or NVA thought it would be a good idea to set an ambush."

Bromhead said, "Shouldn't we deploy the ORF?"

"No need. They have neutralized the threat. Without an order from either of the Green Berets, the NCOIC ordered an attack. They charged the ambush, breaking it up. They killed four, counted two blood trails and found half a dozen weapons. They're bringing those in."

"Then they don't need us?"

"Nope. They handled it perfectly. If we were to have a final exam, or if this was their final, they'd passed with flying colors. We have two wounded, neither seriously."

Bromhead grinned broadly. "We'll need to prepare an after-action report for Major Gerber. We can tell him that we have completed the training a week early."

"Yeah," said Martin. "These guys really hate the VC. Gave them the incentive to learn what they had to learn."

"Let's do this. Split them up into their original strike force, my guys together and yours together, and let's have a shooting contest. We'll have to think of a prize."

"That's easy. A weekend in Saigon. We get the winner a ride down there and maybe provide a little cash for a good time."

"And we should report to Gerber and Bates that we've about finished this training. The unit is ready to go and we're ready to return to our original strength," said Bromhead.

"In person?"

"Why not? Or have them come down here. Either way."

Major Mack Gerber was always looking for an excuse to get out of the office and into the field, even if the field meant heading to a Special Forces camp. While the living conditions weren't as comfortable as those in Nha Trang, he was doing what he believed was the mission of the Special Forces. Training the local populations in what they needed to survive in a combat arena.

Sergeant Major Anthony B. Fetterman had the attitude of an old soldier. He liked his comfort because he had spent so much time in uncomfortable circumstances. He liked the variety of activities at Nha Trang and the somewhat relaxed attitude of those who were stationed on a large base camp. There was no chance that it would be overrun, and the periodic mortar and rocket attacks posed no real threat to his safety. He believed that he was in more danger riding around in big city traffic than he was at Nha Trang.

Now, they were again on their way to Song Be in what they thought of as a pre-planned conference on the strategy of the situation. Fetterman knew that no Special Forces camp had ever been overrun, with the exception of Lang Vei during Tet of 1968. Now, with the interlocking fields of fire from fire support bases, both helicopter gunships and Air Force and Navy fighters almost on call, the chances of a camp being overrun approached zero.

The plane touched down on the gravel paved runway but without the evasion maneuvers that had been typical not all that long ago. They rolled to a stop, turned, and taxied back to a point near the gate for the camp. Without a word from the cockpit, the rear ramp was lowered, and the cool air of the interior was immediately replaced with the hot, humid air of Vietnam.

Gerber grabbed his weapon and his ruck as he stood up and said, "We have arrived, Sergeant Major."

"That we have," said Fetterman. "Do you know what the movie is for tonight?"

"No, but I hear they have television reception here now. Don't know what's on the tube."

"I think I'd rather sleep."

Gerber walked down the ramp and saw that both Bromhead and Martin were waiting for him. Given they were in the field and on the airstrip, neither man saluted.

Fetterman followed, looked at the two and asked, "Where's the band?"

"Playing in a parade," said Martin. "I didn't think you'd mind the quiet."

At that moment, the engines of the plane roared as the pilot wound them up to full operating RPM and began to taxi to the end of the runway for take off. Fetterman put his hand on his head to keep the propwash from blowing his beret into the jungle.

Martin pointed toward the interior of the camp and said, "Let's get inside."

Gerber glanced at Martin and then at Bromhead. "What's changed?"

Martin repeated, "Let's get inside."

Gerber nodded as Martin and Bromhead led them into the interior of the camp. He saw a formation of strikers near the gate, but they looked as if they had just returned from patrol.

Fetterman held a hand up to shade his eyes and asked, "What is going on here?"

Bromhead said, "We had a patrol ambushed this morning. Early on."

Gerber stopped walking. He turned to look at the strikers. "Bad? Casualties?"

"We're set up so that you'll have a chance to talk to the patrol leaders." Martin then grinned. "I think you'll be pleased with the results."

Bromhead said, "We have everything arranged in the team house."

"If this isn't pressing," said Fetterman, "I'd like a moment to get settled, drop my ruck, wash my face and hit the head."

"Twenty minutes in the team house," said Martin. He started walking and the others followed.

"Fine," said Fetterman.

Gerber turned toward Bromhead. "You seem awfully quiet, John. Something on your mind?"

"No, sir. I just don't like meetings."

"Is that meetings with us or meetings in general?"

"It's meetings in general, but your sudden appearance suggests a lack of confidence in what we're doing here."

"Not at all," said Gerber. "We're not here to inspect or criticize but to gather information. Things are in a state of flux and the time frame that we had in mind is no longer in our hands. Things change."

"Such as?"

They were now inside the compound. They were near what was considered the guest quarters. Martin opened the door for them. "Team house in twenty minutes?"

Before entering, Gerber said to Bromhead, "We'll get into that later."

Inside, they dropped their gear. Gerber sat on one of the cots and looked around the spartan room. Not much there other than the two cots, two chairs, a single table and a slight alcove that was sort of a closet. Neither Gerber nor Fetterman had anything to hang up. To one side was a small sink.

"Wash up, Tony."

"Washing wasn't what I had in mind, Major. I'm going in search of the latrine."

"Then I'll meet you at the team house."

Fetterman left and Gerber sat for a moment on the cot, looking down at the dirty plywood floor. Overhead was a ceiling fan, but it was motionless. There was a slight breeze blowing through the screened upper half of the walls. The quarters were typical of those built by the Army throughout South Vietnam.

Finally, he pushed himself up and headed to the door. He wondered why he suddenly felt so tired. It wasn't that the workload had been particularly heavy, and it wasn't as if they had been deployed into the field for long stretches. Maybe it had to do with knowing that he and Fetterman, and none of the other Special Forces soldiers would be used for the mission. The whole plan was to train the Vietnamese and then send them out. They were the ones who were going to be responsible for the conduct of the mission, but Gerber had always believed in leading from the front. Don't send the soldiers out to do something that he, himself, wouldn't do.

Of course, that didn't apply here. Gerber would go on the mission if it was appropriate. He was ineligible based on his size and ethnicity. He wasn't Vietnamese and that was the deciding factor.

He reached the team house and went inside. Not much had changed other than some of the furniture had been rearranged. Now there was a long table on one side of the room with four chairs behind it. In front, arranged in something of a semicircle, were another half dozen chairs. To Gerber, it looked as if it was a court of inquiry, and he was sure that was not the impression that either Bromhead or Martin had intended.

Gerber sat down in a chair and waited. He wasn't sure what was going on now but figured it had something to do with the ambush.

Both Bromhead and Martin entered together. Fetterman arrived a minute later.

Bromhead said, "Why don't you and Major Gerber take seats behind the table?"

"Is this some sort of court of inquiry?" asked Fetterman.

"Not at all, Sergeant Major. I think of it as more of a debriefing or the collection of information for an after-action report. Neither I nor Captain Martin believe the patrol acted improperly. However, your arrival here adds a little bit of importance to our information-gathering."

Fetterman pulled out a chair at the end of the table and sat down. Gerber joined him and both Martin and Bromhead sat down. When they were settled and almost as on cue, the senior Special Forces NCO, Master Sergeant Gottlieb entered with four Vietnamese strikers.

Gerber waved them into the room and said, "Please take a seat. Will you be remaining with these strikers, Sergeant?"

"As sort of moral support and a translator, sir, if that is okay."

Gerber gestured at one of the chairs. "Have a seat. I believe everyone here, on this side of the table, has a working knowledge of Vietnamese."

"Yes, sir, and these strikers have a working knowledge of English."

"Then we are set," said Gerber. As senior officer present, he assumed the role of the chairman. He waited as the others took their seats and then said, "This is not a court of inquiry though it might look like that. This is not a hearing. This is what I think of as a debriefing. We're interested in what happened today during the morning patrol."

Gottlieb stood up and started to speak, but Gerber cut him off. "Please, keep your seat sergeant. Were you with the patrol this morning?"

"No, sir. There were three Americans with them, but I was not one of them."

"Is there a reason that none of them are here?"

"No, sir," said Gottlieb. "I thought you might like this from the perspective of the strikers who were leading the patrol rather than the interpretation of those who were there as observers."

"Okay," said Gerber. "If we need them, we can get them later. Sergeant, which of the strikers will be describing what happened?"

Gottlieb pointed to one of the strikers. "Trung Si Nhat Quang was in overall command of the patrol."

Quang was a slight man with jet-black hair and an olive complexion. He stood just over five foot six and was wearing American-style jungle fatigues. He started to stand but Gerber said, "Keep your seat."

He sat back down and said, "Thank you, sir." He had an English accent. Most of the Vietnamese who spoke English sounded like they came from the American Midwest, unless they learned their English from the French. In that case, they had a French accent that was sometimes almost impossible to understand.

Gerber prompted him. "In your own words, tell us what happened this morning."

"Yes, sir. We left the compound about an hour after first light. We thought of this as a training patrol, but we did carry a basic load, water, some rations, and little else. We were planning to be back here just after noon. We'd be on patrol for about five hours. We weren't going very far."

"About how far?" asked Fetterman.

Quang turned his attention to Fetterman. "No more than seven or eight klicks. I was watching their patrol techniques, how they moved in the jungle, did they avoid the trails, how was their noise discipline, that sort of thing."

Gerber waved his hand. "Continue."

Quang looked at the floor. "I felt there was something wrong. The jungle didn't feel right. Maybe it was the lack of noise from the animals and insects. There was something not quite right, so I passed the word to be on the alert."

"It's the little things that are important," said Gerber. "We see or hear things on a subliminal level. It's good and proper to pay attention to those feelings."

"Yes, sir," said Quang, nodding. "I was about to change direction, loop around and head back. The patrol would be a little short, but I didn't think that would be a problem. Just as I had signaled the change in direction, there was a shot to the right. My first instinct was to drop to a knee to see where it had come from and figure out if it was just one man. The weapon didn't sound like an AK. It was something older and I wondered if it was a weapon that had been taken from the Japanese long ago."

He took a breath and said, "At that moment, there was more firing, this time from AK-47s on automatic. My guys didn't hesitate. Without a command from me, they began firing in return, charging into the ambush. The enemy fire was poorly aimed. We ran toward them, firing carefully to avoid friendly casualties. It was good, aimed fire."

"You didn't think about calling for artillery?" asked Martin.

"No, sir. No time. The charge broke the ambush, and the VC were running. We didn't need artillery and I don't know how we could have called it in. The VC were on the move, rapidly."

"Okay," said Martin.

"We passed their position and I saw two bodies there. When we came back, we found two more. They had left the weapons behind which told me that the VC were not well trained."

"They had AKs," Fetterman reminded him.

"We found six weapons, five AKs and an SKS. The SKS was old and didn't seem to be in good shape. The AKs were rough, which might have explained their lack of accuracy. We chased the VC for about a klick but then I halted that. I was worried that we might run into a larger, better trained group and I didn't want to risk the men with me."

Gerber said, "You had secured a victory over the ambush. There was no need to pursue the VC unless something of military value could be accomplished."

Quang said, "That was my thought as well, sir. We had killed four, we found two blood trails telling me that we had wounded two others. We have recovered their weapons. Not exactly a major victory. A small one that would tell the enemy that we were a solid force."

"So, you treated your wounded, grabbed the weapons and left the bodies where they fell?"

"Yes, sir. I didn't know what else the enemy might have there. They did set up the ambush in a place where they could engage us. That told me that they had been watching us. We ordered the men to head back to the camp, but to maintain proper military discipline."

Gerber said, "Anyone have any questions?"

Martin asked, "Did you search the bodies?"

"Yes, sir. They had no papers or identification. They were wearing black clothing. They only had their weapons, water, and spare magazines. Nothing else. Not even a knife. They weren't planning on staying there very long."

There was silence. Gerber broke it, asking, "Anyone have anything else?"

When no one said anything, Gerber said, "Okay. That's it then. Thank you, Sergeant Quang, for your after-action report. Most professional."

As the debriefing was breaking up, the commo sergeant entered and handed Gerber a note. He read it and then handed it to Fetterman, who said, "We need to get back to Nha Trang."

"Yes, we do."

"What are we going to do?"

"I thought we'd go over to commo and arrange a flight. There are enough helicopters flying around here that someone will be able to divert to us, or at worse, get us to a place where we can catch a flight into Nha Trang."

"What do you think happened?"

Gerber shrugged. They had reached the door of the temporary quarters. "Why don't you wait here while I go see if I can get us a ride."

"Is there something that you're not telling me?"

"Tony, you know as much about this as I do. You read the message."

"Sometimes, Major, you have an insight into these things."

Gerber chuckled and then said, "If I had to guess, I'd say that the Soviets have done something in Laos that requires our expertise."

"You mean the recon missions have spotted something?"

"That's my guess, though I don't know why we have to get to Nha Trang ASAP. Bates knows the score and if there is something on fire, the striker force is here. They'll have to arrange to move it and that will take a little coordination."

Gerber checked his ruck, but he hadn't taken anything out of it. All he had to do was strap it on. "You haven't moved to pack."

Fetterman pointed at his ruck and said, "I haven't had the chance to unpack. I'm ready to go."

Gerber left the hootch and made his way to the commo bunker to arrange transportation.

Colonel Alan Bates had made his classified office as secure as possible. It was set in the middle of the hootch so that no one outside could listen to what was being said inside. He had a double layer of plywood that had a dead space between the sheets filled with dirt and gravel so that there should be no vibrations that a hidden mic might detect. He had an air conditioner and given the climate in Vietnam, it was a necessity in a room that had no other ventilation. He also had a large fan that when turned on created a wall of white noise. With an armed guard on the door and one watching the corridor, no one was going to be able to put an ear to the door. He'd done it so that he could discuss classified material without having to move the discussion into a bunker somewhere else. It was a convenience for him. Besides, in Vietnam, the sometime icy atmosphere was a welcome change from the nearly lethal heat and humidity.

Bates was sitting behind his desk which looked like most of the others in Vietnam, meaning it appeared to be a refugee from the Second World War. It was battered and painted a sickly green for some reason. Bates didn't care because it worked just find and he didn't plan to entertain any generals or politicians in the room. It was strictly for classified discussions except when Bates wanted to cool down.

Major Mack Gerber sat in a chair in front of the desk. He held a Pepsi in his right hand and looked as if he hadn't shaved in a day or two. His jungle fatigues were smudged and one of the pockets was unbuttoned.

Sergeant Major Anthony Fetterman sat in the other chair. He looked as if he had shaved recently, his uniform was pressed and there was no evidence of dirt on it. His boots were shined. Fetterman had taken time to clean up while Gerber had gone to begin the process of getting airlift capability. He didn't have a date or time, but wanted to see what was available.

Bates lifted a folder off his desk. There was a "Secret" cover sheet on it. He handed it to Gerber.

Gerber leaned over and put his Pepsi can on the floor. He opened the folder, looked at the top picture. He sorted through them quickly and asked, "What am I looking at here?"

"That is the camp that we dropped the HALO team on."

"Okay."

"It seems to be deserted."

"Deserted since our team was there?"

"Yes."

Gerber handed the folder to Fetterman who shuffled through it carefully. He stopped at one of the pictures and studied it carefully. "Are those tire tracks?"

"That was the conclusion of the photo analysts at MACV. They thought they might be Soviet-made copies of our six-bysixes. I'm not sure how they reached that conclusion, but it really doesn't matter. It seems that they moved everything out of the camp."

"I don't suppose you know where they went."

"Well," said Bates, "I was hoping that they returned to the Soviet Union, but I don't think that's what happened. I think they just moved to a new location, closer to the border."

Fetterman picked up on that and said, "Then you know where they went."

"We suspect. It was an interesting bit of detective work by the photo analysts along with some HUMINT from sources in Laos. They are at what was a small village about seven or eight klicks from where they had been."

"That makes very little sense," said Gerber.

"Actually, it was a mistake on their part," said Bates. "According to the intel, we know they moved and where they went, but more importantly, they told us that they had something to hide."

"So, what are we going to do?" asked Gerber.

Bates held out a hand and motioned to Fetterman. He surrendered the folder and photographs. "Nothing really. They moved to just the right place for us. We have assets there that can feed us information."

"Do we know the purpose?" asked Gerber.

"I suspect they are now training some of the locals in guerrilla activities as opposed to standard military tactics. They are uncomfortably close to the border."

"Then we should go after them," said Fetterman.

"That's the problem, Sergeant Major. While we have engaged in cross-border ops in Cambodia, there is no way that we can do that in Laos. You might say it's just a step too far and would be considered widening the war when the political climate is to reduce combat operations."

"Then we do nothing," said Gerber. "You called us here for that?"

"Just what have you been doing these last few weeks?"

Gerber said nothing and he considered the question. Then he realized the ultimate purpose for creating the striker force they had put together. He knew that an A-Team couldn't be sent into Laos. If a Vietnamese strike force was sent, then it could be claimed that it was a South Vietnamese mission.

"Then we just watch," said Gerber. "We put patrols out where they are likely to cross the border to intercept them."

Bates said, "I'm not sure about the patrols. We can use Mohawks flying along the border. Their people-sniffers will tell us if a force has moved from Laos into South Vietnam."

"I'd like a little warning about that. Like when they move out of their camp."

"We have to be careful about that. We don't want them to know that we know they have moved. Our HUMINT source might be able to give us a couple of days warning, but we only need to know when and where they cross the border. We can intercept them there."

"By we," said Fetterman, "you mean me and the major?"

"By we, I mean the strikers that you have been training. You should be in the C and C, calling the shots on the ground."

"What happens if we need to reinforce?" asked Gerber.

"We have a battalion of U.S. infantry that we can call on. I can't see where we'll actually need them, but we have them. I'm sure that your strike force can handle it with either artillery or gun support."

"Our strikers are not conversant in calling in artillery."

Bates raised an eyebrow. "I thought there were Americans who would be accompanying them? Don't they know how to do it?"

"Yes," said Gerber. "They know and if Fetterman and I are in the C and C, we can do it as well."

"Then we're set here. Stick close in case we have to launch this strike rapidly."

"You think they're going to try it soon?"

"I think that was the purpose of the move."

CHAPTER 17

Captain George Smith, U.S. Army, having returned from Southeast Asia, was sitting in what they all thought of as the reading room. It had no windows and a single door. The desks and chairs were arranged in a specific pattern so that someone entering the room would be unable to see any of the documents being read no matter how careless the reader might be. The desks had a similar arrangement. If anyone attempted to peek, he would be obvious. Of course, given that situation, there weren't many places to sit and read the classified documents. It was to keep those without a need to know from seeing something to which he was not cleared and had no need to know.

Smith was reading a boring, top-secret document, that described the logistical support for the elements engaged in stopping the Soviet Army if that army, in their T-64 battle tanks, shot the Fulda Gap in an invasion of Western Europe. This was a replacement for the old report and contained few updates. It supplied an Order of Battle, little information about the logistical support, a table of contents that hinted at the information contained there and a few paragraphs that Smith thought of as either an abstract or an executive summary. The full report had not been given to him for review.

He had just about finished when the sergeant major stepped through the door. When he spotted Smith, he said, "The general wants to see you."

"Thank you, Sergeant Major. Let me put this back in the vault and I'll be right there."

"I'll alert the general." He spun and left the room.

Smith walked into the vault, filed the report, and then left. He didn't close the vault because there were others in the area, and they were reading other classified documents. The last one out had the responsibility for closing and locking the vault.

At the general's office, the sergeant behind the desk said, "You can go right in, sir."

There was something about the way the sergeant had addressed him that worried Smith. When he entered the general's office, he marched to a point about three feet in front of the desk, came to attention and saluted. "Captain Smith reporting as ordered, sir."

The general looked up at him and said, "It took a while for this report to climb the chain of command and reach my office. As you might guess, it is not a glowing assessment of your time in Vietnam. What in the hell got into you?"

Smith wasn't sure that the general wanted an answer. He stood quietly as the silence built and became uncomfortable. Finally, he said, somewhat lamely, "I was attempting the assess the use of HALO on a clandestine operation in a foreign country."

"You mean they jumped into Laos. You thought that it was somehow an illegal operation and because of that created a report accusing them all of violating international law."

"Colonel Bates sent my report up the chain of command. I thought it had died in Vietnam." It wasn't really a statement of fact but more of a question.

"You don't know when to keep your mouth shut, do you, Captain? The mission was authorized. You were not there to comment on such missions. You were there to learn about HALO operations in a combat arena. You were fortunate enough to be there for the process that went into that. Instead of learning about HALO, you attempted to turn it into an international incident, as if we don't have enough trouble with our own press without suggesting to the world that we had engaged in illegal operations."

"Sir, I was —"

"Shut up, Smith. You know your career is over at this point. You exhibited incredibly poor judgement by first flying down to Bragg without adequate authorization. I don't know why you thought they would bring you into their operation and tell you about HALO. Then, we send you to Vietnam to take a look at the operational aspect of HALO and you get into a pissing contest with senior officers and the enlisted experts in HALO. Your OER, which is my responsibility to write, is not going to reflect well on either of these episodes. I hope your college education has provided you with another career field."

"General, I freely admit that this wasn't my brightest hour, but I was doing what I thought was the best way to understand my overall assignment. I didn't know that the mission was authorized. It seemed to me that those local guys were taking it upon themselves —"

The general interrupted again. "You should have asked them a few pertinent questions. That would have saved you from the embarrassment of your current situation. Before you go, be advised that your assignment here is concluded. Your transfer orders will be cut in a few days. Take a week of leave and then contact the sergeant major. He'll have your orders ready for you then."

"General, if I might —"

"No. There is nothing that you can say. You are being reassigned and given that the President is about to announce a reduction in force, I would be surprised if you weren't caught up in that. You are dismissed."

Smith stood there for a moment, stunned by the turn of events. Finally, he saluted and left the general's office.

Major Leonid Semenov spent the morning walking through the new camp. The changes they had made were nearly invisible. The peasants no longer saw them as dangerous. They might not be friends, but they were tolerated. The peasants were left alone to come and go as they needed. The recruits and especially the Soviet soldiers kept an eye on them, but they never did anything that was suspicious.

The recruits were no longer sitting around, waiting for something to happen, but were engaged in various training activities. Some of those activities were now taught by the recruits. Those who had grasped the finer points of military training were helping those who were having some trouble.

When he reviewed the marksmanship scores, he saw that many of the recruits were proficient with the AK-47. A few were very good with it. They had expanded the weapons training to include pistols and the RPG. Each of the recruits was familiar with those weapons and could use them with some accuracy.

He watched a group of four recruits who were sitting in the shade sharpening their knives. They were talking and laughing, but they continued to work on the blades.

Volkov had another group of ten or twelve recruits watching him demonstrate hand-to-hand techniques. It was basic martial arts, but they were watching with interest and when Volkov asked for a volunteer, several of them jumped up, wanting to learn as much as they could.

As he returned to what he thought of as his office, which wasn't as big as the one in the old camp, he spotted Petrov. He waved him over and said, "Let's go inside to talk."

Once inside, Semenov pointed at one of the chairs. "Have a seat. I think it's time to move on with the mission."

"You are pleased with the training?"

"The recruits seem to have come around. I didn't see anyone who was not engaged in either military training or working to improve his equipment. The recruits are turning into soldiers."

Petrov grinned. "I noticed it as well. It happened about a week after we moved here. I believe the peasants saw the recruits as some sort of an improvement of their own lives. It boosted the morale of the recruits."

"What I want to do," said Semenov, "is move the majority of our force into South Vietnam. We'll leave a rear detachment here to operate the lines of communication and to ensure that the recruits have what they need in Vietnam. I want to establish our base just over the border, close to one of the terminuses of the Ho Chi Minh Trail. That would provide us with additional access to supplies that we might not otherwise have, and it would provide us with an opportuning to use the NVA soldiers to further our training."

Petrov had known that eventually they would move into South Vietnam, but there had been no timetable. The move was left to the discretion of the commander. He was just beginning to relax here and now it was time to move again. He had hoped that they would be replaced by a new team before that happened. Now they were going to move again. He asked, "Who will be leading the movement into Vietnam?"

"You will, of course. You'll take the recruits with you and carry what you need to create a camp. You will have to be discreet, and you'll have to disguise what you are doing. You'll use the jungle rather than building out in the open as the Americans do. Everything you will need is here. However, you won't have the benefit of much motorized transport. Even though most of your travel will be in Laos, any large convoy will be spotted by the Americans. A truck here or a car there will not be noticed."

"This seems to be an impossible task. The distance to travel is too great for any real support here."

"What you need to do, is take a strong force and survey the areas close to the border but in South Vietnam. Once you have selected the site, then we'll begin infiltrating more of the recruits and the equipment to build your forward base."

Petrov sat for a moment, thinking. "Are you suggesting a reconnaissance in force?"

"Something like that. I want you to identify a location in which we can establish a presence without tipping our hand. Once that is done, we'll begin to move in the equipment and supplies."

Petrov nodded. "And how soon do you want me to leave?"

"Take a day or two to select the recruits you want. We can transport you close to the border so that you don't have to spend a week getting there. We must be careful about that and do it in small numbers to avoid detection. Once you have finished you mission, we can arrange an extraction."

Petrov pushed himself out of the chair. He said, "I'll want to take Volkov with me. He'll be important for communication with the recruits, though I have learned some of the language and some of them have learned to speak a little Russian."

"Let's do this," said Semenov. "Put together a plan along with the names of any of the cadre that you believe will help. Then we'll assign the recruits based on their training evaluation."

"Yes, Comrade." Petrov left to search for Volkov.

Gerber was reviewing the latest intelligence. There wasn't much to it. He had the new location of the Soviets, and he knew that the training was being wrapped up. The training schedule was being relaxed and the patrolling around their camp was being increased. They weren't finding any enemy because neither the ARVN nor the Americans were running any cross-border operations into Laos. But the enemy was gaining some experience in moving through the jungle without making noise or disturbing the animals. At least, that was in the assessment that he was reading which was based on HUMINT resources inside the Laotian government.

Fetterman walked in the door and said, "Do you think it is time for an aerial recon?"

"For what purpose, Tony?"

"I'm a little concerned about that group moving closer to the border."

"What group might that be, Sergeant Major?"

"The one you're reading about now, sir."

"I see nothing here to suggest they have crossed the border or even neared the border and if they stay in Laos, there isn't much we need to do about them. We have them under surveillance."

"Haphazard surveillance. I bet they're about to move into South Vietnam."

"What's really on your mind?"

"I just want to get out of here for a while. I thought a recon flight would be the way to go."

"You understand that I can't just whistle up a helicopter on the spur of the moment. It takes a little coordination."

"Yes, sir. So, coordinate."

"When would you like to take this excursion?"

"This afternoon works for me, sir."

Gerber stood up and rubbed a hand through his hair. "Well, I was getting a little bored myself. I dislike this waiting. Let's head over to operations and see what's on the board there."

"Now you're talking."

As they walked toward the operations bunker, Gerber said, "I don't know what you hope to see. We've got surveillance aircraft monitoring the area. They have movement along the Ho Chi Minh Trail. I don't think they have much from very deep in Laos."

"Well, we can check."

They descended the stairs into the bunker. It was brightly lit. Off to one side was a scheduling board that showed aircraft assignments. Gerber pointed to one of the aircraft tail numbers and asked the clerk, "What's the deal with that chopper?"

"It's designated as Spare Two. If the flight loses an aircraft, Spare One replaces it and Spare Two becomes Spare One."

"What if I need it for a recon?"

"Have to schedule it through the aviation battalion commander and with Colonel Bates. The colonel wants an aircraft standing by if he needs it. Privilege of being a colonel."

"Since I'm working with Colonel Bates on his project, I believe he'd want me to use that aircraft. You can verify that with him."

The clerk picked up the field phone, spun the crank on the side, blew into the mouthpiece and said, "Connect me with Colonel Bates."

Fetterman leaned close to Gerber and said quietly, "This is going to be easier than I thought."

"Don't count your chickens, Sergeant Major."

The clerk hung up and said, "You can have it for two hours subject to recall as needed."

"Alert the flight crew. We'll meet them on the airfield."

"Yes, sir."

Petrov stood in front of the recruits. The recruits had their weapons, they had spare magazines, and rucksacks that contained their rations and some of the squad equipment, and were prepared to be in the field for four to six days. These were the best of the recruits. Petrov had selected them with the help of Volkov.

On the southeast side of camp were two trucks. The trucks would take them within five kilometers of the border. Once they were away from the camp, they would use a dirt road that had been cut through the jungle. The thick jungle canopy hid most of the road. It was the same as driving through a solid green tunnel. Pilots flying overhead would not be able to see the traffic on the road and reconnaissance aircraft would have a difficult time photographing them. Petrov had picked the route for that reason. It meant that the patrol would begin much closer to the border than originally thought.

After providing the final instructions, translated by Sidorov, Petrov climbed into the cab of the lead truck. The driver was a Soviet NCO. He had a map spread out on the steering wheel and a compass set on the dashboard. He looked at Petrov who asked, "You know where you're going?"

"Yes, sir. The markings on the map suggest the road is a little rough and there are two streams that we must ford. The information I have is that neither is very deep or very wide, but I have found that these maps are sometimes inaccurate in the finer details."

"Well, we'll worry about that later." Petrov turned around, opened the door, and looked back at the other truck. Volkov was standing next to the passenger door, talking with one of the Soviet NCOs. He waved a hand, signaling that they were loaded and ready to go.

The trucks started with a belch of black diesel smoke. They lurched forward, bounced across an open field, and turned to the east. After a kilometer, they found the road and turned onto it. The driver was right. It wasn't much of a road. In places there were deep puddles and Petrov wondered if they would have to abandon the trucks. Each time they made it through and continued, he worried about the next one. They weren't driving very fast, but Petrov didn't mind. It was better than walking and the ride was somewhat relaxing. Not exactly a tour through an enchanted forest but more pleasant than thrashing around in the jungle on foot.

The first stream was narrow and not very deep. They crossed it easily. The second was wider and looked to be deeper. The road entered in front of them, and they could see the other side that climbed a steep bank. Petrov said, "Stop here for a moment."

He got out of the truck and walked to the water's edge. From that vantage point, it didn't look all that deep. He took a step into the water. There wasn't much of a current. Carefully, he walked to the other side. The water was never more than knee deep. He signaled the driver to pull forward. The truck had no difficulty and once it had driven up the bank, Petrov got back in.

As the sun began to set, they came to a wide place on the road. They pulled off to camp for the night. They were not allowed to start fires, to smoke, and they were on half-alert even though they were still in Laos. Petrov had learned his lesson back at the first camp when they had discovered the spies had been close. They took four-hour shifts and when the sun came up the next morning, they continued on their journey.

CHAPTER 18

The map was spread out on a table. It was a detailed map that showed buildings, gaps in the jungle, small, intermittent streams, and other fine details. It was based on aerial reconnaissance, on-site examinations, and other observations. A plastic overlay covered the map and marked on it were grease pencil notations showing enemy locations, friendly forces, enemy trails, and any obstacles that had been created after the map was printed or that were temporary.

Major Mack Gerber was leaning forward, both hands on the table as he studied the map. Next to him was Sergeant Major Anthony Fetterman. Opposite them was Colonel Alan Bates. He was holding a grease pencil and had added a few notations to the map overlay.

With them were two Special Forces senior NCOs. Both spoke fluent Vietnamese and were of smaller stature so that, from a distance, they were often mistaken for Vietnamese. They were designated as the leaders of the assault force. They were dressed in the uniforms of the People's Army of North Vietnam.

Staff Sergeant Bill Sanchez was slightly taller than the normal Vietnamese but was as thin as most of them. He was wearing the PANV uniform of a sergeant and had a Soviet-made 9mm Makarov pistol in a holster on his web gear, which was also of Soviet manufacture.

Staff Sergeant Diego Lopez stood next to him and was almost a mirror image except he was stockier than Sanchez. He was dressed the same but, in addition to the pistol, he had an

AK-47 slung over his shoulder. Sanchez had left his AK-47 in his quarters. He would grab it later if he needed it.

Bates was standing at the top of the map so that he was looking at it upside down. "We have identified the probable location of the Laotian camp on this side of the border. Photo recon helped and a flyby in a single Huey did draw small arms fire. Although the aircraft took five hits, mostly in the tail boom, no one was injured, and no real damage was done." He grinned and said, "That is sort of typical. I have wondered if the tail boom wasn't designed to take that small arms fire."

Gerber took over and pointed at a heavy jungle area three klicks from the border. "They have taken up a position about here. We have intel suggesting the construction of bunkers hidden among the trees. They don't have a good, clean field of fire. I think they are more interested in hiding their camp than they are in the defense of it. They have not occupied any of our lines of communication. They are able to receive support from the other side and from those moving along the Ho Chi Minh Trail. Intel suggests that there are fewer than one hundred men in that camp, but they are close enough to the border and to a segment of the Ho Chi Minh Trail that they could be reinforced quickly if necessary."

Lopez leaned forward to look at the map. "If they're in the trees, then we can approach very close before they can spot us."

"I would suspect," said Fetterman, "that they'll have listening posts out. You should try to find those and eliminate them before you begin the attack."

"Well, we do have them outnumbered three to one, which is standard doctrine for attacking a defensive perimeter," said Lopez. He had read about that the night before and couldn't help dropping that nugget of information into the planning session.

"Moving on," said Bates, ignoring him. "The best approach is from the north, or from the deep jungle. On the south, only a couple of hundred meters from their camp is a large, open field that is perfect for helicopter operations. They probably know that as well as we do and will have it guarded. However, if you require reinforcements, this is the site to use. We can bring in a large force. They won't all have Soviet or Chinese Communist weapons and uniforms, but that won't be a problem."

Gerber asked, "Sergeant Sanchez, have you worked out your operational plan?"

"I conferred with Captains Bromhead and Martin and, of course, Sergeant Lopez here. There is a good landing area for helicopters about twelve klicks to the northeast of their position. That should be far enough away that they wouldn't hear the helicopters in the camp and certainly couldn't see them given the terrain and the jungle. We should land about dusk, and we'll make our way into the jungle and set up a perimeter. We'll eat and rest there through the next day. I'll have some small patrols out, moving closer, looking for signs of those listening posts you mentioned, Sergeant Major."

"That could give you away."

"We'll be dressed like them, carrying weapons like theirs and we all speak Vietnamese. We can talk our way out of it."

"You don't think that will alert them to possible trouble?" asked Bates.

"Given the intel we have, there is no indication that they have been coordinating their activities with either the VC or the NVA. They'll just assume we are another communist unit operating in their AO."

"And if your ruse doesn't work?" asked Gerber.

"Then we'll kill them, return to our main force, and wait to see what happens. Worse case, they might attack us. It'll make an interesting fight given we outnumber them and they have no air support."

"Okay," said Bates. "Submit your battle plan to Major Gerber and a timetable to begin."

"Yes, sir. I'll have it to you this afternoon."

With that Sanchez and Lopez left the briefing. When they were gone, Bates asked, "You approve of the plan?"

Fetterman spoke first. "Both Major Gerber and I worked with them on it. The plan is solid, but you have to remember that good battle plans change when the first shot is fired."

"If the plan begins to go south?" asked Bates.

"We have another strike force on standby, along with aviation support. We can reinforce rapidly."

"From that large field?"

"Yes, sir," said Gerber. "We do anticipate that the enemy might, when under attack, attempt to block any rescue force by taking up position near the field, but that would weaken their ability to defend their base, which would shift the momentum back to Sanchez and Lopez in the north."

Bates said, "I feel like we're getting into a proxy fight here. We're using Vietnamese strikers dressed like North Vietnamese to attack a camp manned by Laotians apparently working with the Soviets and dressed as either Americans or Vietnamese." He grinned and added, "This is a crazy way to fight a war."

"You can call it off," said Gerber.

"No. We need to destroy that camp. I don't want them fleeing back across the border. I want them destroyed."

"Then you'll want a blocking force placed between them and the border," said Gerber.

"Can we infiltrate that area without alerting the bad guys?"

"We can attempt it, Colonel, but there is always a chance that we'll be spotted."

"Can you and Fetterman put that together?"

"Of course, but I thought you wanted us in the C and C?"

"I can do that. How long would it take you to get into position?"

Fetterman said, "We'll need to study the map to pick out an LZ and we'll need time to assemble the force. I suspect you are looking to use ARVN or American soldiers."

"I want to use Americans. That blocking force had got to be well trained and professional, but I don't want it over the border in Laos. They are to stay in South Vietnam. I don't want any mistakes."

"Yes, sir," said Gerber. "Sergeant Major, you're with me."

As they left the meeting, Fetterman said, "I don't like the idea of bringing in an American infantry unit. We haven't trained them and many of them have been in the Army for less than a year. They've had basic training, advanced infantry training, and ten they're sent here."

"On the other hand," said Gerber, "they have combat experience. They'll have worked as both the blocking force and as the main thrust. We'll be there and we can bring in our own NCOs. As a blocking force, all they have to do is remain in place and engage the enemy when they show up."

"So, who are you going to call?"

"Let's get to operations and take a look at what is available. There are some good battalions in the Twenty-Fifth Infantry Division. And, I have to say it, but the First Cavalry has experience in this. I was going to say that the First Cavalry has its own aviation but so does the Twenty-Fifth."

"You've thought this through?"

"No," said Gerber. "Just my first thoughts, though both those divisions are headquartered close by."

"I would rather use a Mike Force. Keeps it as a Vietnamese mission, with a little help from us."

"Let's see what is available on short notice and who we can get on standby once we have a time frame."

They reached the operations bunker and ducked inside. The air-conditioning was a welcome change to the heat and humidity outside. Gerber stopped to talk with the senior NCO while Fetterman noticed the situation map.

He studied it for a minute and spotted a problem. He turned to the clerk and asked, "How up to date is this map?"

"Intel guy comes in first thing in the morning to update it. Information is only a couple of hours old."

"Thanks." Fetterman looked over, but Gerber was engaged with the NCO. He just stood there wondering if there were any other problems. Finally, he asked, "What can you tell me about this unit here?"

The clerk looked at the map and said, "It is designated as a headquarters. It means there is cadre in the area, but it is not considered much of a threat."

"Size?"

"As I understand it, it is rank heavy. Lots of officers including a colonel or two, and senior NCOs. They gather their force from the surrounding villages. Total of military-age males runs about a hundred to a hundred and fifty. Takes several hours for them to gather the force. They don't have much training."

Gerber approached. "I've got the aviation assets and have both Bromhead and Martin standing by with their Mike Forces. We can move with only a couple of hours' notice."

Fetterman didn't comment on that. Instead, he said, "You notice anything on this map?"

Gerber stood back and then saw the problem. "They've got an NVA unit identified to the northeast of our landing zone. How fresh is the intel?"

"This morning."

"Well, that complicates the issue. How big a threat?"

"Less than two hundred men. Probably no more than twenty or thirty. They say it's a headquarters unit which means they are not fighting men and that they'd have to gather their people before they could do much."

"Shit." Gerber reached out and touched the map. "We could put arty down on those guys."

"It would be landing awfully close to our guys."

"It's what? Five, six klicks? Not all that close. Arty works or we could use the Air Force to take it out after we start the attack. If nothing else, it would keep them pinned down until we withdraw. I'll talk to Colonel Bates about it." He thought about it and then said, "But it's probably not a big threat, especially since we know they're there."

"Then we're set?"

Gerber nodded. "It's now just a matter of coordinating the various units, getting them in place and launching the assault."

Gerber and Fetterman were at the landing strip as Sanchez and Lopez began loading their strike force on the helicopters. It would take two lifts that would land approximately twenty minutes apart. They would hold in place waiting for nightfall, then make their way through the jungle and launch the attack just after midnight.

Fetterman said, "That's a change of the plan."

"I didn't like them hanging around all day before launching the attack. The longer they are in the field, the bigger the chance they're discovered."

Fetterman raised his eyebrows. "That a good change? I don't think those guys are patrolling."

"It adjusts the timing by about twenty hours and lessens the opportunity for discovery. We ready to go?"

Fetterman grinned and said, "I'm always ready to go."

Gerber turned to Sanchez. "Good luck. Avoid early contact if at all possible."

"We're set, Major. We know what we need to do."

"I'm sure you do," said Gerber. "I just don't like standing on the sidelines as the game begins."

Fetterman held out a hand. "Good luck. You and Lopez have the important role in this."

Sanchez shook Fetterman's hand and then headed to the lead helicopter. He turned and waved as he climbed aboard.

Fetterman said, "Well, the die is cast."

"We can call it off right now, if we want." Gerber grinned and added, "You know that military plans never survive the first shot."

"That won't happen for about fifteen hours."

Sanchez waited until the helicopter had lifted off and then crouched between the pilots' seats so that he could look out the windshield. The sun was just coming up, but the jungle was still wrapped in darkness. There were wisps of fog rising, looking as if parts of the jungle were on fire. They were flying at about fifteen hundred feet in the air.

There was a tap on his shoulder. One of the strikers leaned close and yelled in his ear but Sanchez couldn't understand what he was saying. The sound of the turbine and the rotors made communication nearly impossible.

They began a rapid descent and Sanchez saw a gunship approaching. They were near the LZ. Sanchez moved back, away from the pilots and maneuvered toward the cargo compartment door. He wanted to be the first off the aircraft. As the skids touched the ground, Sanchez leaped out, ran forward and then crouched in the tall grass. He was followed by the others. An instant later the helicopter took off. They were alone now with no sign of the enemy and no shots had been fired.

Without giving an order or making an arm motion, Sanchez began to walk toward the jungle. When he reached the trees, he stopped and watched as the rest of the company followed. They were spread out, on line, and were moving rapidly. Once in the trees, they waited until Sanchez began to work his way deeper into the jungle. He walked slowly, carefully, looking for signs of booby traps. He doubted there would be any, but once in the field, Sanchez treated everywhere as a combat zone that had been booby trapped.

They had gone a klick into the jungle when he heard the second lift landing. Those strikers would be led by Lopez. They would follow Sanchez but would make better time because Sanchez and his company would have cleared the way for them.

They came to a small, shallow stream that wasn't on the map, but it didn't stop them. They just stepped over it. Sanchez consulted his map and compass. When he suspected they were about five klicks from the enemy camp, he halted. They waited for Lopez to reach them and once the two units were joined, they set up a perimeter for security. Half the strikers would rest while the others kept watch. After two hours they would switch positions. Neither Sanchez nor Lopez had to issue an order.

With security set, Sanchez pointed to three of the strikers and motioned for them to join him. Together they left the security of the perimeter and began to head for the enemy camp. They spread out so that they could barely see one another, stepping carefully to avoid making a sound. They were searching for a listening post. Sanchez didn't think there would be one north of the camp because the obvious route to it was from the southeast.

They stopped frequently and listened for the sounds of the animals. They were watching for birds taking sudden flight — anything that would suggest a human presence — but everything seemed to be normal.

When Sanchez estimated they were within three hundred meters of the enemy camp, they halted. For ten minutes, they rested. Sanchez tried to spot any sign of the enemy, but the jungle was too thick. He thought he heard a voice but couldn't make out any words. Without speaking himself, he signaled that they should withdraw. They slipped a hundred meters to the right, spread out, and started for their own perimeter.

It was afternoon before they rejoined the rest of their company. They approached carefully, but the strikers knew that they were out there. No one opened fire as Sanchez and his team approached the line.

Sanchez found Lopez sitting next to a large tree, his canteen in his hand. He took a swallow and held the canteen out to Sanchez, who shook his head. Sanchez said, "We made it close to their camp. We encountered no listening post."

"They could put it out at dusk," said Lopez.

"True enough, but I don't think they will. They think they're safe in there."

"No sign that they heard the helicopters?"

"If they did, they made no effort to find out anything about it. Hell, there are helicopter operations in the area all the time. Since no one had come close to them, I think they just feel safe."

"How long did it take you to get there?"

"Couple of hours, but we were moving slow, trying to avoid any traps they might have set. We leave about eight tonight; we should be in position to kick off at midnight as planned."

Gerber, Fetterman and Bates were all in the operations bunker when they heard the call from the aviation company saying they were inbound. Gerber said, "That's our cue."

Bates held out his hand and said, "Good luck."

"It isn't luck," said Fetterman. "It is professional competence. We make our own luck."

"I'll be up in the C and C in about thirty minutes," said Bates.

"We'll be on the ground with the blocking force," said Gerber. "Do we have artillery or air strikes to take out that headquarters?"

"I thought we'd keep this an Army operation. We'll let the artillery do their job. They had registered the site a couple of weeks ago, but they haven't fired on it. Just waiting for a good reason. They won't need spotters, though Sidewinder Control might have an aircraft overhead in case it's needed."

"That adds an Air Force element."

Bates laughed. "I can call them off it'll make you feel better."

"No, sir," said Gerber. "Just making an observation."

The ops sergeant yelled, "Flight's on the ground."

"Guess I'll see you tomorrow," said Bates.

Fetterman looked horrified for a moment and said, "You're going to jinx us with that kind of talk."

Bates turned his attention to Fetterman. "Are you superstitious, Sergeant Major?"

"No, sir. I just don't like tempting fate."

"Well, then," said Bates. "You had better get a move on it."

As they left the operations bunker, Gerber asked, "You're not really superstitious, are you, Tony?"

"No, sir. Just pulling his chain."

They reached the airfield. The helicopters were lined up in a staggered trail formation with their engines shut down. They found the company commander standing near the lead aircraft. When they walked up the man started to salute and then thought better of it.

Quietly, Fetterman said, "That doesn't bode well."

"He caught himself. Besides, his jungle fatigues look as if he's been here for a while. He'll be okay."

"Major Gerber, I'm Captain Daniels. Captain Andrews came down with galloping trots. He's unavailable for tonight's mission."

"You have been fully briefed?"

"Between runs to the latrine, yes, sir. I understand our mission. It's not the first I have been on."

"We have about thirty minutes until lift-off. C and C will be on station, and we should have gunships to lead us in. The area is fairly open, but we'll be close to the border."

"With that triple A threat up to eleven thousand feet."

"You've heard about that?"

"Yes, sir. Those of us who work close to the border have seen the notations on the maps."

"You have any questions?"

"No, sir. The first sergeant is well briefed as are the platoon leaders. As I say, we've been here before, so to speak."

Gerber glanced at his watch. "Let's wind them up or we're going to be late."

The company commander waved his hand in a circular motion over his head, telling the flight to crank their engines. He asked Gerber, "Where will you be, sir?"

"I'll be in lead and the sergeant major will be in trail."

"Yes, sir."

"See you on the ground, Tony."

"Trying to tempt fate, sir?"

"Nope, just making a statement of fact."

Colonel Bates met the C and C on the VIP pad near the center of the base. It touched down and the crew chief jumped out. He was trailing a long communication cable and had a small black button in his hand so that he could use the intercom. As Bates approached, he warned the pilots that the colonel was on his way.

"This way, Colonel," he said unnecessarily.

Bates climbed into the cargo compartment. The helicopter had been set up for both the air mission and the ground mission commanders. There was a bank of radios in the cargo compartment that allowed Bates to listen to the communications between the gunships, slicks, and the C and C. There were also radios that allowed him to talk to the commanders on the ground.

He wore a headset handed to him that plugged into the radios. He switched to the intercom and said, "I'm set. We can take off whenever it is convenient."

"We're on the go, Colonel."

The helicopter came up to a three-foot hover, turned into the wind, and lifted off. They crossed the perimeter wire and climbed to three thousand feet, well above the small arms range.

Bates checked the map and then looked out the cargo compartment door. The ground was dark with few lights visible. There was a silver ribbon below them, but Bates knew it was a river rather than a road. Farther away was a dark mass that was the beginning of the jungle.

They turned and began to orbit. The air mission commander said, "We're a bit early. Thought we'd orbit for ten minutes until we're back on schedule."

"Roger," said Bates.

He heard the air mission commander say, "Winchester, Winchester, this is Six. Say location."

"We're near the LZ. To the north and can be there in five."

"Hold for ten and then turn toward me."

"Roger that."

Bates leaned back against the gray insulation that wrapped the transmission. He closed his eyes and rested for a few minutes. He knew that things were going to get exciting in a very short time.

Over the intercom, Bates said, "Let's head in."

"Roger."

The helicopter banked sharply, then leveled off. They stayed at three thousand feet. Through the cockpit window, he saw another helicopter coming straight at him. It was the gun team leader.

Over the radio, he heard, "Winchester, I have you in sight."

"Roger. Making a one eighty."

"Flight lead, where are you?"

"Orbiting to the south as noted. I have you in sight." He thought the mic was off and said, "I hope."

Bates grinned but didn't comment. He switched to the Fox Mike for the attack force. He said, "Mike Six, where are you?"

There was a quiet hiss of the carrier wave and he heard, "We are in position. We have not been detected."

"Hold."

"Roger."

"Flight lead, do you have the gunships in sight?"

"Roger."

"Winchester, take him in."

Bates looked in time to see the gun team leader approach the flight, turn and lead them to the LZ. As the flight disappeared, Bates knew they were close to the ground.

He heard, "Lead, you're down with nine."

The gun team lead climbed out and joined the other two gunships of the heavy fire team.

"Winchester, proceed. Orbit until I clear you."

"Roger."

"Lead, you're unloaded."

"Lead's on the go."

A moment later he heard Gerber on the ground. "We'll be set here in ten minutes. Scouts are out."

"Roger," said Bates, then, "Go, all teams go!"

CHAPTER 19

The LZ was cold. Not a shot was fired at the flight as they landed. Gerber jumped out of the helicopter, ran four or five yards, and then crouched. Around him the strikers did the same thing. As the helicopters lifted off, Gerber moved to his left, toward the center of the landed forces.

When Fetterman and the Vietnamese officers came close, Gerber said, "Let's get into position. The sergeant major and I will be on the wings of the spread V, and you two will be in the center with the majority of the force. Remind everyone to identify their targets. We don't want any friendlies shot."

There was a distant rumbling. Fetterman said, "Arc light?"

"Yeah."

"Should have had the B-52s drop the bombs on that camp."

Gerber was surprised by the comment. "Can't do that. Need this to be a Vietnamese operation. Politics."

Fetterman shrugged and knew this was not the place for a political conversation.

Gerber said, "Let's all get into position. Make sure of our rear security — I don't want us hit from the back."

Without another word, the soldiers took off. Gerber consolidated those with him and moved off, placing the strikers, telling them to take cover. They were not to fire unless they had a target they knew was the enemy.

He took a position at the end of the line, knowing that Fetterman was opposite him. They were separated by two or three hundred meters. He couldn't see him, and he could hear nothing around him that would alert the enemy if they attempted to escape in his direction. The blocking force was set.

Gerber peeled back the black Velcro cover hiding the face of his watch. The glowing numbers and hands were barely visible, even in the dark of the jungle. If everything went to plan, the attack force would move toward the enemy camp and would hit it in about thirty minutes. The exact timing of the attack didn't mean much to Gerber. His job was to stop those fleeing from the attack. This was the most likely route, but he was in place now. The execution of his end of the plan depended on what the enemy did.

He thought he could hear explosions in the distance. These weren't the almost subliminal rumbles of the huge bombs from the B-52s but sounded more like the rockets from helicopter gunships. That was probably the attack on the headquarters. It was far enough away that the attack wouldn't alert those in the camp.

Sanchez was leading half the strikers and Lopez was leading the other half. Their attack was not a straight on, human wave assault. It was more sophisticated than that and the cover provided by the jungle let them creep close to the camp without being spotted. There had been no listening posts set and that surprised Sanchez. The only thing he could think of was that the enemy felt safe in the camp that close to the border.

They had crept to within a hundred meters of the perimeter and Sanchez could see no sign of guards. There was a single strand of wire but that was there to mark the perimeter of the camp and was not meant as a deterrent. They had either not gotten more wire strung, or they believed that they had snuck in under the radar and didn't need it.

He looked at the time. The plan called for an attack at midnight, or if they were late, to radio that information to the C and C. Sanchez decided it was time to go. They would approach as close as they could without firing a shot. He hoped to overwhelm the enemy before they knew they were under attack.

He waved to the men to the right and left of him and then stood up. He bent forward and moved cautiously, searching for any sign that the enemy had seen him. He was within fifty meters of the camp when there was a single shot. He didn't know if it was one of his strikers or someone in the camp but that didn't matter. The shot would alert everyone in the camp.

Without a word, he began to run, not caring if he was making noise. He reached the wire, dropped to his hands and knees and was able to crawl under it. Around him the strikers were opening fire, but there weren't many targets. The enemy was still hiding in their bunkers and their shelters. They were slow to respond.

To his left, near one of the new bunkers, a man stood aiming his rifle, but not firing. He was barely visible in the darkness. Sanchez took a kneeling position, raised his one weapon, and looking over the sights rather than through them, aimed. He squeezed off a short burst, the bright muzzle flash nearly ruining his night vision. The man was nowhere to be seen. Sanchez didn't know if he had hit the target, or the man had disappeared into a bunker.

There was sporadic firing now, most of it aimed at the camp. There were shadows running around inside the perimeter. Sanchez reached one of the new bunkers. There was a firing slit in the front with a square in the back as the main entrance. Sanchez grabbed a grenade, pulled the pin, and threw it in the rear door. He ducked back and the grenade detonated. Smoke and dust boiled out the door.

Sanchez saw his strikers swarming into the camp. He saw there was chaos all around. Firing was intensifying, much of it was on full auto. There were screams as men were hit and fell. There were more explosions as the strikers destroyed the bunkers.

Kapitan Aleksei Petrov was awakened by a single shot. To him, it sounded like an AK-47. His recruits had been issued with M-16s and he didn't think any of them had an AK. He grabbed his web gear that held his pistol and left the tent erected in the center of the camp. He saw some shadowy figures moving around but thought they were his recruits. There had only been a single shot which suggested carelessness rather than something more important.

He yelled, "Volkov, where are you?"

Before there was a response, there were more shots. Petrov turned toward the sound of the shooting. He saw the muzzle flashes, lighting the area. Men, outside the camp, were visible in the strobing effect of the muzzle flashes.

Firing broke out around him. The recruits were shooting at those men rushing the perimeter. Petrov dropped to one knee and realized that he was still too exposed. He stood and ran toward the nearest bunker, but he didn't enter. Instead, he used it as cover. He leaned across the top so that he would look like part of the structure in the dark.

The jungle, near the wire, was now sparkling as if a thousand fireflies were out there. He heard an explosion and knew by the muffled sound that someone had thrown a grenade into a bunker.

Now he spun and ran back toward his tent. He wanted his AK-47. But the firing was growing in intensity. He wasn't sure if he should grab his weapon or if he should run for the west side of the camp. The attack was coming from the north, not the direction he had expected. He saw no evidence of anyone on the west side and the border wasn't all that far away.

Volkov appeared out of nowhere. "We are under attack."

"Throw up a defense around the bunkers. Tell the recruits to fire at anything that moves out there."

"Yes, sir. Where will you be?"

Volkov was little more than a gray smudge in the dark, but Petrov felt as if his gaze was burning through him. He said, "I need to plan our withdrawal if we can't turn the attack."

There was another explosion. This one wasn't muffled. It was a grenade thrown into the center of the camp. Petrov ducked instinctively. He said, "You need to get the defense set."

Volkov didn't respond. He just turned and ran off, disappearing into the dark that was now alive with red and green tracers. Petrov thought that they shouldn't be using tracers. It gave away their positions. He didn't think about the muzzle flashes.

One of the recruits ran at him, as if he was the enemy. Petrov waited for the man to stop and when he didn't, Petrov shot at him. The man stumbled and fell. Petrov checked the body and knew that he had killed a recruit. He didn't know if the recruit had thought he was the enemy or if he wanted to kill Petrov because they were now under attack. He didn't care. The recruit shouldn't have been running at him.

The north side of the camp was where the fighting was going on. Petrov realized it was inside the wire. The wire had been set to mark the perimeter and would have been reinforced in a couple of days. They just hadn't gotten to it.

The fight wasn't going their way. He could see the line being pushed back and breached. They weren't going to hold. They were about to be overrun. Petrov decided that his mission was to get away before he was killed, or worse, captured. The international news media would have a great story if a Soviet officer was captured inside South Vietnam working with the Laotians. He knew that he could not be captured. He had to either escape or die in the attempt.

He spotted one of the recruits, kneeling in the middle of the camp. Petrov approached him, grabbed his shoulder and using one of the few words he knew in the recruit's language, said, "Come."

He pointed to other recruits. "Come."

The recruit understood and yelled. Three or four of them, who had been shooting into the dark, stopped firing and came forward. Petrov wanted to find more recruits. He wanted a larger force to break out of the trap he felt they were now in. He pointed to himself, and with a hand swept the camp. He said, "Come."

There was a quick exchange, and the recruits began shouting at their fellows. They were trying to disengage. Even in the dark, the strobing of the weapons provided a picture of what was happening. The enemy, whoever they were, had taken the bunkers on the north side of the camp and were using them as cover to pick off the rest of the recruits.

Petrov was now surrounded by twenty or more of the recruits. Volkov staggered up. He didn't look right somehow and then Petrov realized that his left arm was hanging limp at his side. He held his AK in his right hand, but it was pointed down, at the ground, as if it was too heavy to hold.

Petrov said, "I want to break out. We must get back across the border. We can't be caught here."

Volkov understood perfectly. He nodded and said, "We are going to fall back to the border."

He didn't have to repeat the order. The recruits began scrambling in that direction. Volkov yelled, "Form into a column. Point man out. Patrol formations as we've shown you. Go!"

Petrov took the point position, not out of courage but because he believed the main threat was behind them. He wanted to get to the border as quickly as he could. If he was the only survivor, he didn't care. The sergeant would take the heat for the failure. It was his job to get away. He'd try to take Volkov with him but if he couldn't, then Volkov would not survive the attack. Someone, on either side, would kill him.

Lopez and his team hit the eastern side of the camp about the same time that Sanchez hit the north. He had gotten closer, under the wire and nearly to the first bunker before anyone fired. Like the rest of his team, he dropped low, surveying the situation. He saw no motion anywhere near him. Firing broke out on the north side of the camp. Most of the shooting was Sanchez and his team trying to overrun that part of the bunker line.

With the enemy's attention drawn to the northern side of the camp, Lopez and his force were able to reach the bunkers and tents without a shot fired at them. They crossed into the camp and then spread out. Lopez and his strikers knew that their fellows were at the perimeter.

Lopez stood for a moment and then saw the enemy moving through the camp. He fired on them and those around him followed his lead. They saw the enemy coming from the south and western sides of the camp. Lopez turned his force to meet the threat coming from there.

They opened fire, first on single shot and then switching to full auto. Those rushing them began to fall and others, rather than returning fire, turned and ran back the way they had come. Lopez moved forward and joined forces with Sanchez. They were now herding the enemy to the south and west, hoping they could force the retreat toward the blocking force.

Lopez pointed at a bunker that was now manned. He turned toward it, firing from the hip, trying to put his rounds through the firing port. The strikers with him engaged the bunker and in moments the enemy there fell silent.

"Take it," he ordered.

Half a dozen of his soldiers ran to the bunker. One tossed a grenade through the firing port and turned away. It detonated. Another of the strikers dropped through the rear opening. There were no enemy left alive in it. He took over, searching for more of the enemy.

The firing from the enemy was tapering. Now the shooting was from the strikers, attempting to secure the camp. Lopez saw the enemy fleeing to the west. He thought about giving chase but decided against it. Gerber and his blocking forces were there to stop the retreat.

Sanchez came up and said, "They're on the run."

"Let's make sure that we have the place secure." He looked at his watch. The assault had started only twenty minutes earlier.

"You have any wounded?"

"I saw a couple of our guys fall. Don't know how badly they're hurt."

"Let's get a head count. And we need to check all the bunkers."

One of the strikers ran up and said, "We've got about a dozen of these guys wanting to surrender."

"Put guards on them and move them off to the east, away from the camp."

"Sure."

"Let's swing through the camp, working toward the west side."

"Medevac?"

"Let's see what we have. We need a head count."

There was a sudden shot. Lopez heard the round snap by his head. He ducked to the right and then knelt. There was a wild burst of firing from his strikers. He saw the muzzle flashes, giving him an idea of direction.

"You hit?" asked Sanchez.

"No. It was just too close. You see where that came from?"

"From the west side of the camp. I think your guys neutralized it."

"We need to be sure we have this place secure."

"And let Gerber do his thing."

When the attack started, Gerber knew it. He heard the shooting from the enemy camp. He listened as it grew in intensity and then began to taper. A green star cluster flare was fired. That was the signal that the camp was in the hands of the strikers. It also meant that some of the enemy might have escaped. It put Gerber and his team on alert.

Gerber said nothing. He knew that Fetterman was waiting for the enemy. With luck, they would run straight into the blocking force. It wasn't long before he heard them crashing through the jungle. They were making no attempt to sneak by. They were just running, trying to escape the disaster of the primitive camp. They were fleeing for their lives.

As the noise grew, Gerber flipped off the safety, selecting single shot. A shadow ran past him, but he didn't fire. He let several of the enemy run by, knowing that those at the far end of the ambush would catch them.

Then, suddenly, several of them were running right at him. He raised his rifle and squeezed off a shot. The man fell but a second took his place. Gerber fired again and then was aware that others were shooting. He saw red tracers and the yellow-orange of the muzzle flashes. It all seemed to be coming from his own soldiers and not the enemy.

There was a wild burst of firing and the men stopped running. One of them threw down his weapon and raised his hands, screaming something in a language that Gerber could not understand. Gerber kept his weapon pointed at the man but didn't say anything. He waited for the shooting to stop.

Someone fired a flare, lighting up the whole scene. The jungle here was sparse with waist-high bushes and a thin canopy. There was a bright moon dropping toward the ground. The shapes resolved themselves. There were men standing in the kill zone of the ambush, their hands high over their heads. They were making no hostile move and seemed more scared than dangerous.

Fetterman emerged from the shadows, his weapon pointed at the surrendering men. He shouted at them in Vietnamese, but they didn't seem to understand. They didn't move, holding their hands out, so that they could be seen.

Fetterman pointed, moving the men toward the other end of the ambush. They were corralled there as the soldiers moved among the enemy, searching for hidden weapons. It was clear that the fight was over. They hadn't been interested in fighting. They were more interested in getting away.

Petrov had slowed his retreat because he didn't hear any pursuit. The fighting at the camp had slowed. There had been a few explosions from grenades. He dropped to one knee, but he couldn't see much ahead of him. There was a helicopter somewhere overhead. He couldn't see it and figured that the lights had been turned out.

The recruits who had escaped were running by him. He watched them go and thought they would trigger any ambush that might be out there. If he was patient, they would lead him to the safest path. It was no longer about training or strategy. It was now all about getting out of South Vietnam alive.

To his left there was a sudden ripping sound as someone fired an automatic weapon. There were screams and then silence. Petrov wasn't sure who had been firing, who had been hit, or where they were. He bent lower, attempting to hide in the tall grass around him, using the few small bushes for cover.

He was breathing hard and realized that he was frightened. The emotion surprised him. He hadn't been afraid as they chased Americans through the jungles in Laos or when the helicopter began spraying the jungle around him with machine-gun fire. He had recognized it for what it was. Suppressive five, designed to cause people to take cover. They hadn't been interested in killing anyone, just forcing them to stop shooting at them.

This was different. As the firing increased, he knew that he had run into an ambush so some kind. The Americans anticipated their line of retreat and had designed the attack carefully. Petrov didn't know if there were other ambushes out there, or if someone had figured out the strategy.

He dropped to his belly. He saw tracers flashing overhead. Red tracers from American weapons. There wasn't any return fire from the recruits. He looked up to see several of them standing straight up, hands over their heads, screaming at the men shooting at them.

Slowly, he began to crawl to the left, away from the shooting. No one knew that he was here. All he needed to do was move slowly, quietly, away from the enemy to his right. If he was patient, he should be able to slip away in the darkness. It was four or five hours until sunrise and he didn't think they would be searching the area until the sun was up. By the time they began their search, if he didn't lose his bearings, he could be back in Laos. He didn't believe the Americans would cross the border to chase one man. He would be safe.

Slowly he worked his way to the south, away from the ambushers. He had left his rifle behind but kept the pistol in its holster. He reached out with his right hand, and pushed carefully, with his right foot moving about two feet forward, and then did the same thing with his left hand and left foot.

Behind him was a sudden wild burst of shooting. He didn't bother to look back. He no longer cared what happened to the others. His mission now was to get out of South Vietnam and back into Laos. That was all he could think about.

Suddenly, someone stepped on his hand. He looked up and saw someone pointing an M-16 at his head. The man said, in Russian, "Where do you think you're going?"

For a moment, Petrov thought about drawing his pistol, but realized that would be a fatal error. Another soldier appeared. This one was obviously a South Vietnamese soldier who held an M-16 pointed at him. Even if he could draw the pistol and shoot the first man; he'd never be able to kill the second.

Sergeant Major Anthony Fetterman shook his head and said, in Russian, "This is the end of the line. We've got you."

With the sun now up, they pushed the captured men back toward the camp. It was a slow process because Gerber didn't want anyone to get hurt. The ambush had suffered no casualties and killed a dozen of the enemy. Gerber hung back and began to inspect the bodies. He found one Caucasian man, bigger than the others. Gerber was sure that the man wasn't an American, but he wanted to be sure. He searched for anything of intelligence value, but the dead men had almost nothing on them. One had a thin wallet that held a black and white picture of a young man and woman and a small child.

As Fetterman came close, Gerber asked, "You get rid of our Russian friend?"

"Turned him over to the strikers. They'll take him in and turn him over to counterintelligence. We won't have to worry about him." He then asked, "You find anything of value?"

"No. Just the one Caucasian man. Nothing on him to tell us who he was."

"You going to the camp?"

"Yeah. That should be interesting."

"You and I should probably get out of here," said Fetterman. "This is supposed to be a Vietnamese operation."

Gerber shrugged. "No one is going to care about that. Let's take a look at that camp."

In the daylight, it didn't take them long to arrive. There was security posted in the event of a counterattack, but Gerber didn't believe one would be launched, at least in the daylight. The bodies were lying where they had fallen. Sanchez had arranged for the seriously wounded strikers to be medevacked. He was sitting on a bunker, eating a biscuit from a C-ration carton. His rifle was across his knees. There was a smudge on his face, and he had lost his helmet. As Gerber approached,

Sanchez began to stand but Gerber waved him back down. "Stay comfortable. What's the tally?"

"We had four killed and six seriously wounded. I've counted forty-eight bodies here, but there are a couple of bunkers where it's hard to tell how many were in it. Count could run to fifty-five or sixty."

"Quite the victory for our side."

"Yes, sir. You stop the runners?"

"There is another fifteen or twenty, not to mention those who surrendered. There is going to be some interesting interrogation there. I found one Caucasian among the dead."

"We've found two here. They were wearing American jungle fatigues and had American weapons," said Sanchez.

"You seen the Sergeant Major?"

Sanchez pointed at one of the bunkers. "He was in there, but I don't know what he was looking for."

Gerber started to walk toward the bunker and saw Fetterman climb out of it. He said, "Anything interesting?"

Fetterman shrugged. "They have all this US equipment, but I also found some of communist manufacture."

Gerber said, "Some of our guys are equipped with AK-47s."

"I think it's time for us to get out of here," said Fetterman. "We should get some intel guys in here to look around. There are some documents that haven't been destroyed in the fight."

"Let me brief Sanchez on this, and then we'll whistle up a helicopter."

"Really a strange situation," said Fetterman. "Normally, we're defending a camp rather than attacking."

"You think this is a change in the overall strategy?"

Fetterman thought for a moment. "No, sir. I think it was an experiment that failed."

"Yeah," said Gerber. "Me too."

EPILOGUE

The Army Chief of Staff, General William C. Westmoreland, along with Major General David Kincaid and Major General Steven Walker, were back in the hidden room in the bowels of the Pentagon, meeting with Colonel Leonard Lake, who was a senior intelligence officer, and Captain Leslie Newman. This meeting was a follow-up to one that had been held nearly a year earlier. Unlike that meeting, Lake was not standing at a lectern and there were no slides to be shown. There were handouts that contained the information and each of the officers had a copy of it. When the meeting was over, Lake would collect those handouts and they would be destroyed.

Lake said, "I have the latest intelligence from Vietnam. As has been suggested early on, the Soviet Union attempted to establish a camp somewhat modeled after our Special Forces camps in South Vietnam."

"We have proof that the Soviet Union is behind this effort?" asked Westmoreland.

"Yes, sir. There is no doubt about it."

"Proceed."

"If you'll turn to page three, that is the beginning of the report. It is an assessment based on the retrieval of information from the camp inside South Vietnam. The Soviets did what they could to hide their involvement, but some of the material picked up after the battle was clearly Soviet. No, not the sort of equipment that you'd expect in an aid package, but the kind of material that a Soviet soldier might have with him. And, in one case, they found a letter written in Russian addressed to the man's wife in the Soviet Union."

"We have that letter?" asked Westmoreland.

"Yes, sir, though I'm a bit ambivalent about it."

"Why's that, Colonel?"

"It was a personal letter to his wife. He shouldn't have written it at that camp for the very reason that it could fall into enemy hands, or, in this case, ours. The letter makes it clear that he was involved in training Laotians in various combat techniques."

Kincaid said, "I can expand on this later, if you need me to, General."

"Let's see where we are when we're finished here."

Lake flipped through the briefing document. "The other evidence, that is, the best evidence, is the testimony from those captured during the fight. Most of them were Laotian conscripts, that is, military-age males, who were ordered from their homes to beginning training. They were not volunteers, and they were not enthusiastic about finding themselves in a military organization. They provided additional information including evidence of war crimes."

"Elaborate," said Westmoreland.

"They told of men being executed for disobeying orders or for attempting to return home. All of them have asked for asylum here, citing the real possibility of execution if sent back to Laos."

Kincaid said, "We have transcripts of the debriefing interviews. The training described tells us they were going to infiltrate teams of these men into South Vietnam to begin a program of indoctrination and intimidation of the Vietnamese. Sort of a Vietnamization in reverse."

Walker took over. "I'm not clear on their thinking. They did not have the lines of communication to do this sort of thing. We saw in that first camp that the recruits, if you want to call them that, did not have a will to fight. They were not zealots who embraced the communist system but men whose one desire was to go home."

Lake said, "There is evidence that they had set up training camps in several locations in southern Laos. Our HUMINT sources provided more information, including pictures of high-ranking Soviet brass touring some of those camps. What we don't know is why this one group moved into South Vietnam when they did. They just didn't have the capability to support such an action at that time."

He looked up and grinned. "But the best evidence we have are the two Soviet soldiers captured in the fight. We believe one was an officer, though he had been reluctant to tell us much. He even refuses to give name, rank, serial number and date of birth as required by the Geneva Convention."

"Why is that?"

Lake hesitated and then said, "I suspect he fears retribution by the Soviets because he failed in his mission. He shouldn't have allowed himself to be captured but the circumstances prevented his suicide. I don't believe he wants to be repatriated and thinks by refusing to provide any information, we won't send him to Moscow to be shot."

"And the other?"

"He was, or rather is, an NCO. He is cooperating after a fashion. But he has refused to identify the other prisoner."

Kincaid said, "The interrogations are continuing. Frankly, I think both are waiting to be offered sanctuary in the United States. They both fear the firing squad."

Westmoreland closed his briefing book and looked up at Lake. "There is no doubt that this was completely Soviet inspired. It wasn't the North Vietnamese or the Chinese."

"We thought about that," said Lake. "We ruled out the Chinese simply because of the centuries of animosity between the Vietnamese and the Chinese."

"Two communist agencies working together to bring the benefits of communism to the South Vietnamese," said Westmoreland.

"Except, sir, the North Vietnamese would fear a push by the Chinese to drive Uncle Ho and his minions out of power, making Vietnam little more than a Chinese satellite."

Westmoreland looked at his watch. "What is the final analysis here?"

Lake flipped to the end of the briefing book as if he needed the reminder of the conclusions. "The Soviets were attempting to set up a proxy force in Laos to exert their influence over the region. They set up training camps to train the locals in the ways of asymmetrical warfare, overlooking the necessity of having a force of volunteers who believed in the mission. That was a major flaw in their plan."

"Did they have permission from the Laotian government for all this?"

"No, sir, I don't believe they did. I believe, based on some of the intel, that they sold this as a way to prevent the South Vietnamese and by extension, us, that is the American Army, from operating in their territory. The Laotians thought of it as a preventative measure and the Soviets thought of it as expanding their influence. So, there was something of a misunderstanding, probably intentional on the part of the Soviets. They were just going to train the locals to defend themselves and the Soviets thought of it as a force to be used against the South Vietnamese."

"And it has failed?"

"In my assessment, and with the concurrence of General Kincaid, yes, it has failed. Their other camps have been closed and the recruits have, for the most part, returned to their farms and villages. There are hints that a few of the recruits were convinced of the benefits of communism. They went on, into the Soviet Union, when the soldiers left."

"From what you have said here today, Colonel, I take it that you believe that this threat has been neutralized without the involvement of American soldiers."

Lake couldn't help grinning. "There is no evidence that American forces had anything to do with the attack on the Soviet-Laotian base. That was carried out by Vietnamese Special Forces."

"There were Americans involved?"

"Oh, yes, sir. There were helicopters involved in landing the military force and the extraction of the soldiers later. They provided gunship support and medevac support. But there were no American soldiers wounded or killed in the battle. While we can prove Soviet involvement, no one can prove American involvement. The Soviets know we were there, but they have no evidence. All the evidence is on our side."

Westmoreland stood up and said, "Then this never happened. I want everything destroyed so there is no paper trail and no leaks." He shook his head. "We actually did nothing wrong here, but the world might not agree with that. Gentlemen, thank you for your time. Let's get back to work."

With that he left the room. Lake slumped in his chair, relieved. He was sure that somehow this was going to end his career. The bullet had been dodged.

GLOSSARY

AC — Aircraft commander. The pilot in charge of the aircraft.

AIT — Advanced Individual Training. The school soldiers were sent to after basic training.

AK-47 — Assault rifle normally used by the North Vietnamese and the Viet Cong.

ANGRY-109 — AN-109, the radio used by the Special Forces for long-range communications.

AN/PRR9 and **AN/PRT4** — Intrasquad radio receiver and transmitter used for short-range communications. The range is something under a mile.

AO — Area of Operations.

AP — Air Police. The old designation for the guards on Air Force bases. Now referred to as security police.

AP ROUNDS — Armor-piercing ammunition.

APU — Auxiliary Power Unit. An outside source of power used to start aircraft engines.

ARC LIGHT — Term used for a B-52 bombing mission. Also known as heavy arty.

ARVN — Army of the Republic of Vietnam. A South Vietnamese soldier.

ASA — Army Security Agency.

ASH AND TRASH — Refers to helicopter support missions that didn't involve a direct combat role. They hauled supplies, equipment, mail and all sorts of ash and trash.

AST — Control officer between the men in isolation and the outside world. Responsible for taking care of all the problems.

AUTOVON — Army phone system that allows soldiers on one base to call another base, bypassing the civilian phone system.

BDA — Bomb Damage Assessment.

BODY COUNT — Number of enemy killed, wounded or captured during an operation. Used by Saigon and Washington as a means of measuring the progress of the war.

BOONDOGGLE — Any military operation that hasn't been completely thought out. An operation that is ridiculous.

BOONIE HATS — Soft cap worn by a grunt in the field when not wearing his steel pot.

BROWNING M-2 — Fifty-caliber machine gun manufactured by Browning.

BROWNING M-35 — The 9mm automatic pistol that became the favorite of the Special Forces.

C AND C — Command and Control aircraft that circled overhead to direct combined air and ground operations.

CARIBOU — Cargo transport plane.

CHECKRIDE — Flight in which one pilot checks the proficiency of another. It can be an informal review of the various techniques or a very formal test of a pilot's knowledge.

CHINOOK — Army aviation twin-engine helicopter. A CH-47.

CHOCK — Refers to the number of the aircraft in the flight. Chock Three is the third, Chock Six is the sixth.

CLAYMORE — Antipersonnel mine that fires 750 steel balls with a lethal range of 50 meters.

CLOSE AIR SUPPORT — Use of airplanes and helicopters to fire on enemy units near friendly troops.

COLT — Soviet-built small transport plane. The NATO code name for Soviet and Warsaw Pact transports all begin with the letter C.

CONEX — Steel container about 10 feet high, 10 feet long and 10 feet deep, used to haul equipment and supplies.

C-RATS — C-rations.

DAI UY — Vietnamese Army rank equivalent to U.S. Army Captain.

DEROS — Date of Estimated Return from Overseas Service.

DIRNSA — Director, National Security Agency.

DZ — Drop zone.

E AND E — Escape and Evasion.

FEET WET — Term used by pilots to describe flight over water.

FIELD GRADE — Refers to officers above the rank of Captain but under Brigadier General. In other words, Majors, Lieutenant-Colonels and Colonels.

FIRECRACKER — Special artillery shell that explodes into a number of small bomblets that detonate later. The artillery version of the cluster bomb, it was employed as a secret weapon tactically for the first time at Khe Sanh.

FIREFLY — Helicopter with a battery of bright lights mounted in or on it. The aircraft is designed to draw enemy fire at night so that gunships orbiting close by can attack the target.

FIRST SHIRT — Military term referring to the First Sergeant.

FIVE — Radio call sign for the Executive Officer of a unit.

FOB — Forward Operating Base.

FOX MIKE — FM radio.

FREEDOM BIRD — Name given to any aircraft that took troops out of Vietnam. Usually referred to the commercial jet flights that took men back to the World.

GARAND — The M-1 rifle that was replaced by the M-14. Issued to the South Vietnamese early in the war.

GRAIL — NATO name for the shoulder-fired SA-7 surface-to-air missile.

GUARD THE RADIO — Stand by in the commo bunker and listen for messages.

GUIDELINE — NATO name for the SA-2 surface-to-air missile.

GUNSHIP — Armed helicopter or cargo plane that carries weapons instead of cargo.

HALO — High Altitude, Low Opening.

HE — High-explosive ammunition.

HOOTCH — Almost any shelter, from temporary to long-term.

HORN — Term that referred to a specific kind of radio operations that used satellites to rebroadcast the messages.

HOTEL THREE — Helicopter landing area at Saigon's Tan Son Nhut Airport.

HUEY — UH-1 helicopter.

HUMINT — Human Intelligence resource.

ICS — Intercom system in an aircraft.

IN-COUNTRY — Term used to refer to American troops operating in South Vietnam. They were all in-country.

INTELLIGENCE — Any information about enemy operations that would be useful in planning a mission.

KIA — Killed in Action.

KLICK — Thousand meters; a kilometer.

LIMA LIMA — Land line. Refers to telephone communications between two points on the ground.

LLDB — Luc Luong Dac Biet. The South Vietnamese Special Forces.

LP — Listening Post. A position outside the perimeter manned by a couple of soldiers to give advance warning of enemy activity.

LRRP — Long-Range Reconnaissance Patrol.

LSA — Lubricant used by soldiers on their weapons to ensure they will continue to operate properly.

LZ — Landing zone.

M-3A1 — Also known as a grease gun. A .45-caliber submachine gun favored in World War Two by GIs because its slow rate of fire meant that the barrel didn't rise and they didn't burn through their ammo as fast as they did with some other weapons.

M-14 — Standard rifle of the U.S. Army, eventually replaced by the M-16. It fired the standard 7.62mm NATO round.

M-16 — Became the standard infantry weapon of the Vietnam War. It fired 5.56mm ammunition.

M-79 — Short-barreled, shoulder-fired weapon that fired a 40mm grenade. These could be high explosives, white phosphorus or canister.

M-113 — Armored personnel carrier.

MACV — Military Assistance Command, Vietnam. Replaced MAAG in 1964.

MEDEVAC — Medical Evacuation. Also called Dust-Off. A helicopter used to take the wounded to medical facilities.

MI — Military Intelligence.

MIA — Missing in Action.

MONOPOLY MONEY — Term used by the servicemen in Vietnam to describe the MPC handed out in lieu of regular U.S. currency.

MOS — Military Occupation Specialty.

MPC — Military Payment Certificates. The Monopoly money used instead of real cash by the U.S. Army.

NCO — A noncommissioned officer. A noncom. A sergeant.

NCOIC — NCO in Charge. The senior NCO in a unit, detachment or patrol.

NDB — Nondirectional Beacon. A radio beacon that can be used for homing.

NEXT — The man who said it was his turn to be rotated home.

NINETEEN — Average age of the combat soldier in Vietnam, as opposed to twenty-six in World War Two.

NVA — North Vietnamese Army. Also used to designate a soldier from North Vietnam.

ONTOS — Marine weapon that consists of six 106mm recoilless rifles mounted on a tracked vehicle.

ORDER OF BATTLE — Listing of units available and to be used during a battle.

P (PIASTER) — Basic monetary unit in South Vietnam worth slightly less than a U.S. penny.

PETA-PRIME — Tar-like substance that melted in the heat of the day to become a sticky black nightmare that clung to boots, clothes and equipment. It was used to hold down the dust during the dry season.

PETER PILOT — Copilot in a helicopter.

PLF — Parachute Landing Fall. The roll used by parachutists on landing.

POL — Petroleum, Oil and Lubricants. The refueling point on many military bases.

POW — Prisoner of War.

PRC-10 — Portable radio.

PRC-25 — A lighter portable radio that replaced the PRC-10.

PULL PITCH — Term used by helicopter pilots to mean they are going to take off.

PUNJI STAKE — Sharpened bamboo hidden to penetrate the foot.

PUZZLE PALACE — The Pentagon. It was called the Puzzle Palace because no one knew what was going on there. Puzzle Palace East referred to MACV or USARV headquarters in Saigon.

RLO — Real Live Officer. Term used by warrant officers to refer to officers who were commissioned.

RON — Remain Over Night. Term used by flight crews to indicate a flight that would last longer than a day.

RPD — Soviet-made 7.62mm light machine gun.

RTO — Radio Telephone Operator. The radioman of a unit.

RUFF-PUFFS — Term applied to the RF-PFs, the Regional Forces and Popular Forces. Militia drawn from the local population.

S-3 — Company-level operations officer.

SA-2 — Surface-to-air missile fired from a fixed site. A radar-guided missile nearly 35 feet long.

SA-7 — Surface-to-air missile that is shoulder-fired and has infrared homing.

SACSA — Special Assistant for Counterinsurgency and Special Activities.

SAFE AREA — Selected Area For Evasion. It doesn't mean that the area is safe from the enemy, only that the terrain, location or local population make the area a good place for escape and evasion.

SAM TWO — Refers to the SA-2 Guideline.

SAR — Search and Rescue.

SECDEF — Secretary of Defense.

SHORT-TIMER — Person who had been in Vietnam for nearly a year and who would be rotated back to the World soon. When the DEROS was the shortest in the unit, the person was said to be *Next*.

SINGLE-DIGIT MIDGET — Soldier with fewer than ten days left in-country.

SIX — Radio call sign for the unit commander.

SKS — Soviet-made carbine.

SMG — Submachine gun.

SOI — Signal Operating Instructions. The booklet that contained the call signs and radio frequencies of the units in Vietnam.

SOP — Standard Operating Procedure.

SPIKE TEAM — Special Forces team made up for a direct-action mission.

STEEL POT — Standard U.S. Army helmet. The steel pot was the outer metal cover.

TAOR — Tactical Area of Operational Responsibility.

TDY — Temporary duty, temporary assignment.

TEAM UNIFORM OR COMPANY UNIFORM — UHF radio frequency on which the team or the company communicates. Frequencies were changed periodically in an attempt to confuse the enemy.

THE WORLD — The United States.

THREE — Radio call sign of the Operations Officer.

THREE CORPS — Military area around Saigon. Vietnam was divided into four corps areas.

TO&E — Table of Organization and Equipment. A detailed listing of all the men and equipment assigned to a unit.

TOC — Tactical Operations Center.

TOT — Time Over Target. Refers to the time the aircraft are supposed to be over the drop zone with the parachutists, or the target if the planes are bombers.

TRIPLE A — Antiaircraft Artillery or AAA. Anything used to shoot at airplanes and helicopters.

TWO — Radio call sign of the Intelligence Officer.

TWO-OH-ONE (201) FILE — Military records file that listed all of a soldier's qualifications, training, experience and abilities. It was passed from unit to unit so that a new commander would have some idea about the capabilities of an incoming soldier.

UMZ — Ultramilitarized Zone. Name GIs gave to the DMZ (Demilitarized Zone).

UNIFORM — Refers to the UHF radio. Company Uniform would be the frequency assigned to that company.

USARV — United States Army, Vietnam.

VC — Viet Cong, called Victor Charlie (phonetic alphabet) or just Charlie.

VIET CONG — Contraction of Vietnam Cong San (Vietnamese Communist).

VIET CONG SAN — Vietnamese communists. A term in use since 1956.

WHITE MICE — South Vietnamese military police who all wore white helmets.

WIA — Wounded in Action.

WILLY PETE — WP, white phosphorus. Called smoke rounds. Also used as antipersonnel weapons.

WOBBLY ONE — Refers to a W-1, the lowest of Warrant Officer grade. Helicopter pilots who weren't commissioned started out as Wobbly Ones.

WSO — Weapons System Officer.

XM-21 — Name given to the Army's sniper rifle. An M-14 mounted with a special ART scope.

XO — Executive Officer of a unit.

X-RAY — Term that refers to an engineer assigned to a unit.

A NOTE TO THE READER

Dear Reader,

If you have enjoyed this novel enough to leave a review on **Amazon** and **Goodreads**, then we would be truly grateful.

Sapere Books

Sapere Books is an exciting new publisher of brilliant fiction and popular history.

To find out more about our latest releases and our monthly bargain books visit our website: **saperebooks.com**